I0691793

THE FIRM

First Edition

\

Published by The Nazca Plains Corporation
Las Vegas, Nevada
2010

ISBN: 978-1-61098-019-7
E-book: 978-1-61098-020-3

Published by

The Nazca Plains Corporation ®
4640 Paradise Rd, Suite 141
Las Vegas NV 89109-8000

PUBLISHER'S NOTE
The Firm is a work of fiction created wholly by *Bill Smith*'s imagination. All characters are fictional and any resemblance to any persons living or deceased is purely by accident. No portion of this book reflects any real person or events.

Cover Photo, Joshua Blake
Cover Design, Ian Ray
Art Director, Blake Stephens

DEDICATION

"To the many, many readers who celebrate the renaissance of vivid fantasies regarding the ownership of one person by another for often the ultimate benefit of both."

THE FIRM

First Edition

Bill Smith

CONTENTS

CHAPTER I

SIGNING ON WITH THE FIRM

"Are you looking forward to the sale tonight, David?" Forrest asked as the two men in their late twenties entered the taxi from their 91st street address.

"Depends," David answered languidly.

"Depends on what?" Forrest sharply cut back. "Sometimes I think you'd be bored at your own funeral. I went to a lot of trouble to make sure you'd get invited – those invitations don't come easily I'll have you know."

"I know, I know," David replied in a low voice. "I appreciate all the trouble you go to keeping me in polite society," he added with a chuckle, "but, Forrest, we were at a sale just a month ago in Rio and if you weren't into primitive types, there really wasn't much to look over. And the level of training evident was just atrocious. Of course, this is New York – things will undoubtedly be at a much different level tonight. And I'm sure we won't have to worry too much about the level of training if THE FIRM is sponsoring this one. No doubt it will be more interesting than Rio – at least THE FIRM has definite standards to uphold. So it'll be interesting from a technical viewpoint if nothing else. But I can't get too motivated when there is no conceivable personal need at this point – what in God's name would I do with yet another one?" Davis sighed as he rolled his eyes upward in feigned frustration.

"Don't be so damned selfish," Forrest retorted. "If you're not looking for yourself, you can help me with some potential purchase. Besides, you're never blind to picking one up for a quick profitable resale if the price is right. Don't tell me you've forgotten already where most of that legendary wealth of your's actually came from! Your memory can't be that short, David."

David laughed softly as he said, "Calm down, Forrest. I haven't forgotten where my 'old money' comes from anymore than you know where yours is coming from lately since I 'dragged' you into the respectable world of commerce and trade, legitimate or not. But 'drag' is hardly the right world, is it, Forrest, as I recall. You couldn't wait to make those first purchases and I thought you'd die of excitement when you realized the huge profits you made on your first sales. It's been a sad day ever since I 'dragged' you into this – I've hardly had a day's rest since. You don't have to go to every sale, you know – a few good ones a year is all you need to enjoy a nice lifestyle. But, damn it, Forrest – now that you've got the fever – it's like we have to go to every damn sale in the world to matter when or where it's at, what's for sale, or who's doing the selling. I'm just getting tired, that's all. I never dreamed my best friend would get 'slave fever' after the first sale or so. Now's there's no stopping you."

"There you go exaggerating again, David," Forrest responded. "You make me sound like a 'slave junkie' or something!"

"Look, Forrest. Let's face facts. Five years ago we bought the townhouse. Then I quietly bought Adam to help out with the house and brighten up our sex life and we put the cages and the slave training and maintenance areas into the basement and made some other improvements. Although you certainly took advantage of having Adam around, it didn't seem to change you much even after I bought Sergei in Moscow and added him to the staff. But when you decided to buy Abdul that time we were in Northern Africa and actually owned a boy yourself, I could see you were rapidly getting 'slave fever' as I call it. When you sold Abdul for – what was it – five times what you paid for that little stud – your eyes got a greedy glare that hasn't left yet. How many boys have you turned over since then? Twenty? Thirty? You must be worth at least several million by now on those profits alone. And our basement is so crowded most of the time two to the cage is more the rule than the exception nowadays.

Sergei and Adam spend more of their time managing your stable than helping around the house anymore."

"Bitch, bitch, bitch," Forrest shot back. "I'll admit I've made a little money over the past two or three years since you introduced me to my calling, David, but to claim I'm addicted to the slave trade is ridiculous. I don't mind making money and the trade is about the most interesting occupation I've explored to date, but you hardly have grounds to complain. First off, David, I offered to buy both Adam and Sergei from you because I know my stock is taking up most of their time, but you wouldn't hear of it and who else can I get that knows exactly what they're doing like those two. They wield those whips I gave them both at the first sign of any resistance by a new slave and the slightest hesitation in total and complete compliance after that on the part of any slave, old or new. It's obvious they enjoy beating the slaves until they're practically whimpering masses of bruised flesh, but it sure helps speed up the training, I'll tell you. But, what's so great about them, they always stop just short of permanently damaging the value of the merchandise. Overseers like that are hard to find – it just seems to come natural to those two! So I gave you Marcos outright after I saw you drooling over that hot Latin the first time I showed him to you. And then I gave you that good-looking American black – what was his name – LaBradford – that was it – after I found you poking his butt the day after I first brought him home. And you know you can have any of the others you want anytime. So don't bitch to me – you've benefitted too, you know. But, David, you're right – we are going to have to add another room of cages down in the basement – it's just too crowded down there most of the time."

"Well, Forrest," David said with a big smile, "you've made your point. I remember Marcos and LaBradford fondly – great gifts really – and when I tired of them and sold them off – well-trained as they were by that time – I made enough to stagger by another year or so," David laughed. "Who knows what lurks behind the shadow of THE FIRM tonight," David mimicked in the dramatic tones of the old 'Shadow' radio show. "Forrest's ideal of the perfect male body? David's concept of the perfect bedmate? Everyone's perfect slave? Who knows what lurks in the great unknown of THE FIRM?"

"Well, David," Forrest grinned. "I can see you're beginning to get in the mood. You'll probably end up buying out the house even before we get those new cages installed."

"Only if you don't beat me to it, Forrest," David said as he sat up in the taxi seat and began to seriously think about THE FIRM's first sale this year just a few minutes ahead of him.

— — — — —

THE FIRM's sale was being held in a totally private warehouse located near the pier for the Cunard Line. The warehouse facility had long been owned by Matthew Broadley, one of THE FIRM's best known directors and was well equipped for its sole purpose anymore: the maintenance, training, and sale of slaves. Since tonight's sale was probably going to constitute one of the largest single venues for THE FIRM this year, numerous preparations had been made for the offering of 183 well-trained and highly selected stock – the majority male at this particular sale but a variety of females were also available. Over 500 highly screened repeat customers, some reputable well-known dealers from throughout the world, and a few highly-trusted wholesalers were invited and, knowing THE FIRM, anyone lucky enough to get an invitation was almost sure to attend – such opportunities were too hard to come by to treat in a cavalier fashion. Staff slaves owned by THE FIRM had been working for months in preparation for this first sale of the year. Additional cages, showers, and toilets had been installed for the stock offerings, last minute training had been accelerated, and the gymnasium equipment groaned from all the use it was getting as the overseers made sure the slaves were in top physical condition for the sale.

Three main areas had been defined in the huge warehouse: the holding facilities for the slaves; the inspection and demonstration area for convenience of the customers prior to the sale; and the sales arena itself with luxurious seating accommodations for the 800 visitors expected to attend. In addition, a final holding and shipping area had been set aside near the rear of the warehouse for disposition of the slaves once they were sold.

As would be expected with any of THE FIRM's activities, everything was spotlessly clean, odor-free, and pristine within the luxurious accommodations offered potential customers. For the slaves in holding, however, things were more Spartan: cages and the naked bodies in them were hosed down just once a day; the smell of raw fear, uncertainty, shock (among those just being initiated into their new status), semen, blood, vomit, urine and sweat prevailed the air. Whips, manacles, chains, dildos, harnesses, gags, body rings of various types, butt-plugs and other implements of control and decoration lined the walls and were often strewn about the floor. Groans from the insertion of unbelievably sized 'stretching' dildos, screams in reaction to a corrective intense lashing, shrieks caused by the punishing application of electrical prods and shocking devices, and the low moans, gasps, gagging and grunts from the steady intrusions inherent in perfecting the slave's sucking and fucking skills filled the air as last-minute training proceeded right up to the time of the slave's pre-purchase inspections.

The inspection area was a different story, however. Here thick plush carpets covered the entire area around the marble sales pedestals with the holding chains discretely anchored into the pedestal bases. Mirrors adorned all walls and divans were strategically placed near the pedestals for the comfort of prolonged viewing. Beside each pedestal was a small chromium stand with the log book for each slave displayed outlining his or her history, health records, and training record; an assortment of whips and lashes to test reaction; a rack of dildos of various lengths and widths, various lubricants; small silver bowls filled with perfumed water to cleanse after various probings and strokings were completed; and a supply of soft cotton towels to dry one's hands.

By contrast, the shipping area was stark and practical: mainly consisting of shipping cages, wrist and ankle manacles, gags built into head harnesses, shipping collars, and temporary clothing mainly consisting of one-size-fits-all knee-length coveralls and a few tunics made out of cheap thin cotton where clothing might be required prior to final delivery. THE FIRM's shipping overalls, complete with the company logo, were cleverly designed in that Velcro tabs at the chest, waist, and crotch made sure each slave's physique and physical attributes was well displayed, even in shipment.

— — — — —

The two young men presented their engraved invitations through the small peephole in the iron entry door to the huge warehouse. After careful inspection, the door quickly opened into a dimly limited anteroom and, once inside, the door was swiftly shut. After adjusting to the low light level, the two could make out the personage behind the heavy door. A naked male slave, towering over them as he shut the door with his heavily muscled 6'4" frame glistening in the light from his sheen of sweat and body oils, appeared to be about 25 years old. He was a Latino of superb proportions who epitomized raw sexuality in such an exaggerated fashion it reminded you of a cartoon drawing. Two-inch rings adored each tit on a mass of pectoral muscle, his high neck collar forced his head into a straight ahead upright position which made his ear and nose rings display well, and, most impressively, a one-inch band in back of his scrotum forced his massive genitals outward for obvious display – made all the more impressive by his rigidly erect penis dripping pre-cum copiously.

"Welcome to THE FIRM, masters," he intoned with a basso voice reeking of humility and respect. "Feel free to use me or any other FIRM slaves at any time as you see fit for your enjoyment and pleasure. We, like all slaves of THE FIRM, are here to serve totally – with no restraints on your part and no reservations on our part," and with that he gracefully fell to his knees, now wide spread, leaned forward and kissed our feet in greeting.

"Wow!" David laughed. "THE FIRM sure knows how to put on a show!" as he reached down and twisted one of the slave's tit-rings.

"Thank you, master," the slave humbly responded as he jerked back into a kneeling position with his pectorals thrust out so THE FIRM's customer could have easy access to his nipples.

David pulled the tit out by its ring a good inch, massaged it roughly between this thumb and forefinger as he twisted it again a good 90 degrees or so, and then let loose so it snapped back, making the slave jerk slightly in his reaction as the tit visibly turned red and started to swell.

"Thank you, master," the slave said out of habit as he struggled to maintain the correct kneeling posture despite what was being done to his tit.

"Nice tits," David said more to himself than to anyone, as he continued fondling and massaging the sensitive pierced nub.

"The boy likes to have his titties played with," Forrest laughed. "Look at the cum leaking out of his prick now!"

David let loose of the abused nipple. "Position, boy."

The slave instantly lifted himself from his knees, spread his legs wide and placed his hands in back of his head as he tightened every muscle and thrust his pelvis out for inspection. He kept his head in a straight-ahead position and bent his legs just slightly so that his ass muscles were tightened and his genitals were thrust out as much as possible.

"Well, the boy knows how to display himself, anyway," David said as he casually reached down, grabbed the boy's ballsac and squeezed tightly with one hand while stroking the long smooth shaft with his other hand. "Don't you shoot, boy," he cautioned as he increased his stroking.

"No, master," the slave boy whispered between clenched teeth as he moaned from the ball squeezing. But his display posture, including his pelvis being thrust out as much as possible, remained perfect no matter what was being done to his body.

"The boy's well-trained," David said as he suddenly let loose of the boy and slapped him sharply across the ass as a sign of dismissal. "But that's what I'd expect of any slave THE FIRM owned. Can you imagine, Forrest, what this boy will go through before the evenings over if we're representative of most of the invited guests? He's going to be a mighty sore boy before the last guests have been welcomed," as he reached over and pinched the boy's swollen tit again.

"Most of the guests are going to play with him a lot rougher than we have," Forrest commented as he stepped behind the slave and thrust his finger up the boy's ass as far as it would go in a single thrust and then proceeded to twist his finger back and forth in a pumping motion as a low moan escaped the boy's lips. "He's still tight," Forrest exclaimed as he continued his probing up the boy's asshole. "The right exercises keep these boys tight no matter how much they're used. At least, I've found that's true with my stock. You would assume THE FIRM would know every slave exercise there was by this time!"

Forrest removed his finger only after pushing it into the boy's hole all the way and then presented it to the slave's mouth for cleansing. The boy sucked the finger in and gave it a through cleansing without hesitation. "Thank you, master," came out of the boy as soon as he could talk.

"Only 500 more customers to go tonight, boy," David laughed as he slapped the slave on the rump and guided Forrest into the next hall: the pre-inspection room. "Keep up the good work!" but by this time the slave had dropped to his knees to kiss the feet of the next arriving customer.

But apparently at least half of the customers had already arrived in that the hall was filled with all 183 offerings that night as well as at least 250 customers strolling around inspecting the available goods. The slaves were all manacled into display positions at the pedestals scattered throughout the huge inspection area. All goods were displayed so that total access to all parts of their bodies was convenient and various 'tests' could be run by potential customers, yet the slaves' were highly restricted in their movement. As the two men glanced around the inspection area, they saw slaves being butt-fucked with huge dildos as the slaves bent over grabbing their knees or ankles, other slaves on their knees swallowing down huge dildos or the customer's own tools, some slaves bent over the pedestals receiving a violent lashing to see how well they responded to pain, some slaves receiving a "test fuck" from a potential purchaser, while many others were trying to hold inspection posture while customers pinched and squeezed their balls and tits, stroked and massaged their pricks, and ran their hands over sleek arms, legs, chests, and stomachs to feel for musculature and skin texture. Occasionally, a slave's head would be sharply jerked back by his hair to test reaction, fingers were inserted into slave's mouths to check out teeth and suctioning potential, while still others were in the throes of being "milked" to test semen quantity, texture, consistency, smell, and taste. Judging from past pre-sales inspections the two men had attended, most slaves could expect to shoot off at least three or four times prior to the end of the inspection period. Despite their training to not discharge unless they had their master's permission no matter what was done to them, in this case the 'master' wanted the discharge, so all the slave could do was try not to shoot off until he was ordered to do so to save himself for the sale. No matter how well-trained, few slaves left the sales without having their balls drained dry somewhere along the line. Ironically, dependent on who bought them and for what, for many it might be the last time they could expect relief for months since most owners wanted their slaves kept in a state of constant need to unload knowing this kept the boys interested and motivated in what was expected of them at all times.

Some slaves looked exhausted from what had been done to them already although they knew they would have to endure to the end of the inspection period no matter what. Some were already crying from the frustration of their helpless position, but the crying was often mixed with a sexual excitement clearly evidence in their chronically erect organs. Other slaves sweated profusely, not from the heat which was kept at a very comfortable level, but from their continual state of arousal and the sheer excitement of being on display as a possession for sale. Most dripped cum incessantly, no matter how short a time since they had last discharged, and, as they were almost continually fondled, stroked, pinched, and caressed in their most sensitive areas, there was little they could do to escape the perpetual arousal so evident in their bodies at all times. Even the frequent lashings, slaps, whippings, and electrical probes to elicit pain reactions only seemed to heighten their sexual response rather than hinder it – a sure sign of good slave training THE FIRM, of all groups, would insure. Most slaves displayed the angry red stripes and numerous skin burns across their backs and asses caused by the ever-handy whips the customers were encouraged to use to test "reaction". A few who had failed to "display" to THE FIRM's standards for one reason or another were now bleeding profusely in that THE FIRM's own slave handlers brooked little nonsense when it came to customer inspection, and the special whips they carried tore into the flesh for maximum intense pain despite the obvious risk of scarring the goods being sold and the terrified screeches that occasionally rent the air.

"Looks promising," Forrest said excitedly. "I have a feeling I'm going to part with a little investment money tonight!"

"Slave fever," David laughed as he offhandedly reached down and hefted the prodigious balls of a strikingly handsome and incredibly muscular African boy of about 20 as if to weigh them. The African, banded behind his scrotum for maximum protrusiveness, thrust his pelvis out for utmost access.

"This boy's equipment alone will certainly bring a good price," David added as he strongly massaged the huge balls which led to an instant erection of the slave's equally big shaft. "If he's well-trained, some owner could use this boy quite well for years and years." The boy kept his eyes properly downcast and remained mute as he was being discussed as if he wasn't even there, reflecting a degree of decent voice-training in his past.

"Let's see what his ass is like," Forrest asked as he grabbed a 12-inch thick dildo from the convenient stand. "Bend over, boy. I want to see your asshole."

The African promptly bent over placing his hands on his wide-spread knees so his asshole was exposed for inspection and easy entry. Assuming the boy had been lubed prior to being placed up for inspection, Forrest jammed the huge dildo all the way up his hole with no preliminaries.

"Uhhhhh," the boy groaned loudly as the dildo tore into his body until he thought he was being split in half and the pain caused tears to flow down his cheeks as he struggled to maintain position. Forrest started ramming the ramrod in and out as fast as he'd first forced it up the boy's channel and the boy's moans, despite every effort on his part, grew in intensity.

"You like that, boy?" Forrest asked as he increased the tempo of his pounding.

"Yes, master," the boy whispered between gritted teeth.

"You lie well, boy," Forrest laughed as he stepped up the intensity of the ass pounding and slapped the boy so hard on his ass check even his black skin turned a bright maroon. "But you'll learn to like it real well once you're properly broken in," and he chuckled as he pulled the dildo out almost all the way and then plunged it back in as far as it would go as the boy's moaned even more loudly and the tears spilled to the floor more copiously.

"He's not lying, Forrest," David said as he reached down and grabbed the swollen penis dripping steadily by now. "Here's the real test – this boy's even bigger now than when we started – so he likes it all right. And he'll like it even better once he gets used to a little size up his butt. This boy's a natural born slave I tell you. The proof's right here – as he squeezed the swollen penis tightly. He'll be easy to train."

Forrest reached down to the boy's mouth and stuck three fingers down his throat as far as they would go. The boy gagged but then recovered quickly and swallowed the fingers down into his throat and proceeded to give them a massage with his well-trained throat muscles.

"This fucker's mouth is trained to all get out," Forest exclaimed, "even if his ass isn't. He sucks like a vacuum cleaner I tell you."

"Where's he from, anyway?" David said as he stopped stroking the boy's dripping shaft and opened the log book. "Says here he's from the Cameroons, captured at the age of 18 by the rebel forces there, family wiped out by the war, and readily agreed to be sold as a slave to a French trading house in Yaoundé when given the option of that or remaining a prisoner of the rebel forces. Smart move there I bet – at least he's been well fed and sheltered, looks like. Had his basic slave training by those original French owners, completing obedience, subservience, body maintenance, and voice-training to their complete satisfaction. Sold to agents of THE FIRM at age 19 for advanced training and subsequent resale potential. Has completed training in physique development, universal sexual usage, and customer appeal enhancement. Says here that due to his looks, youth, and training, he will not be sold for under the Level 1 sales price and that he's guaranteed by THE FIRM for the first 30 days with 100% purchase price refundable with no questions asked; 80% resale guaranteed over the first six months. No legitimacy questions with signed title papers of ownership guaranteed by both Cameroon and French colonial governments as well as THE FIRM."

"God – Level 1 means 500 grand minimum," Forrest said, "but, you know, this boy's probably worth it," he added as he continued plunging the huge dildo in and out of the boy.

"He'll sell for a lot more than that," David said softly. "He's got 15 prime years ahead of him where he would appeal to almost anyone for anything, but especially doing what he's doing right now – offering up a great fuck!. After that, he'll still be good for another 15 years to a less discriminating buyer who can't afford fresh meat, and then you could work him as a laborer or house servant for a few years after that dependent on what he looked like by then. If all else failed – look at the muscles and physique on that boy – you could easily get your money back just hiring him out as a laborer – he looks like he'd last for the next 50 years doing just that, even at five bucks an hour ninety hours a week – let's see: 52 weeks a year times 90 hours a week times $5 an hour – by the time this boy's 42 years old he would have earned 500 grand. By the time he was 50, figuring in his food and shelter costs, he would have turned a good profit. And that's hiring him out at less than minimum wage. Now let's add his other talents like the one's he is showing us right now. Selling that body for some serious pleasure would earn his price back in just a few years if he were marketed right."

"Yeah, and we'll enjoy him ourselves along the way, David," Forrest smiled as he pulled the dildo out of the boy with a loud plop and smartly slapped the boy's ass with the command: "Position". The boy shot upright with his arms behind his head, all muscles tensed, and his swollen genitals thrust out for display.

"What's his number, David? I'm definitely going to bid up to 700 grand on this one," Forrest said with finality.

"You're a greedy little bastard, Forrest," David laughed as he slammed the log book shut. Now let's get serious and start looking for something to really stuff those cages at home with. By the way, Forrest, this one's numbered 174M-1 – write it down – you know how damn forgetful you are!" Turning to the boy, he slapped him on his ass sharply again and ordered, "Relax, boy. If all goes well, my friend here will be loaning you out to me by tomorrow!"

"Thank you, master," was all the boy could say as he relaxed. But a smile spread across his properly lowered face as the two wandered on.

— — — — —

It was ecstasy to be wanted and valued. Since the advent of the civil war at the age of 8 and the death of his entire family in the massacre of his home village by the rebels, he had known nothing but desperation, overwhelming feelings of loneliness, the chronic anguish of being alien and unwanted, and, finally, the total despair of even keeping alive. When captured by the rebels, it was almost a relief until he realized they had no intention of wasting food and shelter on a personage useless to them, especially one who had every reason to hate them. When he agreed to sign himself over to be sold to the small illicit band of remaining French colonists in the capitol of Yaoundé, he at least knew he was worth enough to be fed. Although he was only 18 at the time, they still valued his willingness to earn his keep by helping out around the house as a willing manservant and when quickly pressed into serving their sexual needs, they actually seemed appreciative between their arrogant commands and dictates characteristic of a first experience in total ownership of another human.

Although he might have preferred freedom in happier, more secure times, the use of his body for their pleasure seemed a small price to pay to be alive – to be cared for – to even be valued. After a while, getting fucked regularly, sucking them off at their whimsy, and sitting quietly while they played with his genitals and tits seemed no different or more demanding than cleaning the house, washing the dishes, serving dinner, waiting bar, and tending the grounds. For all he knew, every other captive was probably doing the same thing – certainly every slave he met was happy enough to do what they could to keep their masters happy. When he heard the Frenchmen tell THE FIRM that he was pretty well slave-trained, he had to agree with them. It was really the only life he had known. And he couldn't say he was unhappy so far – especially compared to his life prior to enslavement. Yes, he had made the right choice all right.

And, now, if those two handsome young men would buy him, he'd be about as happy as he could imagine. They wanted him so bad he could almost taste their need. And to think they liked him so much they were willing to pay all that money for him. He never dreamed anyone could care that much for another human being – let alone someone like him – just a slave to start with. He'd make them a slave worthy of their investment. If only they could be the purchaser. But he knew he had no choice in who bought him – he'd go to top dollar – that was the way things were in the real world of capitalism – and he'd have to cooperate totally with whoever bought him. But he could dream!

– – – – –

"Position," the middle aged woman commanded in her shill voice. The boy placed his hands behind his head as he thrust his pelvis out for inspection. He felt a cold bony hand with sharp nails encircle his balls and churn them through the vein-lined fingers.

"Gladys, why don't you get something like this?" her companion, even older, asked. "He'd sweeten you up, you ol' bitch!" the companion laughed as she grabbed his prick and starting stroking and squeezing. "Looks like he's hung well enough to tickle your tubes, you ol' hussy, and he's young enough to outlast even you!"

The cold hand hefted his balls as if weighing them and then moved to his right tit pinching it painfully between the nail of her thumb and forefinger. "Well, these tits have been worked on plenty – look how they're all swollen. That's the trouble of getting here a little late – the merchandise is pretty well picked over by this time," and she grabbed his whole tit with her knuckle and twisted until he gasped in pain. "Jesus, his tits are so swollen they're almost as big as mine," she exclaimed as she reached over with her other hand and twisted the other tit until the boy groaned deeply and thought he just might pass out from the extreme pain right here on the inspection pedestal. "Has he got any juice left in those balls?" she queried as she continued twisting the swollen nubs.

"The way's he's dripping I would think so," her companion said as she stroked his shaft so hard he could feel the skin chaffing and he again gasped from this new source of pain.

"Ah, the hell with him," the first lady said as she slapped the nipple she'd been twisting. "He's not my type anyway. I want something a lot smaller and a hell of a lot whiter – fucking this would be like falling into a dark abyss – I'd feel like I'd mounted a horse or something. Let's keep looking – they've got to have something better than this around here!"

———

"Forrest, look! Identical twins," David said as he saw the pair of 21-year-olds chained to the same pedestal. "Perfect," he continued as he grabbed first one set of genitals and then the other and stimulated the boys to full erection. "Nicely equipped down here, good and muscular all over, and I love that tapered look of theirs with those big shoulders and those tiny little waists – and those muscular little globes for a butt are a nice touch too," he said as ran his hands over the features he was describing. "Don't you love their cute looks with those big eyes and smooth skin and how refreshing to have some small bodies for a change – why, they couldn't be a touch over 5'4" – compact but very well-built," he continued, as he felt the boys' tits until they too became erect. "Bend over, boys, and grab your ankles – I want to see those assholes of yours."

Both slaves promptly complied and their widely spaced legs assured their assholes were open for full inspection. David jammed a finger into each proffered hole without hesitation and noted the lack of resistance from either twin.

"Great, Forrest," David said. "They're used to it and the way they're massaging my finger now with their butt muscles shows they've had considerable training."

"What's their numbers, David?" Forrest said with a tone of resignation. "I can tell already you're going to bid on these two. More crowding of the cages," he laughed.

"I can't reach the log book while I'm finger fucking them, Forrest. Would you mind looking it up, and, while you're at it, where did these two cuties come from, anyway?"

"The numbers are 144-M2 and 145-M2, so THE FIRM is not expecting top dollar on them – probably because of their size, but it says if you buy both together they'll give you a 25 percent discount since they feel their guarantee will hold up a lot better if the two have the same owner. That makes sense – THE FIRM always seems to know what it's doing all right. David, it sounds like a real buy if you take the both of them. You could always sell them off separately later if you wanted and had the right buyer in hand. Let's see," Forrest said as he thumbed through the pages of the log, "the boys are of French-Canadian birth, orphaned before three, raised in an unbelievable number of foster homes, runaways at 14 to Mexico, and imprisoned in Mexico City for public prostitution in the tourist areas. Upon release, they were working out of a pimp's stable in Acapulco and arrested a few months later for soliciting, public prostitution, and drug dealing. This time they were sentenced for life in a Mexican federal prison, but the warden sold them to THE FIRM to enhance his retirement fund after the boys agreed to sign the necessary papers. THE FIRM's had them for two months intensive training, but feels, with their background, that's plenty to withstand the rigors of their new life. Sold together, they're fully guaranteed for the 30 day money-back guarantee, but THE FIRM will extend the 80% guarantee for five years since these boys took to their training so readily. – sounds like they don't expect one drop of trouble out of these boys no matter where they end up," Forrest commented on the log summary report.

"They're mind!" David said with some finality as if he intended to outbid any and all for this handsome pair.

— — — — —

As the evening progressed, Forrest really did "slave fever" and selected a 25 year-old Mexican with the body of an Aztec god and the sleek good looks usually seen in cologne ads, a couple of blond Germans in their late teens who were all muscle and prick but were covered in blood in that the slave overseers had intervened when they had balked once while on display (an old man kept "cracking their nuts" with his incredibly strong grip and they had the audacity to break position), a devastatingly handsome Pole who, at the tender age of 21, was going to his fifth owner through a bizarre set of circumstances, an Arab boy no more than 18 who had a swimmer's build: willowy and slim – almost effeminate – but unbelievably sexy, and an American black sold to THE FIRM out of the Mississippi penal system who was pure black, pure muscle, and pure stud, but totally compliant and always willing as a result of extensive slave training both at the prison and by THE FIRM. With the African he'd originally selected, he was facing a total expenditure of close to 3.5 to 4 million before the night was over.

David, in addition to the French-Canadian twins he already selected, added a Polynesian slave of 18 from some obscure island only THE FIRM knew about, an handsome 19-year-old Cambodian boy bought out of a refugee camp by the FIRM, a devastatingly beautiful Czech boy of 19 who THE FIRM had bought out of a male brothel in Prague, and two of a brand new breed just being introduced by THE FIRM: slaves bred to specifications on some new breeding station THE FIRM had set up a number of years ago on an uncharted island in the Indian Ocean. The latter two were 18, considered by THE FIRM to be the idea age for first sale of this new line of trained-since-birth and fully developed slaves. Like Forrest, he could expect to hand over close to 4 million to THE FIRM if he got his first choices of stock. David, however, was usually one who didn't let money stand in his way.

— — — — —

"Those cages are going to be crowded! All these new ones will have to be double-caged until we get at least 30 new cages installed as soon as possible!" David said to Adam and Sergei as they handed the truckload of new slaves over to the two seasoned slave overseers as soon as THE FIRM had delivered them in their unmarked truck. "Save those shipping overalls from THE FIRM even though they are covered in sweat and blood right now. Jesus, Forrest, look at those German boys – the way their overalls are half blood by now, I imagine their backs are still bleeding from the beating THE FIRM gave them while they were being inspected. Well, that may be the only way they can learn some slave lessons until they get a little older," David sighed. "After they're laundered, we can use those overalls again to ship some of our boys out as we find a good owner for them. Clean them up thoroughly inside and out – three enemas for each one – God knows what's been up their butt the past 24 hours – scrub that hide of theirs until they turn bright red, body shave every damn one of them with the exception of their head hair, lube them fresh, get them started on their slave feed – they probably haven't been fed for at least 18 hours since I know THE FIRM never feeds before a big sale, butt-plug them with the standard 8-incher and then cage them for a good well-earned 15-hour rest. These boys are tuckered out after that long inspection time and the sale itself. But send that African boy up to Master Forrest when he's been cleansed and fed and send those twins up to me, Adam," David said. "After all, I've waited half the night to really try out those twins to see if they're as good as they look. And Master Forrest here needs to get milked himself after all the goings on tonight!"

"Yes, Master," Adam said with lowered eyes and motioned for Sergei to start giving the first boys their enemas.

"And Adam," David added, "remind me to get those new cages ordered as soon as I awake tomorrow. With two in a cage, these boys really can't rest up too well and you be sure and shackle them good before caging them. Otherwise, they'll spend all night playing with each other, knowing slaves the way I do," he chuckled.

"Yes, Master," Adam said, adding, "you sure know how slaves think, Master David, if you will allow me to comment so brazenly," matching his tone of humility with lowered eyes and his head bowed as low as his high neck collar would allow.

— — — — —

Two days later the twins both had mighty sore butts from the repeated fucking they'd gotten from first Master David and later Master Forrest. In addition, their throats felt dry and stretched after sucking both their new owner and his friend off too many times to remember. They had only been allowed to leave their master's bedroom once to be fed, cleansed out inside and out, re-shaved and re-lubed. Since they hadn't been allowed any release themselves, they both sported perpetual hard-ons. But this was heaven compared to the constant abuse they got from those ugly old guards and even uglier warden in that filthy Mexican prison. And both their master and his friend were good looking, and sure knew how to fuck a boy properly. They had to admit that since being enslaved they'd actually learned to enjoy having their bodies used and found significant satisfactions in pleasing their owners no matter what the demands were. So, all in all, they sensed a marked improvement in their life so far and smiled inwardly at their good fortune.

—————

The African smiled as he lifted his legs over the shoulders of his new owner and placed his butt in the best position for his master to fuck him for the tenth time in the two days he'd spent in the upstairs bedroom. After his master entered him all the way, he tightened his butt muscles and began to gently massage his master's prick with the kneading motion he'd been taught by his French owners years ago. As he did all the work required for a good fucking with the pumping movements of his chute muscles, his owner sucked his tits until they were swollen twice their normal size and the tingling feelings of intense tension from the tit-sucking added immeasurably to the boy's pleasurable excitement of being fucked, expressed primarily by his rigid dripping penis caught between the two bodies. Inevitably, he again felt his owner tense up, and with a loud moan, empty his seed deep into the boy's body once again before collapsing on top of the boy's sweat-coated torso. The African remembered to squeeze the erupting prick as hard as he could with his ass muscles so his owner could receive maximum pleasure in his discharge.

"Good boy," his owner commented as he withdrew his shaft from the boy's ass and presented it to the boy who quickly scooted down to perform a thorough month cleansing of the still-dripping prick while fighting hard to keep himself from discharging without his master's permission.

"Uh," the boy answered since his mouth was now stuffed.

His owner reached down and felt the slave's rampant prick between them dripping considerable amounts of leaking cum. "Don't you shoot, boy," he warned as he playfully stroked the black shaft a few times for emphasis. We want to keep you motivated and interested at all times now that you belong to this house," he laughed as he moved down and began to massage the swollen balls rather forcefully. "Jesus, these balls feel full. David's going to love them that way – he always claims a slave's balls should be packed full all the time," he chuckled as he continued his vigorous massage. He abruptly jerked his prick out of the boy's mouth, let loose of the African's balls, and said, "You douche that butt out good in the bathroom, boy! I'll see if Master David wants to fuck you again – he sure reveled in it the last time – but he'll want you freshened up in your hole, I'm sure. I'll tell him to play with those packed balls of yours – he'll enjoy that I bet! You like it when Master David fucks you, boy?"

"Yes, master," the African answered with lowered head and a tone of intense gratitude.

As the warm water of the douche filled his bowls, he sighed in contentment. It was the happiest he'd ever been.

— — — — —

But the African wasn't to get fucked by Master David that afternoon as it turned out. Both David's and Forrest's exploration of their new property was interrupted by a visit from one of the owners of THE FIRM – Mr. Broadley himself who had arrived in his usual style. A shiny black Rolls-Royce limousine with matching black liveried chauffeur stood at the curb. The two possessions seemed to compete for attention: the gleaming rare car itself vs. the incredibly handsome black done up in a skin-tight uniform tailored to show off every attribute of his magnificent physique but hiding his thick slave collar from public view. Both objects stood at rigid attention while their owner entered the house.

"David," Mr. Broadley said warmly as he shook his hand, and "Forrest," he repeated the gesture. "So good of you to see me without notice. I thought you'd be at home what with all that new stock on hand," Mr. Broadley smiled knowingly. When the two men smiled back, he ventured, "With the looks of some of that Level 1 stock you bought, I'm surprised you have the energy left to make it down the stairs," chuckling as he sat down in the comfortable chair offered him by David.

"I'd like a drink," David said. "Could I offer you one, Mr. Broadley, and I bet Forrest could use one too," as he clapped his hands lightly and Sergei, naked, freshly shaved, and gleaning with body oils, suddenly appeared in the doorway with his head properly bowed for taking instructions. "Martinis OK, Mr. Broadley, or would a Scotch be better?"

"Scotch on the rocks, thank you," Mr. Broadley responded.

"Sergei," David switched to a commanding tone, "A Scotch with plenty of ice for Mr. Broadley here and two martinis for Forrest and me, and then I want you to offer yourself to Mr. Broadley here if he's so inclined this afternoon."

"Yes, master," Sergei said humbly as he left to prepare the drinks.

"I'll take a rain check on using that big Russian," Mr. Broadley laughed. "I remember when you bought him from that wholesaler in Moscow, David. Working out OK despite the lack of THE FIRM's guarantees?" Mr. Broadley teased. "You always take a chance buying from these foreign up-starts," Mr. Broadley cautioned.

"You're probably right, Mr. Broadley, but in this case it worked out fine. Sergei seems to like his slavery better than any other options and we've never had the slightest bit of trouble with him since we've had him – been almost five years now – and he's invaluable as an overseer – takes to shaping up the new stock with a real lust it seems," David replied with a broad smile.

Sergei reentered with the drinks, fell to his knees to properly offer the drinks to each party, and humbly invited Mr. Broadley to use him in any way with an almost pleading look in his eye.

As Mr. Broadley reached down and felt Sergei's ringed tits, he said, "I can see what you mean, David. He does seem to be well-trained as you say. That's what I'm here to talk to you two about," he changed tone but continued to play with Sergei's nipples who, arching his back, thrust out his beautifully sculptured pecs for the convenience of his master's guest.

"THE FIRM has noted, as you'll not be surprised I'm sure, that both of you have bought considerable stock over the past few years – at least enough to get into the upper 10 percent of our customers. But we've also noticed that you have managed to resell a lot of that stock at considerable profit after further acclimation and training. Frankly, we're impressed. But I know that you can't extend yourself too much further with your own capital. So, right to the point, we want to extend an invitation and I'm sure you two will take it in the right way. We want you to consider becoming agents of THE FIRM, especially finding and buying the type of stock that would meet our very high quality standards and, with a lot of training once they're purchased, THE FIRM could guarantee fully. You'll use our money – you'll find our resources are almost inexhaustible – with no questions asked. All expenses will, of course, be covered in the type of travel and lodging accommodations you two are accustomed to – first class in all respects – any legal problems will be handled by THE FIRM's own lawyers throughout the world – the best legal minds in the business I might add – and we'll give you all the help you need to reach your goals – both our own hired staff as well as the considerable permanently owned staff we keep at the main slaving depots around the world – 16 of them now – Stockholm, London, Moscow, Berlin, Tunis, Riyadh, Beirut, Abidjan, Dar Es Salaam, Nouakchott, Palermo, Rangoon, Buenos Aires, Mexico City, and, of course our two in this country. And we're going to open pilot operations in Rio, where I understand the supply is most plentiful but the local operators there are pretty pathetic with practically no training taking place prior to sale – and another one in a business-friendly African or Middle Eastern country if the supply keeps increasing like it has over the past few years – probably the Sudan, Zanzibar or the Congo – we're trying to strike a deal with the governments there as I speak." Sergei moaned softly as his tits swelled even larger in the continuing simulation from Mr. Broadley's busy fingers. "Does this boy have a well-trained mouth?" he continued without changing his tone.

"Try the Russian boy, Mr. Broadley," David said softly. "You won't be disappointed."

Turning to Sergei, he said, "Suckle our guest and be quick about it. The slave twisted quickly and placed his open mouth in front of Mr. Broadley's crouch, lowered the zipper on the expensive trousers, and swallowed the guest's penis to its base in one quick gulp.

"Um," Mr. Broadley responded, as he shifted around in his chair a little to better accommodate the sucking. "This boy is well-trained, it seems. May I offer the use of my chauffeur just wasting away out on your sidewalk? I think you'd especially like him, Forrest, with your appreciation of dark-skinned boys."

Forrest stepped over to the window and glanced out at the astonishingly handsome black, still ramrod straight. "It's tempting, Mr. Broadley, but I'll take a rain-check. I'm pretty played out right at this moment," he said sheepishly with a blush.

"I understand, but I'll make sure you enjoy the pleasures of that big hunk of meat at the first opportunity. He loves to be loaned out – I imagine because it's the only possible chance he ever gets to unload. I haven't let him shoot in over three months now and he's actually beginning to smell like cum he's in such need all the time," Mr. Broadley laughed. "But he's still the best fuck I've ever owned and I just can't part with him – despite the fact I've been offered over a cool million for him just last week. Well, heart over pocketbook, I guess," he laughed again.

Sergei was breathing heavily through his nose as he continued the oral massage of his master's guest combined with deep suctioning. His throat muscles were clearly outlined above his slave collar as his stretched throat adjusted to the swelling penis inside him.

David looked serious and asked, "Mr. Broadley, what sort of commission would we be talking about and how many slaves would we reasonably be able to buy up for THE FIRM over, say, a year's time – assuming we had all the help you indicated and assuming we were working on this rather diligently, despite our activities here in New York in our own trade which, as you are no doubt already aware, would have to continue whether we were working for THE FIRM or not. You can't just walk away from stock, as you well know. The maintenance, the training, and the location of buyers – all of that has to continue until either our stock is completely sold off or we just wholesale it."

"Your last question first, David, and a good one it is," Mr. Broadley replied as he ran his hand slowly through the slave's long blond hair that was sucking him. "You and Forrest can continue the same level of slave trading you are currently engaged in and work for THE FIRM as you have time, or, if you prefer to go full time with this, THE FIRM will buy up all your stock at a profit you couldn't begin to expect from private buyers and simply add your stock to that already marked for the next big sale. That part is your choice and up to you – you can't lose either way. If THE FIRM buys up all your stock, I imagine, without even knowing exactly how many you have on hand or having looked them over myself, I'd say that we're talking close to a 10 million transaction for both of you. That's a nice little kitty if I do say so myself. Now to your first excellent question. If you went into this full-time, and with the new sources I mentioned, THE FIRM's board thinks you could obtain 500 to 700 top quality new stock a year between the two of you that would cost us roughly $200,000 each at point of origin on the average. Being conservative and saying the first year you could only buy up 500, that's $100 million expenditure on our part the first year alone. We would offer you a five percent "finder's fee" on THE FIRM's retail sales of your stock – not wholesale, mind you – but the actual price THE FIRM would get at their sales after the body enhancement and slave training has been successfully completed. The average price of THE FIRM's fully trained slaves is around $410,000 currently. That's over $20,000 "finder's fee" on each slave we sell. Multiply that by 500 head and we're talking $10 million profit a year between the two of you. That's as much in one year as either one of you could cash out for now. In two years, each of you could double your current capitol. And I'm assuming you can only buy 500 a year. If you could up that to 700 or 800, you'd be clearing a cool $15 million a year. Of course," Mr. Broadley warned – he briefly got a glassy-eyed look and paused as Sergei reached his goal and Mr. Broadley's seed spilled into the slave's throat – "it really wouldn't work out to quite that much. Some stock, no matter how good you are in the business, will not reach THE FIRM's high standards in either training or body development and have to be sold to wholesalers dealing in inferior stock before the training is completed – a few get sick and die on you – then we invariably lose one or two a year to overzealous slave overseers who occasionally go just a bit too far in their training efforts. We've even had one or two who turned out to be untrainable even for our excellent trainers – probably the best in the world – no matter how much they were beaten, starved, shocked, humiliated, and tortured. I hate to admit it, but it seems there really are a few people in the world – damn few let me assure you – sort of like 'martyrs' or the dumbest, most rigid people on earth dependent on your point of view I suppose – who simply cannot be made totally subservient and under the complete control of someone of the same species and we simply sell them off for medical experiments or spare parts. Either way, that's the end of them! Overall, we figure in a three percent loss factor even with our agents. Your job, of course, is to make sure your purchases don't exceed that three percent leeway and that the stock delivered to THE FIRM for training and development will bring top price at final market." Sergei waited patiently for permission to remove his mouth from around the guest's now flaccid penis.

"Put it back after you've made sure you've cleaned it properly, boy," Mr. Broadley commanded as he patted Sergei on the head. As Sergei quietly zipped Mr. Broadley's pants, he never moved his muscular highly tapered torso from the position he'd assumed for the guest's manipulation of his tits which now resumed. "This boy's well-trained and good-looking enough to be sold by THE FIRM," Mr. Broadley stated in a congratulatory tone. "You found this slave boy in some obscure market – you can do the same for us and make a lot more money in the process," he added as he took a tit in both hands and squeezed hard until Sergei tensed and moaned deeply. "You sure you wouldn't like to use the blackboy out there?" he added gesturing toward the front door. "He's American and has equipment sized like you rarely see, even among THE FIRM's offerings that, as you know, almost always have that attribute as a prerequisite for any slaves they purchase. At least take a look?" he urged.

Without further ado, he stood up and headed for the door which he opened with a flourish, eyeing the black slave still rigidly at attention by the Rolls-Royce, and ordered him inside with a simple gesture of his finger. The black instantly complied and before we knew it, the large liveried chauffeur was in our living room, hands in back, with lowered head and his feet spread wide apart.

"Strip and posture," Mr. Broadley said sharply. The slave shucked his high leather boots and simply peeled out of the skin-tight uniform. He was devoid of any under clothing whatsoever so he was stark nude within seconds, it seemed, and was standing in front of us in 'posture': hands in back of his head, every muscle tensed, pelvis and chest thrust out, and head lowered as far as his thick slave collar would allow. His jet-black skin gleamed from a light sheen of oil spread over his totally hairless body. The first thing you noticed was his massive musculature everywhere – then his truly gigantic circumcised manhood, now arching out at a straight angle from his body dripping copious amounts of pre-cum – and, finally, the fact he sported slave rings everywhere his uniform covered: two-inch gold rings in both tits and his navel and a one-inch ring fitted behind his huge balls so his genitals were constantly thrust out for display. His balls, stretched tightly from the close-fitting genital ring in back of them, looked like large oversized black mangos and were obviously hard and swollen from lack of draining over a period of time. And, as Mr. Broadley had said, the prick was awesome: 14" hard and at least 4" thick as I tried to fit my hand around it and found I couldn't.

"I was offered over a million for this boy just last week," Mr. Broadley repeated himself proudly. "And he fucks even better than he looks," he added as he plowed his middle and forefinger up the boy's asshole and moved it around vigorously but the boy didn't flinch one iota from the anal assault. "Now this is the type of boy THE FIRM's looking for, David and Forrest. Go out and look for them and we'll make some real money," he exclaimed as he reached in front of the black with his free hand and started vigorously stroking the rampant shaft.

"Don't you shoot, boy," he said menacingly.

"No master," the black slave answered through clenched teeth, whether from the vigorous finger-fucking of his ass or his attempt to keep from cumming due to the stroking of his shaft, it was difficult to ascertain.

"Mr. Broadley, Forrest and I are used to – how should we put it – certain amenities available at all times," David said firmly.

"I said all expenses and first-class everything – travel, lodging, food, you name it – first class on THE FIRM," Mr. Broadley said as he increased the tempo of stroking the monstrous shaft, now dripping volumes on the beautiful Persian carpet on the floor.

"No, I understood that, Mr. Broadley. I'm talking about other amenities more important."

"I'm afraid I don't understand you, David," Mr. Broadley looked perplexed as his slave gasped in desperate efforts to keep from shooting off as the stimulation front and rear continued unabated.

"He's talking about getting serviced regularly and promptly by some interesting slave meat like the boy you're playing with now, Mr. Broadley," Forrest interjected. "Both of us are spoiled rotten in having our pleasure available at any and all times. It's been our life style for the past decade now. If we're always on the move looking for brand new, but untrained, meat for your market, what about the experienced, highly trained meat we're used to around the clock?"

"How thoughtless of me," Mr. Broadley laughed as he watched his black slave break out in a deep, dripping sweat all over his body as he frantically tried to comply to his owner's demands to not ejaculate.

"Master," the slave finally spoke, "I can't hold it anymore," he pleaded as cum began leaking a steady string out of his bursting prick.

"Of course you can, slave," Mr. Broadley said in a flat unsympathetic tone as he continued his manipulation of the boy's body, but within a minute he finally let loose of the slave's penis and withdrew his other hand out of the boy's asshole.

"Would it be all right if your Russian fucked this slave of mine for our amusement while I explain the details," Mr. Broadley asked as he bent his slave over for accessibility.

"Sure," David said. "Sergei doesn't get the chance to fuck anything very much as a slave. He'll especially enjoy fucking something as pretty as your slave boy there, won't you Sergei?"

"Oh, master, thank you, master," Sergei blurted out as he rose from his knees, grabbed the black slave by his hips, and, in one long thrust, entered the black's hole completely before his owner changed his mind. He started vigorously pumping to the accompaniment of low groans as the black slave totally complied with his master's wishes: subservient acceptance of being fucked by another slave simply for his master's amusement.

"Forrest, I'm glad you spoke up because there's a simple answer. THE FIRM will provide you at least two or three well-trained and experienced slaves of your choosing out of their own stock to accompany you wherever you go. They will serve as chauffeurs, valets, secretaries, and boy-Fridays in addition to their continual devotion to fulfillment of your pleasure needs whenever and wherever you choose. THE FIRM provides that small fringe benefit to all its agents. I apologize for not mentioning it earlier. No cost to either of you of course. Each time you swing into New York, you'll probably want to look over THE FIRM's new stock to see if you want to trade them in on some new meat. We certainly don't expect you to have to survive in the wilds without well-trained and experienced slave boys available to you. What did you think, David?" Mr. Broadley asked with a huge smile, "that THE FIRM expected you to just meet your needs the best way you could with the totally untrained stock you'll be buying up along the way? Why, that new stock you'd be buying are total virgins compared to anything we're used to like this blackboy here and that big blond humping him!" He laughed at the absurdity of the question as he watched his slave accommodate himself to the stalwart fucking he was receiving from the Russian slave now hunched over his back.

"Well, I didn't know," David explained, "but it would be a requirement after our 'spoilage' as Forrest puts it. But I have another question, Mr. Broadley. What sort of training are we to give slaves we're buying up? That could take up a lot of our time, especially if we got into some markets offering slaves who didn't sign themselves over to their new status. I understand some of those markets in Rio, the Sudan, Dar es Salaam, Abidjan, and even the markets in this country are increasingly receiving life-term government prisoners, street people, war prisoners where there's civil wars going on, chronic welfare cases including those termed unemployable, abduction and kidnapping cases, and some orphans, many of whom, when first placed into slavery, are anything but willing and compliant. All you can do with those slaves is let them know their lives are permanently and inalterably changed before you can even begin the simplest levels of basic slave training. We wouldn't have time for that if we're to locate 500 plus bodies a year who really would, with complete slave training behind them, bring top dollar at New York or another discriminating marketplace."

"Another excellent question, David," Mr. Broadley said as he reached over and began to play with the black slave's balls as the black's fucking continued. THE FIRM'S Board of Directors was dead right about you two – you're naturals or you wouldn't even know the right questions to ask and both of you certainly do."

"THE FIRM realizes you need full time to locate the right kind of quality stock we demand and that search alone, along with the time to conclude purchase and proper legal papers, is a full time job for any team. Therefore, we don't expect you to have any responsibilities beyond purchase and conclusion of sales transactions. Slave custody, maintenance, health issues, inoculations, security, and the original basic compliance and obedience training are all the responsibility of our slave depot staff who are specialists in this sort of boring detail, and that includes shipment for subsequent training, advanced training and eventual sales venues. You look over the raw material, buy it up, get that sale iron-clad from a legal viewpoint, and get on with it. The 'dirty work' of shaping those minds and bodies to what will ultimately be displayed at THE FIRM's markets – the sales-ready stock that you and Forrest are so use to – is the job of some other specialists on THE FIRM's payroll. They work on commission and salary – you work on commission and expenses. But, take my word for it, your job is the most important in THE FIRM's operations – getting the stock we can train to our standards and will have almost universal sales appeal – and THE FIRM is willing to pay for that important job well done."

Sergei, panting heavily, looked at his master and asked, "Master, do you want me to unload into the slave?"

"Would you like to, Sergei?" David teased.

"Yes, master, yes," Sergei gasped for air as he increased the pumping into the black's butt.

"When did you last shoot?" David deliberately prolonged the agony knowing his slave hadn't been allowed to discharge in several months as Sergei broke out in a total body sweat as he tried to control cumming while continuing fucking the slave as ordered.

"Two months ago, master," he gasped. Risking his master's wrath and knowing he was exceeding the limits of good voice-training, he added, "I'll sure like to, Master."

"You're not on this earth to do what you like, you impertinent bastard," David answered. "It's what your owners like that matters. Why can't you get that through your thick slave skull?" he shouted. "Didn't they teach you anything when you were being trained?"

Sergei continued the fucking since he hadn't been ordered to stop, and tried every trick he knew to keep from discharging since he assumed he had exceeded the boundaries of slavery in asking to fulfill an immediate want and felt apprehensive about the strong punishment for impertinence he would no doubt receive in the very near future. This new anxiety helped him gain considerable self-control, he noted with satisfaction, and he accelerated the pounding into the black's ass to try to make up for his transgressions, hoping his good performance would mitigate the promised punishments.

"You're good with slaves," Mr. Broadley commented as his continued to stroke the black being fucked so thoroughly.

"Thanks for the compliment, Mr. Broadley, but, risking impertinence myself, may I ask that you place something under that boy's dripping penis. The way he's leaking cum, he going to ruin that carpet I just purchased for a king's ransom. That carpet cost almost as much as one of THE FIRM's boys," he joked.

"Don't worry, David, cum doesn't hurt a good Persian – and I'll have the boy lick up every drop before we leave. Believe me, I've had cum all over carpets like this for hours and I've not had one stain yet." Saying that, he jerked the boy's head down to the pool of his own cum and ordered him to lick the mess up which he did without hesitation as his fucking continued.

"OK, Sergei, shoot!" David ordered unexpectedly. Sergei tensed, trying his best to mute his scream of ecstasy as he shot deep into the black's ass – the first time he'd been allowed to unload, as he'd told his master, for over two months or so.

David looked at Forrest and said, "What do you want to do? Think it over a while? Sell our stock to THE FIRM right now and start making some real money? Take it on half time and see how we do, keeping all our stock around until we can profitably dispose of it? Or tell Mr. Broadley how much we enjoyed his visit, seeing his beautiful black slave, and working on our own as free-agents like we've been doing so well for the past five or six years?"

"Ten million each for our present stock, a probable $10 million minimum in commissions next year, and THE FIRM paying all expenses and loaning us two or three trained slaves of our choice for our private use? David, I'm ready to have a new employer!" Forrest said with conviction.

"Well, I'm glad you feel that way, Forrest. That way we can work together as a team! I made up my mind some time ago, but wanted to make sure you'll go with me. We're at our best as a team."

"Well said," Mr. Broadley said. "Let's celebrate by giving my boy here the treat of a lifetime and milk him properly for the first time in months."

"Sergei, withdraw and freshen our drinks," David commanded and the Russian instantly slipped his softening oversized shaft out of the black's ass and picked up the used glasses before leaving the room. As he returned and handed each man their new drink, David was now stroking the black slave's shaft, Forrest was massaging his swollen ballsac, and Mr. Broadley was continuing to fuck the boy with his cum-coated fingers.

"I'll take Sergei for my own use as a house steward rather than place him up for auction with the rest of your stock," Mr.

Broadley said. "That way, when you come back to your townhouse between buying trips you can pick him up and have him available for your use when you're back in town. You'll need someone who's good at handling slaves when you're home. And I'll keep him in good practice when you have to be gone."

Sergei beamed at his good fortune in not being placed up for auction at this time. He realized he could still service his two former masters when they were in town and service the obviously powerful Master Broadley when they were gone.

"Ah–AH-AHHH," the black screamed as he unloaded fully for the first time in months and he shot clear across the room onto a valuable antique armoire before heaving quarts of cum in load after load onto the Persian carpet below.

"This boy must have had a gallon of cum stored up in those balls," Forrest laughed as he squeezed the slave's balls to get the last drops out.

"Well, I guess I can stop my masterful stroking," David chuckled. "It seems to have had the desired effect."

"This boy has supper all ready for him," Mr. Broadley laughed. "By the time he cleans up that armoire, and slurps up all that juice on the floor, his tummy will be full for awhile, I'll wager."

The black slave slumped in total relief as the last string of cum dripped out and temporarily looked blank as he just stood there with, for once, no hands in or on any part of his body.

"Get that tongue busy, boy," Mr. Broadley cracked out. "Start over there with your cum on the armoire and get every drop, you hear me boy, every drop off that rug and where it's spilled over onto the floor. And don't tell me you're full either. Just think of this as supper, boy," as he slapped him on the ass sharply.

"Yes, master, thank you master," the boy got out with a tone of immeasurable gratitude for his unexpected relief before bending to the task at hand.

"And, Mr. Broadley, how about loan of this black boy here as one of our first personal servants?" David shyly asked.

"I just knew you'll ask for him first, David. But a deal's a deal – you can have him as long as you take good care of him and don't sell him at any price – I want this boy back," Mr. Broadley said almost affectionately as he stroked the boy on his head. The thrill of being owned by a truly caring master caused the boy to shiver all over as he busily slurped up and then savored the taste and texture of his own still warm cream.

CHAPTER II

PRINCE RASHID

"Good to hear from you again, your Highness," Mr. Broadley said cordially as soon as he recognized the voice on his Rolls-Royce's car phone. "Where are you calling from?"

"I'm in my jet heading to New York as we speak," Prince Jamel ibn Ibrahim ibn Saloman Rashid answered in his usual deep polished British English accent. "I have some business affairs to attend to at the New York office of OPEC but, Mr. Broadley, I also have some needs THE FIRM may be able to help me with. If past experience is any indicator, I'm sure we can do some business during my visit and I always prefer to deal with THE FIRM's top man if you don't mind the intrusion on your time, Mr. Broadley."

"Not at all, not at all, your Highness. THE FIRM is always eager to do business with you. I just hope we will be able to accommodate your needs this time as well as we have been able to in the past," Mr. Broadley said with confidence. "I know we charge a bit more than some other markets, but quality always costs a bit more."

"Yes, yes, you old rascal. Already jacking up the price, I see. But I will admit my last few purchases have proven to be satisfactory, even though one of THE FIRM's products is beginning to suffer some stamina problems as it gets older."

"Although all of THE FIRM's products are fully guaranteed, we never claim they last forever," Mr. Broadley laughed. "How long have you had this product, anyway, Prince Rashid?"

"About twenty years now," the Prince laughed, "so I suppose I've gotten my money's worth. Still, he brought more on the open market in Umm al-Qiawan than I paid two decades ago, so I can't complain. Even at 40, he's still in perfect shape and his training both at THE FIRM and later under my tutelage made him invaluable to the merchants in Umm al-Qiawan, all of whom are looking for a mature, experienced slave who can mold their own primitive stock into something sellable."

"Sounds like a good market for us to investigate, Prince Rashid, if we could ever get enough excess stock to expand our operations. What about your other purchases from THE FIRM?" Mr. Broadley inquired. "Have they worked out satisfactorily?"

"No complaints, Mr. Broadley. But my stock is getting rather depleted, what with one thing and another. Let's see, the last time we did business, I bought a huge Malaysian from you along with an American black, a blond from one of your breeding farms, two dark-haired olive-skinned Italian boys, and a young Czech muscle-boy with fantastic equipment. I've still got the blond, the Czech, and the American black, but the others are long gone, I'm afraid."

"I can see where you and I probably will do some business," Mr. Broadley chuckled. "Prince, just out of curiosity, what happened to those FIRM products you no longer have? You don't have to answer, of course Prince Rashid, in that it's really none of my business, but my curiosity exceeds my good manners, I'm afraid. I suspect your generous nature has once again benefitted your many friends," Mr. Broadley laughed.

"Well, you're partly right," the Prince chuckled along with his long-time friend from THE FIRM, Mr. Broadley, "The Malaysian died after I'd had him only a few years. Heart attack, I suspect. But I admit we tended to overwork him a bit. I used him to entertain all of the many oil company representatives on their visits to my kingdom and I'm afraid they were very demanding in their use of him. At one point, he was assigned to fifteen of them in a given night and the strain seemed to have taken its toll. He always gave everything he had to fulfilling his duties – maybe too much so. Perhaps THE FIRM over-trained the boy – who knows? But, as you suggested, his demise was probably due to my generosity in his use with the oil representatives, certainly not anything to do with his condition when I bought him from THE FIRM. And the two handsome Italian boys – ah – what beauties they were and so exquisitely trained – were gifts to favored sheiks in my own land that were most appreciative, after having expressed their admiration of their dark good looks and beautiful bodies every time they laid eyes on them in my palace. After those gifts, some oil exploration and production grants were quickly signed by the recipients of the gifts, as I'm sure they will be in the future – as long as those boys please their new masters as well as they were pleasing me. I'm sure they will, as their new masters were quite handsome in their own rights and even younger than they were." The Prince paused, reflecting, and then added, laughingly, "You should have seen their pricks spring up when they first saw their new masters. I thought they might shoot off right then and there before the Sheiks had even had a chance to look them over thoroughly. Those Italian slaves were always eager anyway no matter what use you had in mind for them – are all Italians that way?"

"All Italians THE FIRM deals with are," Mr. Broadley laughed. "If they're not when we get them, they will be when their training is completed."

"I'd like to look at some new Italian material," Prince Rashid injected, "as well as some new products off your breeding farms. That bred blond has a certain quality other slaves don't have, regardless of your fine training efforts – I suppose being born into service does something no amount of training can compete with."

"Bred slaves know nothing but slavery and have nothing to compare slavery with. They know they are slaves from the time they are born and will never be anything but vassals of service until they die. I suppose it does make a difference, although we have remarkably little trouble with slaves we break into perpetual servitude in our training programs. That's why we are able to guarantee each and every one," Mr. Broadley said proudly.

"I agree you have fine products, no matter where they originally came from or what they did before THE FIRM got hold of them. But bred slaves have definitely had a longer training period – from birth on!" Prince Rashid laughed.

"Sounds to me like I'm going to sell you at least four or five out of our pens," Mr. Broadley laughed. "With customers like you, I can plan to retire early."

"Get some likely prospects lined up if you will, Mr. Broadley, and I'll call you tomorrow after I finish my business at the OPEC Center. Do you think it would be possible for me to look over some potential stock tomorrow evening, or is that rushing you too much?

"For you, Prince Rashid, we'll make it possible. We'll have some interesting stock ready for display around 7 P.M. tomorrow at our main warehouse – we're in the same location you visited us at before – and I'll have a delicious dinner ready for the both of us so we can enjoy supping together as you shop."

"Excellent, Mr. Broadley. I knew I could count on you to accommodate my busy schedule."

"Prince, will you be taking your purchases with you back in your jet, or should we arrange shipping?"

"They'll go back with me. It'll give me a chance to find out what I really did buy from a wily old flesh peddler like you," Prince Rashid laughed.

"If age hasn't caught up with you, Prince, those boys will do well to crawl off that jet and I can only hope you'll give them a chance to recover before you put them to regular use," Mr. Broadley chuckled.

"Tomorrow for supper, then, Mr. Broadley?" the Prince concluded.

"Seven at the main warehouse, Prince."

— — — — —

"Driver, take me back to the main warehouse immediately," Mr. Broadley commanded as he placed the phone back in its holder. "We have much to do to prepare for the arrival of an important customer."

"Yes, master," the exceedingly handsome black replied, his head held high by the wide silver collar around his neck, only partially hidden by his skin tight brown chauffeur's uniform. He instantly flicked the turn signals on, and at the first opportunity, turned the huge Rolls back in the direction they had come from.

"Perhaps the Prince would like a boy like you," Mr. Broadley said as he studied the back of his chauffeur's head. "The last time he bought stock, he purchased an American black built much like yourself – very similar at least – although as I recall his nipples were a little more pronounced and his shaft was a little thicker than yours although he about equaled you in length. The Prince still has the boy in his service, though, so I don't know whether he'd be interested in you or not – being as you're almost a clone of what he's already got. Of course, you're quite a bit younger – that black boy must be 23 or 24 by now," he mused.

The chauffeur felt his swelling genitals bulging outward in the skin tight chauffeur's pants so that his excitement was totally evident. Although he was happy enough serving in THE FIRM's main headquarters, the prospect of being sold to a Prince who could afford whole stables of slaves intrigued him. And, although Mr. Broadley had turned out to be a good master, his advancing age mitigated against being used much other than as a display object – his main relief now was when Mr. Broadley loaned him out to his friends now and then or had him couple with another slave for either Mr. Broadley's or a customer's amusement. Perhaps a new owner would require his use more frequently.

Within minutes, the Rolls swung into the parking garage underneath a nondescript, unlabeled windowless warehouse close to the New York harbor surrounded with a high, electrified fence, and the electric garage door shut quickly after the car's entry. The chauffeur stopped the car in front of the elevator, quickly ran back to open the rear door for his master and promptly sank to his widely-spaced knees with his forehead touching the ground as his master stepped out of the car.

As his master waited for the elevator, the chauffeur didn't need to be told to quickly peel out of his uniform, remove his boots, cap, and gloves, and store the articles in the front seat of the car. Clad now only in his silver neck collar, his tit rings, and the large silver ring soldered around the base of his genitals to effect maximum protrusion of his sexual equipment, the slave quickly knelt at his master's feet until he heard the leash snap shut on his collar ring. A quick tug on his leash told him the elevator had arrived and he leaped to follow his master into the wood paneled brass trimmed elevator. As they ascended into the warehouse offices, Mr. Broadley reached down and stroked the slave's erect penis with one hand while his other squeezed the slave's large balls.

"I'd hate to lose a good chauffeur, but the Prince may want to purchase someone hung as well as you are," Mr. Broadley said casually, "and you're always ready to go, it seems," he laughed as he wiped some pre-cum off the end of the slave's rampant cock.

"Yes, master," the slave replied as Mr. Broadley moved his hand to his ringed tits and squeezed them until they too were fully erect.

"As soon as we reach my office, I want you on your knees ready for some mouth service," Mr. Broadley said as he began to loosen his belt and unzipped his pants in preparation.

In less than a minute, Mr. Broadley's own endowment was deep in the slave's throat and his moans of pleasure were matched by the slave's muted groaning as he struggled to swallow the entire penis while massaging the shaft with his tongue and his indrawn cheek muscles. "Yes, the Prince may very well be interested in a boy like you," Mr. Broadley gasped as he discharged a full load down the slave's throat who struggled to swallow the entire load without gagging. "We'll let him try you out tomorrow evening for sure," he said, running his hands down the boy's chest and tweaking his nipples hard between his thumb and forefinger.

When the slave gasped in pain, Mr. Broadley jerked him to his feet with his neck leash and, unfastening the leash from the collar, ordered "Now get that Rolls polished inside and out, then report to the slave pens. You can help me sort some of the stock out for the Prince tomorrow."

"Yes, master," the slave said as he quickly turned and headed for the servant's staircase to the garage.

By the time the naked chauffeur reached the slave pens, Mr. Broadley already had the two slaves trained to manage the slave pens busy at work. He had a computerized stock inventory on his clipboard.

"22C, 114N, 231A, 151C, 89C, and 4C in Preparation Cage 4," Mr. Broadley ordered as he studied his list. "That will give us an Asian, a bred black, two bred blonds, a bred Italian, and a Mexican. I don't think the Prince has ever owned a Latino and I think he might be interested. I know he likes our farm bred slaves and we'll offer four of them for his choosing – two blonds, a black haired Italian, and a black – all bred to our exact specifications. He lost an Asian he may want to replace, and we'll offer this black here also," he said, pointing to his slave chauffeur. "You know the routine: four enemas each followed by insertion of a big plug, complete body shaving four hours before display, a through scrubbing one hour before display, no sex outlets, but plenty of stimulation until they're up for display so they'll show hard all the time, and then another enema right after you remove their anal plug. And don't forget the deodorant this time or you'll find a 14 inch plug up you for a week or so to learn some discipline."

"Yes, master," the two slave handlers responded with lowered eyes and a quick look of fear at the mention of the 14 inch plug. One fastened a leash to the chauffeur's collar and led him to the preparation room several levels below, while the other quickly left to gather the other slaves to be put up for sale.

— — — — —

Prince Rashid had arrived exactly as scheduled without his usual entourage of bodyguards, secretaries, and personal assistants. He had driven his rental car himself to THE FIRM's warehouse's parking lots so that both his and THE FIRM's privacy could be maintained. Mr. Broadley led him immediately into the "display room," now outfitted with two low velvet couches, a serving table loaded with Middle East delicacies, the two naked slaves who served as handlers for sales displays like this and who had carefully prepared the evenings offerings precisely according to Mr. Broadley's orders the day before, but who were now outfitted in high leather collars, prominent tit rings, and broad genital bands in keeping with the banquet's ambiance. Both stood in the background rigidly alert with their massive arms folded over their muscular chests; their legs wide apart to best display their semi-erect genitals. Two additional slaves, obviously there to serve as waiters were chained by their metal collars to each of the reclining coaches where they knelt in naked readiness with their knees spread wide and their heads deeply bowed. The fact the two well-muscled chained slaves were not only incredibly handsome, even beautiful, but that they were also identical twins did not go unnoticed by the Prince who promptly began hefting and massaging his slave attendant's massive erect organs.

"I see you haven't lost your taste in beautiful slave boys, Mr. Broadley," the Prince said appreciatively as he became stroking his waiter's long thick shaft. "And you know I have a special weakness for blonds," he added as he ran his other hand through the slave boy's thick mane of shoulder-length hair.

"I thought you'd find him interesting," Mr. Broadley graciously responded, "but the twins will serve us in a special way during this evening's meal. Of course, you can use them anyway you wish at any time," he continued, "but they'll also serve our evening meal. They've had a lot of experience in serving up the special dishes we hoped you enjoy this evening before we get to the business of the evening."

"I'm intrigued," the Prince responded as he continued to pump the boy's shaft, now fully thrust out for his convenience. "But may I suggest we not wait until the meal is over to view the offered merchandise. I'll like to view the offerings while we eat, even though I probably won't inspect them thoroughly until we've supped. And please, call me Jamel," the Prince said with considerable warmth.

"Only if you'll call me Carl," Mr. Broadley responded graciously. "We do go back a few years, don't we, Jamel? And what an excellent idea to have the merchandise on display while we eat." With a curt movement of his finger, he motioned for the two slave handlers to quickly fetch their carefully prepared merchandise and chain them in their display positions. Within a minute, they heard the sharp crack of a whip across bare flesh, a few muted groans, and chains clanking across the floor as a far door opened and seven magnificent specimens of slave flesh entered the room. Each was promptly chained to a display plinth resplendent in their metal collars, wrist and ankle bracelets, and throbbing erect penises, even now glistening with small drops of precum. All had been freshly body shaved, were glistening with oil, and worked their rumps around huge butt plugs inserted just hours before. Upon mounting their display stands, each promptly put their hands in back of their head, thrust their pelvises forward, and tensed their muscles to best display their bodies.

"Yes, that's better, Carl. We can study them as we break bread together. From the looks of them, I see THE FIRM hasn't lost its touch in offering top quality."

"I think you'll find these slave boys to your liking, Jamel," Mr. Broadley smiled, "but we'll get to that later. If you loosen your grip on your attendant's shaft, they can begin serving the meal – if you don't, I'm afraid the boy, well-trained as he is, is going to shoot all over your hand."

Both men laughed as Jamel relinquished his grip on the waiter's shaft and both attendants began spooning the appetizers on their respective guest's plates within the limitations of their neck chains.

"This dish requires a special sauce to bring out the flavor," Mr. Broadley winked as each boy began stroking himself rapidly, holding the plate of delicacies next to their dripping erect pricks.

"Uh, Uh, Uh," the twins moaned as they both simultaneously shot copious amount of hot cum directly on the food ladled out. After six pulsing discharges, their balls were emptied and the plate was offered to each guest as each knelt and bowed their head, their organs still hot and erect.

"You'll find the hot sauce brings out the flavor, Jamel," Mr. Broadley said as he swallowed the first bite of the new delicacy. "Um, it's even better than I remember," he said as he savored the food for a while and then swallowed.

"You're right, Carl, the sauce does bring out the flavor, but I like slave cum anyway as you're well aware. How often can you milk these boys, Carl, before they run dry?"

"I really don't know, Jamel, but we keep them constantly stimulated, so I doubt if we'd milk them dry too often," Mr. Broadley laughed. "I'm sure they're good for two or three more discharges before this meal is over, if past experience is any indicator." Reaching for his own attendant's prick, he pumped it vigorously and it was soon rock hard with precum again evident on the crown. "See, he's ready to shoot again if we want."

— — — — —

Several more courses quickly followed the appetizer course, although the slave's special sauce had only been ordered up once more. Jamel's attendant was now under the Prince's robes, swallowing the royal shaft to its root while gently massaging the shaft with his tongue and throat muscles while the Prince rather roughly played with the boy's tits.

"Watch it, boy…gently now…if you bring me to orgasm you'll get a beating you won't soon forget," the Prince warned as he inserted his forefinger in the boy's asshole for emphasis.

The slave boy's mouth was fully stuffed so his only acknowledgment of the command was muffled groans as he spread his legs to make it easily for the Prince to finger fuck him.

"You understand my reluctance to shoot off so early in the evening," the Prince said. "It would only lessen my interest in looking over your fascinating merchandise."

The 'merchandise' was still posed in perfect display, their erect organs almost quivering in anticipation of the upcoming inspection. Not one had broken stance for a moment in the long wait while Mr. Broadley and his guest dined.

"They're obviously exquisitely trained," the Prince complimented as he thrust the attendant off his shaft and quickly rose from the couch to the closest display stand where the first of the farm bred blonds was chained. The slave was 6'2" tall with a perfectly sculpted well-balanced musculature, possessed a classical face featuring deep blue eyes and flawless dazzling white teeth, and was equipped with a thick 12" smooth penis atop two large and obviously full round balls.

"How old are you, slave boy?" the Prince asked as he hefted the heavy balls and weighed them in the palm of his hands.

"Eighteen, master," the slave said softly, pushing his balls even more into the prospective buyer's hand.

"Are you well-trained, boy?" the Prince continued as his other hand reached up and tweaked the boy's well-formed dark tits atop a powerful chest.

"Yes, master," the slave said humbly. "Perfectly trained," he whispered as the Prince began to massage his balls vigorously.

"Bend over, boy. I want to see your ass."

The slave instantly grabbed his ankle bands and spread his legs as far apart as he could and, taking both hands from the back of his neck, spread his ass so his plugged hole was clearly visible.

The Prince twisted the huge plug out of the proffered asshole and quickly inserted two fingers as far up the boy as he could and then began a rhythmic pumping action as the slave moaned softly and tried to coordinate his ass movements with the pumping of the inserted fingers.

"Does he suck well?" the Prince inquired of Mr. Broadley.

"See for yourself," Mr. Broadley laughed.

The Prince jerked his fingers out of the slave's ass and jerking his robe up, ordered the boy to his knees for oral service. Without hesitation, the slave swallowed the Prince's large shaft to its root and began massaging the full intrusion with his well-trained throat muscles.

"He does suck well, Carl. Have you tried him?" the Prince said, grasping the slave's head down until his lips fully enveloped the entire shaft and his nose was buried in his pubic hair. "And this hair is an asset," he added as he ran his hands freely through the thick long blond strands cut shoulder-length.

"I can't personally try out all of the slaves," Mr. Broadley laughed. "Remember, we usually have over 250 in stock at any given time. A man has limits! As for this boy – no, I haven't used him yet – but I've observed how well he took to his training – he's a natural if there ever was one – there's not a buyer on earth who would be disappointed with that one – unless they wanted a rebellious or resentful slave. This one's been bred to specifications, Jamel, at one of our Caribbean farms so he was born to be a slave and knows no other life. He'll not disappoint you, no matter what you put him to, Prince."

"Can I breed him? You're not the only one growing a crop with their female slaves, you know."

"Of course. All of THE FIRM's slaves are trained to please any potential owner, male or female. He'll know what to do when you pair him with a female and he's young enough to stud for a good 20 to 25 years. Even then you can use him as a trainer for the oncoming crop."

"What's his genetics, Carl?" the Prince said as he pulled the slave off his shaft and indicated he should resume his display position, whereupon he again began stroking the slave's huge cock.

"The brood and sire were both Germanic, as you no doubt guessed. We originally bought the stud from a corrupt German prison warden who faked his death, while his mother was bought out of a Bavarian orphanage by our agents when she was a young girl. After some rigorous training at this very location here in New York, the former prisoner was sold to a Greek millionaire who used him almost exclusively for many years both as his personal bed boy and as an occasional reward to valued employees. When the Greek died, the estate sold him back to us and we put him to stud at one of our Caribbean farms since the demand for big blonds was steadily increasing. The brood was sent directly to our Caribbean farm and has been kept in almost constant foal since her arrival. This slave boy was her 17th issue, I believe."

"Price?"

"I'll let you have him for $900,000. It's a steal considering his size and age."

"I'll take him, you old robber," the Prince said, "if his seed looks good," continuing his pumping of the slave's shaft.

"You have permission to shoot, boy," Mr. Broadley commanded the slave who by now was awash with a thick sex sweat and was noticeably panting in his need.

"Thank...you..., ma...master," the slave gasped as he spelled into the Prince's hand with a steady stream of hot, thick creamy cum. Due to the volume, as much dripped on the floor as the Prince was able to cup in the palm of his hand.

The Prince lifted his palm to his mouth and poured some into his mouth, running the thick sauce around his mouth with his tongue.

"Thick and tasty," the Prince announced and then slowly emptied the entire contents from his palm into his mouth, swallowing it bit by bit as he savored the taste. "I try to drink some cum every day – helps you keep young, you know – and they say it's the best tonic in the world. It sure is the most expensive," he laughed as he cleaned his hands in the slave's hair. "There's enough seed there to impregnate a thousand women," the Prince laughed as he slapped the blond slave on the rump in dismissal.

———

"I can't bear this much longer," the Mexican slave thought as he watched the slave handlers lead the compliant blond slave, bought so casually by this handsome hawk-eyed Arab and now fully emptied, back into a holding cage. The blond had been alongside him in preparation for this sales event and Santos had been curious to see if he was as terrified of being 'sold' to a new 'master' as he was. What he discovered terrified him all the more: the blond was eager to be put 'to use;' welcomed being sold in that it verified his worth; and clearly accepted this sale of human property, probably one of many in his future, as his given destiny. He was, after all, a slave, and slaves were frequently sold to please their new masters in any way those new owners saw fit. Santos' concerns were clearly foreign and beyond understanding to the bred blond slave. He seemed completely undisturbed by being publicly fondled, then finger fucked, mouth fucked, and finally milked by a man he'd never even seen before. The fact he was sold to this same man as mere property for obvious sexual use seemed almost pleasing to him.

Santos knew his status was no different than the bred blond as he stood completely naked in the rigid 'display position': arms in back of his head, chest and pelvis thrust forward with his sex erect and dripping, and muscles tensed for definition. "Why am I doing this? Why am I obeying them? Why don't I refuse them?" was his ever-present thought as he studied the other five slaves displaying themselves on command. They, like him, were all hard and dripping, a heavy sheen on their bodies from the body oil and sweat reflecting off the hot display lights, and all beginning to tire a little from the constant muscle tension. "Why don't we just say, 'I won't do this. I won't let you use my body. I won't let you handle me. I won't obey you in all things.'"

But Santos knew they wouldn't. His rebellious thoughts would never occur to the three bred slaves remaining – boys raised from birth on as slaves just didn't think about a slave's parameters. It was easier for them. He knew, from having been penned with bred slaves on many occasions. And they had taken to their training almost eagerly with little use of the omnipresent strap necessary, let alone the excruciating electric prods, the merciless punishment dildos, the ever present hunger, and the unceasing floggings that was now part of the life of any slave acquired from environments others than breeding farms, i.e., those that had been kidnapped, abducted, delivered from prisons or detention centers, or hoodwinked into slavery. All that pain delivered for no more reason than that they were now slaves and slaves profit from pain.

Yes, Santos thought, I've experienced all of that and more and the lessons learned from pain were now the reason he and the others now stood rigid and hard, completely under the command of their betters. He was a slave now and the many deep welts on his rump and backside reminded him of that even if his thick slave collar and ringed tits didn't. His constant need, revealed by his throbbing pulsating prick, could not be met unless his master ordered it; he couldn't piss until he had his master's permission; every drink, every bite of food was granted only by direction of a master; his body was exercised to meet the specifications of his owners; even his constant nakedness was altered by his owner's desires as all of his man-hair was kept removed and his skin was kept soft and supple with regular oiling. Owners decorated their property at whim as he reflected on the large swollen nipples he sported ever since his tits had been pierced and ringed. He glanced over at the black slave next to him, the master's chauffeur, and studied the tall silver collar which held the black's head rigidly erect, and the large silver genital ring which encompassed his scrotum and protruded his gigantic sex out for easy handling and full display. He too wasn't born to this – he had been carefully trained for many months – trained to the point where he could no longer even think of self-determination or free will. No, the black, like himself, was a totally obedient slave, now and forever. He wondered if the black could even marvel, like himself, at the success of their training or if that too had been trained out of him.

The black caught his appraising look and briefly smiled without breaking poise. His smile told Santos the black shared his thoughts but knew he must obey – he had no choice now that he was a slave – and that he would accept whatever came, just as Santos knew that was his destiny as well. Santos smiled back and he saw a silent tear spill down the cheek of the handsome black – a tear of resignation, even acceptance. A fresh drop of white liquid appeared at the end of the black's quivering shaft and Santos understood: accepting being totally controlled by others was sexually exciting at the most basic human level. It was as arousing as the master's excitement in controlling another's body for their own pleasure – like pain becoming pleasure at a certain level. Santos understood how former masters could enjoy their slavery where fate had reversed their position in life and where slaves like him made excellent masters when the tables were turned in war and social upheaval. Being controlled and controlling were all elements of a basic animal sexuality inherent in every man, slave or master. The thought made him all the harder and he felt another drop of pre-cum drip from his shaft.

"We are trapped by our own bodies," Santos reflected, "and desperately enjoy our most abject slavery. We want to be owned and are easily manipulated into pleasing our masters, no matter what the demands!"

Santos looked at his current owner (and trainer) and at his potential new master, the handsome Arab. In a strange way, he loved his owner: he had taught him pleasure and love and control and compliance and obedience and fulfillment and destiny and acceptance. Yes, he owed him much for the many lessons he had learned so well. And, if the Arab wanted him, he would please him in all ways – perhaps wondering the entire time just why he did it so willingly. But deep down inside his slave's soul, he knew exactly why he did it!

─ ─ ─ ─ ─

"My ally, the Ruler of Ras al-Khaimah, would probably take a liking to that dark-haired olive-skinned boy," Prince Rashid said, "and he always likes blacks," he chuckled. "Only Allah knows how many black slave boys he's given me over the years to seal our friendship. I certainly owe him a few. Let me look your black boys over more thoroughly, and I'll see if I can give Prince Faisal some fresh flesh he seems to like so well."

With a single wave of his finger, Mr. Broadley directed the slave handlers to his chauffeur and two exquisite blacks fresh from the slave breeding farms. The three specimens were quickly kneeling before the potential buyer with knees spread wide, their hands still squarely clasping the back of their necks. Prince Rashid ran his hand languidly over the blacks' massive chests and roughly massaged their swollen tits.

"The boy on your left, Jamel, was bought at a prison sale in Alabama about three years ago when he was 18. After his basic slave training, I made him my personal chauffeur due to his outstanding display qualities and he's worked out splendidly. He gets loaned out a lot for personal service to friends, staff, and customers and I've never had a complaint. He was easy to train, too. That Alabama prison had done most of the training for us. He was, for all practical purposes, turned into a whore in the prison what with his outstanding good looks and great physique. All the staff and half the prison population were either fucking him regularly or using him for mouth service. The warden told me this boy fought them all off for about a month, but after being force raped repeatedly, eventually he just gave in and tried to avoid as much pain as he could. When we got him, he still resented being fucked but he was as opened as they get by that time. He's always willing now, but you can still get a hint of resentment when you fuck him if you look carefully – he doesn't say anything and he gets in position and opens up fast enough – but he still seems to be humiliated by his use once in a while. Sometimes I catch him shedding a few tears – sometimes he blushes when you handle him – and he still quivers a bit when you play with his tits, although he knows better than to ever pull back, as no doubt you've already noticed. He took to driving my car as well as he took to being fucked," Mr. Broadley added rather proudly.

"I appreciate a boy with some spirit," Prince Rashid said as he turned his attention to the chauffeur's tits and roughly pinched them, rewarded with the expected quiver and the slave's desperate attempts to maintain full body control as he furtively smiled at his tormentor.

"Quite a slab of meat here," the Prince said has he hefted the black's massive shaft and ball sac. "To bad it doesn't get used much, according to you," the Prince laughed as he vigorously kneaded the organs. "Ever bred him?"

"Not yet. As much as that boy's been fucked, I guess he'd know what to do once you showed him the right hole and got him pumping – I suppose nature would take over after that. I doubt if he'd fucked much before prison – he was only 14 or so when they first locked him up I understand."

"How much, and don't tell me you can't part with your chauffeur – you've got a hundred potential chauffeurs caged within 500 feet of here, I'll wager," the Prince laughed.

"Eight hundred thousand due to his age. He's 24 now or he'd sell for over a million."

"I bet that Alabama warden was lucky to get 20 grand for him, you old bastard," the Prince smiled.

"That warden had so much flesh on his hands he was happy to get anything," Mr. Broadley confessed, "but he knew we are always discrete in our dealings, we always pay in cash, and the purchase could never be traced back to him. Besides, we didn't just buy this boy from him – actually we bought a hundred boys that same day, so each boy counts up, you know. The warden wasn't going to quibble with his best customer, and he knew the boy would need lots and lots of expert training before he could be properly marketed. Remember, he's guaranteed by THE FIRM now that his training is complete. You name it, this slave will do it – and that's guaranteed or you'll get every bit of the 800 grand back."

"OK, I take him, but I'm not giving him to Prince Faisal for a while. I think I'd like to fuck him myself for a while and try my hand at studding him some. Should produce some interesting new slave stock if I pick his broods carefully.

Prince Rashid squeezed the slave's balls until the boy moaned in pain before he addressed him eye to eye. "I gave my own chauffeur away just last week as a gift to an important oil man who'd taken a fancy to his pretty little butt – a Russian boy I bought at THE FIRM here some years ago. You can replace him at the wheel, slave."

"Yes, master," the slave responded humbly between gritted teeth as his balls continued to be plummeted by his master's hand.

Prince Rashid abruptly pushed the chauffeur away and the slave handlers, appearing out of their hidden stance in the corner, quickly led him away to the holding pen below to be prepared for shipment.

"These remaining two are from our own breeding facility, Jamel," Mr. Broadley said as he quickly reached down and stuck a finger up each of the slave's assholes.

"Ugh," the slaves moaned as Mr. Broadley's finger was inserted up their holes as far as it would reach, their backs arching somewhat in the process so that their ringed tits were practically thrust into Prince Rashid's hands. "Thank you, master."

"As you probably guessed from their looks, these boys are half-twins, Jamel," Mr. Broadley said. "Same sire (and a handsome brute the stud is too as you can tell from looking at these two) on two broods, both conceived on the same breeding day. And trained from birth. I can let you have the pair of them for 1.5 million or 850,000 each. Farm bred slaves are bringing more at market nowadays due to their exquisite training and highly selected genetic traits. And blacks are a sensation in the American market," Mr. Broadley offered.

"Maybe in the American market, but black slaves are common as sand in my kingdom, Carl. You forget slavery is still very open and thriving there and we're so close to the source. Still, farm bred slaves have their definite appeal," he said, wistfully stroking their huge engorged shafts.

"I'll pass on these two – I'm sure you can get that price where handsome black boys are relatively rare. But in my country, practically everyone owns at least one or two by now. They're available in every little dealer's stall, even boys equipped as well as these two," he said as he released their rampant pricks and turned to the display stand.

Mr. Broadley removed his fingers from their stretched holes and nodded to the slave handlers. "Take these two to the sales pens – it won't take long to get their price with Westerners," he nodded to his friend Prince Rashid, who confirmed Mr. Broadley's speculation with a quick nod.

"Let's look at that sloe-eyed yellow boy and the olive-skinned Mediterranean – where are they from originally?" the Prince picked up as the two black boys were scurried below with leashes now attached to their neck collars.

"The Asian is Cambodian – our agent bought him from a Hong Kong wholesaler just a few months ago – just enough time to get him properly trained – and the Italian boy is our own product – the offspring of two Italian slaves we had sold years ago and then bought back for breeding purposes. This boy's father was once owned by the Sultan of Ras al-Khaimah who traded him in for a younger version after years of faithful service in his own personal harem. And his mother served as a concubine for a very prominent Japanese businessman who eventually sold her to us as breeding stock. He'd bought her in an underground Naples market years and years ago when a destitute orphanage was clearing out some of their older wards.

"Another bred slave, Carl? You seem to be moving rapidly into breeding as your main source of supply."

"Well, it's certainly the cheapest and most predictable source, Jamel, and the training possibilities are infinite," Carl proudly replied.

"This boy's background?" Jamel queried as he placed the Cambodian slave over the edge of his couch face down and withdrew his butt plug with a quick jerk.

"Ugh, ugh, ugh..." the boy groaned as the plug was tugged out of his distended hole.

"His parent's handled him over to the Rhymer Rouge in exchange for amnesty and food supplies. The Rhymer Rouge had far too many boys offered to them to effectively use all of them in their

Army brothels, so they traded a large number of the heaviest hung and best looking to the Hong Kong market in exchange for modern guns."

The Italian boy, handsome beyond description, was similarly positioned and had his butt plug removed just as abruptly, reacting with a stifled cry as his well-trained hole was emptied.

"May I test their capacity?" Jamel asked.

"Of course, Jamel," Carl replied and snapped his fingers at the slave attendants standing ever ready. "The phallus collection," he commanded.

Almost instantly, the attendants wheeled in a huge rack of phalluses. They were of all lengths, widths, colors, textures, some with rings, some with tails attached, some of leather, some of plastic, some soft, some rigid. Jamel selected two 12" rods, each 5" thick and molded out of a semi-rigid plastic with definable 'sensation' ridges molded cross-wise into each shaft. Each shaft was as thick as a Coke bottle, insuring the buttholes would be stretched to unimaginable proportions, but the ridges promised even more input into the selected slaves.

The attendants carefully greased each phallus the minute Jamel had made his selection, although the two slave boys had been well greased up their entire chutes in preparation for display. Jamel took one in each hand, stood behind the boys' nicely distended buttholes and forcefully drove each phallus in as far as his initial effort would take it, twisting each one vigorously as he drove it up the wide open holes.

The Cambodian and the Italian responded identically to the invasion. Both turned ashen white, became absolutely rigid as they endured the intense pain, and groaned through clinched teeth as the huge shaft was shoved up their chutes. Their eyes wide in panic, they instantly broke out in sweat, and moaned anew as Jamel regained his strength and shoved again on the shafts with all his might.

"Open up, open up," Jamel commanded as he shoved with renewed effort. The slave's butts churned and they stretched their legs even further apart as they struggled to find a position allowing the huge phallus entry. Despite themselves, they cried out piteously as they felt their chute stretched to the breaking point and were convinced they were being torn in half.

"Quit your squalling, slaves," Jamel said harshly as he smacked their rears sharply. "You should be grateful I'm helping prepare you for your duties," and he smacked them again and again until huge red welts appeared on their rumps. The smacking only added to the slave's agony but finally they felt the base of the dildo on their backside and they knew the huge phallus was fully inside them.

"What do you say to your master, slave boys?" Jamel demanded as he twisted the phallus first to the right and then to the left as the slaves gasped and moaned anew.

"Thank you, master," the slaves whispered as tears flowed from their eyes and they gasped for air in short little snorts.

"I'd think so, slaves," Jamel smacked them again sharply on their rumps. "Next time, I'll put some Tiger Balm on the phallus so you'll be doubly aware you're being properly fucked."

"Yes, master," the two slaves gasped out, unable to stop the flow of tears down their cheeks.

"Look between their legs, Jamel," Mr. Broadley directed. "It's obvious the boys are enjoying your instruction, although they'll need to lick their strains off of the couches the minute you're through playing with them."

Jamel reached between the Italian's stretched legs and saw the white puddle of cum on the couch directly in front of the slave's rigid pulsating shaft. He stuck his finger in it and brought a sticky string of cum to his mouth.

"Fresh and tasty but a little runny," he announced as he savored the slave's output. "But they'll need to be punished for shooting without permission."

"They didn't," Mr. Broadley said as he reached down and sampled the output. "This is pre-cum – zesty in its own right, but hardly the thick heady tang of a healthy boy's cum. When this boy shoots, I'm afraid it won't be a mere stain on the couch – it's going to be a venerable river on the floor," he laughed. "Same for the Cambodian – that boy can shoot a cup at a time, I swear. Both of these boys seem to have the capacity of a cow," Mr. Broadley said as he reached down and squeezed their swollen balls. "But they won't shoot off until we give them permission, Jamel," Mr. Broadley added as he pulled the swollen balls into the palm of his hands.

"How much for the two of them, Carl, and remember I'm one of your best customers," Jamel asked as he again twisted the huge phalluses within each of the slave's chutes and heard them groan again miserably as their pricks pulsated from the constant prostate stimulation.

"I can let you have the Asian at a mere $210,000 in that, frankly, they're glutting the market right now what with the steady supply from the Rhymer Rouge. We picked this boy up for a song and a dance in Hong Kong – all I'm really charging you for, Jamel, is the cost of his careful training since we got a hold of him. But if you pay me the going price on the Italian boy, I may just throw him in for free since you are a good customer."

"I can see you're setting me up for a steep price on the Italian," Jamel laughed. "How much?"

"That boy's been 18 years in the making, Jamel," Mr. Broadley laughed as he smacked the protruding end of the phallus fully stuffed up the boy's ass, causing the Italian slave to yelp as the shaft drove even deeper into him. "And Mediterraneans are popular choices these days – seems like everyone wants a well-trained boy with olive skin and dark flashing eyes – and of course all of our offerings with that coloration are hung bigger than a horse and handsome as they come, We could easily get 1.2 million for him – after all, he just turned 18 and he's always willing and ready now that he's been properly trained – but I'll let you, Jamel, have him for 1.1 mil and throw the Cambodian in for good measure."

"Done, Carl. I've got just the place for these two – in my public brothel. That business has really taken off since the oil money's filtered down to every man on the street and I can hardly keep it properly stocked to meet the demand. Seems everyone wants to fuck or be sucked by a member of the royal harem. I overheard some common peasant on the street tell his friends the other day, 'I just fucked one of the Prince's favorite slave boys.' Apparently, that's worth a great deal to my subjects who are doing well to just own a couple of ugly old work slaves who barely have the strength left to suck their masters off each night."

"You were never one to overlook a new source of revenue," Carl chuckled. "Tell me; are the boys in your brothel really part of the royal harem?"

"Well, some of them were once," Jamel winked. "I still keep a few for my exclusive use, but when I tire of them, their sex lives take on considerably more variety. Most of the boys don't mind being moved over to the brothel – they're pretty bored with harem life by then and only having each other to talk to. In the brothel, they service a lot of people every day and a lot of their customers love to talk to them about their lives as pampered slave boys. Sometimes, a customer even wants the slave to fuck them – you can imagine what a treat that is to a boy usually on the receiving end."

"Aren't you boys lucky," Carl said as he twisted the huge phalluses in their butts once again. "Going directly into brothel service, and a royal one at that. It's what every slave dreams of, I imagine," Carl added as he again twisted the phalluses and motioned for the slave handlers to come get the pair.

"Take them to the holding pen and prepare them for shipment," Mr. Broadley commanded. "Give them a good enema, and then reinsert this same phallus in them and strap it in tightly before fastening their hands to their neck collars. A final stretching period will be good for them in view of where they're going, and, with their hands fastened to their collars; they'll arrive just as fresh and dripping as they are now. And mind you they're shipped out in separate cages – otherwise they'd be sucking each other all the way over to the Prince's kingdom, hands restrained or not," Mr. Broadley chucked. "We want them arriving fresh and interested."

"Good idea, Carl," Jamel added, turning to the slave handlers himself. "I want ALL of my new purchases to receive a series of thorough enemas before shipment with their hands fastened to their neck collars and all in separate cages where they can't get to each other. No need to worry about food and water – the shipment will only take about 11 to 12 hours in my private jet and they can be fed and watered after we get them transferred to their new homes."

"Yes, master," the slave handlers said as they fastened leashes to the neck collars of the Italian and Cambodian slave, the huge phalluses still sticking out of their asses as they were led out of the room on their hands and knees, their own swollen sex swinging heavily between their legs.

– – – – –

"Let's see," Jamel said, counting on his fingers, "that's four so far and two rejects. You're quite a salesman, Carl."

"Our stock sells itself, Jamel," Mr. Broadley replied rather soberly. "Who else in the business offers a 60-day no-questions-asked guarantee of complete satisfaction?"

"Still, at the prices you charge, I'm always amazed your stock turns over so fast," Jamel commented. "You're not the only outfit in the business, you know."

"You underestimate the demand," Jamel, "and it's getting stronger every month. THE FIRM has to really put forth a concerted effort to keep at least 200 to 300 well-trained stock on hand all the time."

"Speaking of stock, I see we still have one of your selections for me left," Jamel laughed as he pointed at the Mexican slave desperately struggling to still maintain his commanded 'display' position. "I know he's a Latino of some type, but exactly where is that big boy from?" Jamel questioned as he spaced his hands a good 15" apart to indicate what he meant by 'big'.

Mr. Broadley snapped his finger and motioned with his hand for one of the slave handlers to bring the remaining slave offering over for the Prince's inspection.

"Over there, Santos, and we quick about it," the slave handler grabbed the Mexican's slave collar and shoved him toward the Prince with a smart smack on his rump for emphasis. The Mexican blushed deep red despite his natural light brown skin, but kept his hands buried in the back of his neck, his fully erect dripping cock waving in front of him as he hurried to the Prince's couch.

"Did you see that, Carl?" Jamel exclaimed. "The boy is blushing. How absolutely charming and so rare in a trained slave these days."

"There's something I need to tell you about this slave boy, Jamel," Mr. Broadley said gravely. "His training really isn't complete yet. Oh, we've tried and tried and tried, and he's already been in our training program half again as long as most slaves, but so far we're still not quite there. There's just that touch of rebellion in the boy, that hint of resentment, that suggestion of a slight hesitation before responding, that occasional defiant look in his eye, that tells me he's still not accepting his slavery in every aspect. In other words, Jamel, I don't think he's totally bought into the fact he's just a piece of meat on the block to do with as his masters please. Look at him – he's humiliated – that's what he is – in just the fact we're talking about him as if he weren't here. And the fact he's stark naked with a collar around his neck and his prick rampant at our command still embarrasses him. He's got a lot to learn yet."

"Jamel, I didn't put this boy on display to sell him to you – he's obviously doesn't meet THE FIRM's standards yet. But I am going to ask you to take him – free of charge – for three months or so – as part of his ongoing training. You'll teach him his place in life if anyone can – at the very least, your demands on him should get him over that silly embarrassment every time he's put to some simple use, like blushing at even being examined. And those petty subtle objections to being used – like crying when he's being fucked – he's got a long way to go to bear THE FIRM's standards for a slave."

"I understand your problem, Carl, and your idea of loaning him out to me may have some merit for the slave's own good, but I think we'll discuss it as I sample what this strange slave has to offer. Mind if I fuck him?"

"Of course not, Jamel. The boy desperately needs to learn compliance."

Jamel took the Mexican's jaw in his hand and jerked the slave's head up until their eyes met.

"Look at me directly, slave boy," Jamel commanded. "So we fully understand each other. I intend to take my pleasure with you and you better do everything in your power to give me that pleasure or you'll certainly learn to regret it. Your owner here is going to loan you to me for some period of time so I can teach you a proper attitude and make you worth something on the market. Do you understand, slave boy?" Jamel grabbed the Mexican's balls and squeezed them hard as he stretched them downward. "Do you understand, slave boy?"

"Yes, master," the Mexican gasped as he winched in pain and a tear trickled down his cheek.

"And how are you going to serve me, slave boy?"

The Mexican slave looked perplexed at first, but managed to stammer out, "Any way you want, master. Any way that pleases the master...," but his response was interrupted by his master's guest pushing his head down to the end of the couch while his other hand remained firmly clutching his balls.

"Ugh…ugh," the Mexican moaned, shuddering as his large butt plug was hastily removed without warning. Before he had a chance to experience any feeling of emptiness, he fell the tip of an erect prick at his now highly displayed asshole and, in an instance, a large shaft pushing on his anal ring and then, with a quick push, enter him steadily, and he heard himself audibly moan between his clenched teeth.

"Open up, you bastard. Open up," the voice above him commanded, and a series of hard slaps rained down on his right rump.

Santos, the Mexican slave, shuddered as the huge intrusion worked its way up his chute until the only way he could keep from screaming at the top of his lungs was to bite his tongue until the blood filled his mouth. The pain was unbelievable but he knew it would eventually go away if he could just hold on a little longer. Flashes of being split in half flashed through his mind as he imagined he felt riverlets of blood trickling down his legs. Again, as in a dream, he felt his butt being repeatedly spanked by an open hand. Or was it a slave strap? He wasn't sure. But the burning sensation was the same – white pain. Tears flowed down both cheeks now as he struggled to cope with the incessant pain. Surely he would pass out, and he knew he'd be punished so severely if he did that this pain would seem pale by comparison. So he struggled to remain conscious and respond to his violator.

"Yes, master," he gasped as he felt his vision fading in and out from the pain. "Please, master…the pain… I can't take it…master…."

"Carl, did you hear that? Did you hear that? What sort of slave is this? By Allah, we'd throw such rubbish to the dogs," as he thrust completely into the Mexican slave with a final powerful thrust and felt the boy underneath him go limp.

"Now what?" Prince Jamel roared as he withdrew a little and plunged back in even further. "Did this untrained mongrel pass out, or die on me, or what?" and he savagely pumped the ravaged hole for an answer.

"Uh, uh, uh,' the slave moaned as a convulsive shudder racked his entire body.

"Oh, he's just getting used to being fucked," the Prince laughed. "Why, this boy must practically be a virgin. You didn't tell me the boy was a virgin, Carl," Jamel laughed as he began slowly but steadily pumping his large shaft in and out of the boy, still catatonic from the pain.

"Oh, he's no virgin," Carl laughed. "Not after all the training he's received. But he's sure acting like one, isn't he? You see what I mean – he's got a long way to go before THE FIRM could ever sell anything like that!"

"Where did you run across him? I know he's a Latino, but he's lighter and more muscular than so many Latinos. And he's certainly hung a lot heavier than most Latinos I've seen put to market." Jamel continued his slow rhythmic fucking of the boy's ass.

"You're right, Jamel. He's a Mexican and he didn't come to us through the usual sources – the national prison system, poverty-ridden orphanages, starving parents selling off excess children. No, this boy was deliberated kidnapped from a middle-class Mexican family. Some greedy goons spotted his handsome physique and prodigious endowment at a local gym, and knew of an agent who would pay well for such boys who also had beautiful faces. So they kidnapped him on his way home, took him to a mountain hideout and contacted one of our agents who arranged for the charred body of another boy of similar build to be found beside the highway in his wrecked car so his parents would conclude he was dead. Practically before this boy got over the trauma of being repeatedly raped by his captors, he found himself caged here in our warehouse in New York with his hands strapped to a slave collar. Incidentally," Mr. Broadley laughed softly, "those rapes were the first time he'd been with a man, so he's had a lot to learn."

"How'd you get him from wherever it was in Mexico to here without being detected?" Jamel asked as the slave under him shifted slightly, leading to a round of smacks on his exposed rump. "Flex those ass muscles like you've been taught, boy. Make my shaft feel like its welcome up your ass. Squeeze that shaft for all you're worth, slave," Jamel commanded as he ground his hips in a fresh round of pumping.

The slave managed a weak "Yes, Master," as he clinched his ass cheeks together and tried to tighten his ass muscles so they would clinch and massage the huge shaft within him.

"Trade secrets, Jamel. Let's just say we have a fleet of private jets all equipped with plenty of soundproof cages that could pass for shipping crates in any airport in the world, and, of course, we drug most of our stock for shipment, just as I'm sure you do, Prince. At least, the stock you don't want to use during the flight," and he laughed. "I'm sure you are going to get your new stock back home in a similar fashion if you're planning to take them home with you in your own jet, or have you changed your mind and want us to arrange the shipping for you?"

"No, no, Carl. I'll be taking them with me but I'll need to borrow some of those soundproof covered cages until we get them on board. And I just assumed you'd drug them for transit – after all, we'll be there in 11 or 12 hours so it's not like putting them in a coma," he laughed. "But this one…," he paused and gasped as he begin the first of his discharges deep into the boy beneath him…"this one we'll keep chained up front with me…he'll be fun to play with during the flight…and I'm sure my attending staff would enjoy his use. My pilot especially has a fondness for willful slave boys with a touch of resentment in them, and I enjoy watching him fuck slaves anyway. He's got a certain style that's quite remarkable. When he's through fucking a boy, that boy knows he's pure property and nothing but a piece of meat for his owner's pleasure."

"Sounds like your pilot could make a good trainer for THE FIRM," Carl replied, almost wistfully.

"Indeed he would, Carl, but you won't get him on this trip at least – I need him to pilot my plane," and they both broke into laugher as the Prince began a second fuck of the slave loaned him, this time flat on his back with both his legs well over his shoulders and his dark panicked eyes starring directly into his possessor.

— — — — —

"I can't endure this," Santos thought as the second assault on his ass began. "This is more shame than any man can survive," But as the shaft once again burrowed its way up his ass, he knew he would endure this, just as it had all the other times he been used by his kidnappers, his 'agent', his handlers, scores of trainers, numerous prospective customers, and now this Arab with a shaft as thick and long as his own. He blushed from head to toe as he thought of his being used like an animal, without his consent, and certainly against his will. His ass had been stretched to accommodate anything, it seemed, and his sex was kept always erect, always primed, without any release, any relief, so that he remained constantly obsessed with sex, in constant need, in perpetual heat, dripping droplets of pre-cum like a stud dog. "I won't be turned into an object of pleasure – a sex machine – an owned plaything – I won't, I can't." And yet he knew that's exactly what was happening to him and there wasn't one thing on earth he could do to stop it. Within a matter of only a few more weeks, the last vestige of resistance would be gone and he would be exactly like all those hundreds and hundreds of other slaves THE FIRM owned. All those slaves who wanted nothing else then to best serve their masters in all the many ways they'd been trained. All those slaves who reveled in their ownership, who gloried in their servitude, who first longed to be sold to a master they could serve, and, once sold, found true happiness in the fact they had a master. Yes, he was but a shade away from becoming a new person – well, not a person really – but a slave. It was just a matter of time. And the person pounding away on his butt now may be the first 'master' he ever really acknowledged. It was just a matter of time... "I can't bear this humiliation – the constant shame – I can't bear it...." and he blushed from head to toe as he realized what was being done to him and he just didn't care anymore – he just didn't care — if only he could get some relief – if only a master would let him shoot – he would do anything to gain relief... only a master could allow relief... he knew that now... he needed to please his master... and get relief...he needed to please those wanting to use him... he was a slave now, not a person...he was a slave..."

––––––

The Prince shuddered as he spelt once again into the Mexican slave. Quickly, he withdrew his long thick shaft with an audible plop as he exited the slave's ass and ordered the boy beneath him, "Clean me properly, slave, and be quick about it."

The slave quickly sunk to his knees and swallowed the Prince's shaft, cleansing first the head and then the long shaft with this tongue, swallowing any remnants of the Prince's cum and his own ass juices in the process.

Mr. Broadley motioned for the slave handlers. "Complete enemas; a fresh lube, shower and oil his body, and plug his ass for the flight. As for the others the Prince has purchased, they're to be thoroughly fed, then douched, body shaved, bathed and oiled, and then drugged for a 12 hour flight before being caged. Then deliver them to the Prince's private jet, located at the secluded airstrip in New Jersey our customer's prefer. As to this slave who remains property of THE FIRM but will be on loan to the Prince, he's not to be drugged and caged as the others. Four complete enemas after all the fucking he's had this afternoon, then a hot bath, complete body shave, a thorough oiling, and a fresh lubing. Check his collar, tit rings, and genital band for tight fit, and make sure all are marked as "Property of THE FIRM" since he won't be changing ownership this time around. But feed him well and make sure he's watered. The Prince will be using him on the long flight home and won't want to bother with those details. And remember, you'll be seeing this slave boy again under your tutelage, so don't let up on the discipline. You handlers, as well as his trainers, have really screwed up with this property, so we still have a lot to do before we can successfully market him at THE FIRM's standards."

"Yes, master," the handlers said, their eyes cast downward in proper respect, looking anxious at the reminder of their failure with this slave. They'll make sure this rogue Mexican slave was prepared to properly service THE FIRM's customer during his long-term loan. And when he returned, they'd make sure they weren't accused of 'screwing up' with this piece of meat again.

— — — — —

The purchased slaves were all somnambulant in their respective cages in the baggage compartment as Prince Rashid watched the 'loaned' boy between his legs struggle to suck his entire length deep into his throat. The slave's beautiful eyes glistened with tears as he fought to overcome gagging from the deep invasion.

Jamel had enjoyed watching his pilot artfully fuck the boy once they were well over the ocean on their way home and was amused when the boy was finally allowed to shoot after being stroked and stroked until every pore in his body oozed a sex sweat and he gasped as he struggled to contain himself. When his new master finally issued the magic command "Shoot, boy," his relief was joyous and he emptied gallons of cum over the thick carpets of the private jet to the amusement of the staff watching him with glee. "Now lick that cum up, boy, before it ruins the carpet," the Prince had laughed as he reached down and squeezed the balls to make sure they were emptied. "And then get your ass up in the air over that chair arm there – I want to see my steward fuck you next."

The Mexican slave felt the last vestige of his old self leave as he once again struggled to swallow the entire length of his master's shaft just as soon as the master's personal slave, as commanded, had fucked him thoroughly while the crew shouted encouragement to the well-hung and seemingly inexhaustible slave who now served as the plane steward. A new persona seemed to possess the Mexican slave – "I am nothing but what my master wants me to be." And the Mexican knew love for the first time – the love a true slave has for his master. And he felt overwhelming happiness. He now belonged to THE FIRM, body and soul.

CHAPTER III

THE RESORT

David and Forest had worked for THE FIRM for three years now as Chief Procurers – work which had taken them to some of the most exotic spots on the planet and which had familiarized them with almost every aspect of THE FIRM's multifaceted operations. When Mr. Broadley, THE FIRM's Chief Operating Officer, had first invited them into THE FIRM's inner circle of trusted employees, they never dreamed of the vastness of THE FIRM's operations or the precise organizational system that now stretched into 66 different nations.

They had certainly profited beyond their wildest dreams. When Mr. Broadley had originally suggested they could expect to make at least 5 million dollars each annually working for THE FIRM's procurement services, they thought he was exaggerating. After one year, they had been paid over 8 million each in commissions; by the second year this had grown to over 10 million each; and the third year had seen their commissions grow to over 20 million each. Between the two of them, they had "acquired" literally tens of thousands of acquiescent new stock for THE FIRM's training facilities – stock that had eventually been sold in THE FIRM's own markets for several billions of U.S. dollars.

Mr. Broadley's judgment as to David and Forest's talent had been totally accurate and he was as pleased with their contributions to THE FIRM as David and Forest were in their success in this endeavor. In fact, both of them felt like at last they had found their true calling. The fact it had made them both multimillionaires many times over seemed almost incidental.

"How'd you like to visit THE FIRM's private resort?" Mr. Broadley asked them as they chatted one day in the New York office.

"As you no doubt are aware, it's by invitation only. And that invitation only goes out to a select few of our long-term customers and a few – very few – of our most favored employees. I'm proud to say you two are certainly in the league of 'most favored' employees now," Mr. Broadley said as smiled, giving both the young men an accepting long look.

"I'm pretty sure you'd find THE FIRM's resort most interesting and enjoyable. But it will be a training experience also in that you'll both probably pick up some new ideas while you're there. At any rate, you'll find it enjoyable. It's a boondoggle at our expense," Mr. Broadley laughed, "and a little vacation to boot. You boys have been working pretty hard lately if the stock rolling in is any example."

David and Forrest glanced at each other briefly and simultaneously broke into a smile.

"We were just about to ask you for some vacation time, sir," Forrest laughed, "but once again you've read our minds."

"I'm all for it – how about you, David?" Forrest glanced at his long time companion.

"I'm packed," David laughed. "Do we need any clothes or will THE FIRM furnish what we need once we're there, Mr. Broadley?"

"Your question tells me once again you perfectly understand how THE FIRM operates, David," Mr. Broadley responded. "THE FIRM will take care of all your needs. All you need to do is step onto THE FIRM's plane which is waiting for you two while we speak."

As he led us to the heliport door, Mr. Broadley added, "Stay as long as you like. You'll find THE FIRM's resort most interesting as well as fully capable of meeting all of your needs. Once you board THE FIRM's jet to the resort, you'll meet some of the other invited guests. Most of them are long-term customers who are paying unbelievable amounts for this privileged sojourn, but I believe you'll meet one or two other employees who have also been invited – a Mr. Simmons who supervises the New York sales outlet, and Mr. Sanchez from our Mexican training camp. Both are valued long-term staff of THE FIRM, but, like you, this will be their first trip to THE FIRM's resort.

The resort's assistant supervisor, Mr. Yamahoma, will greet you the minute you step off the plane and serve as your personal guide during your stay. Mr. Yamahoma has worked for THE FIRM since its inception, first heading up our Japanese marketing unit, and later was involved in the initial planning of THE FIRM's resort. In fact, some of its current operational features are his own ideas I believe. We use him for employee visitations since he knows intuitively what features you should pay special attention to and which would warrant further study, and hurry you through what resort features are quite ordinary to any employee of THE FIRM. THE FIRM's customers on your trip to the resort will be hosted by a lower level guide who is focused on the special interests of purchasing customers."

─ ─ ─ ─ ─

Within 10 hours, the jet, containing all ten of THE FIRM's specially selected long-term customers and the four honored employees had reached the South Pacific resort, located on an uncharted island deep in the outer reaches of the Marshall Island chain, and electronically equipped to ensure total privacy from a prying outside world.

Our arrival was greeted by eight tall beautifully built naked Asian slaves who had been totally body shaved and were properly collared and fully ringed, even to having their noses pierced.

"Welcome, masters," they humbly stated as they sank to their knees and reared back until the back of their heads touched the ground in a novel display of total obeisance. Such a position forced their knees wide apart and totally exposed their large semi-erect organs, heavily banded to ensure prominent display.

As Mr. Broadley had promised, Mr. Yamahoma quickly spotted us and led us to one side while the guide amiably greeted the customers and led them to a 'Welcoming Tent' located nearby.

"David, Forest, Bill, Wade," he said as he vigorously shook each of our hands in greeting. "I'm delighted Mr. Broadley arranged this little visit to THE FIRM's resort for you. It's a high compliment to be invited, as you undoubtedly know, but, more importantly, I think you'll find it a great learning opportunity. Although I'll give you more details later, your visit here will be focused around the 'settling in' of a brand new slave to us – a slave you, David and Forest, first procured for THE FIRM; then trained at our Mexican training camp by you, Wade; and eventually marketed by you, Bill, in New York. It'll give all four of you a good idea of what happens to all that stock you process one way or another and, I suppose, give you some idea of what you're working toward. Focusing in on one new resort slave all four of you have had contact with was Mr. Broadley's idea – it'll make your visit more interesting in that you all have a stake in the object under study. I also hope you'll see this visit as an intrinsic reward – sort of a validation of what you do day in and day out with THE FIRM's operations. I know the staff here at the resort is most appreciative of all you do – all we deal with is the finished product. But we're smart enough to know it took a lot of careful selection and training to get the stock to THE FIRM's standards. You guys make our job easy!" he said gratefully.

"Now we'll join the other guests for our opening auction which will get us right into the heart and soul of what the resort offers. Each guest has been given 10 million play dollars to buy whatever pleases them during their stay at the resort."

We entered a luxurious wheeled cart while a driver quickly fitted the eight naked slaves into harnesses attached to the cart's drawbar. With a sharp crack of the driver's whip, the harnessed slaves pulled the 14 of us toward the resort's center, struggling with the heavy load and the swift pace as their bodies strained into the leather harnesses each now wore over their torso. The oozing sweat from the slave's bodies, the sporadic crack of the driver's whip lacing across their prominent rumps which were constantly churning around deeply embedded butt plugs, and the sound of their heavy breathing gave an exotic air to the occasion, especially since all eight slaves managed to maintain full erections of their incredibly heavy organs the entire time – a result of long and rigorous training as we all knew, especially when it was accompanied by copious discharges of precum as their labors intensified.

Soon we reached a huge square that seemed to be devoted almost exclusively to the sale of human flesh – the infamous slave markets the resort boasted was an exact copy of those of Ancient Rome.

– – – – –

"You'll all recognize the white American slave up on the block. David, he's the oddball teacher from Chicago you procured for us after Forrest spotted him trying to get work in a modeling agency there. And Wade, you'll remember training him down in Mexico – it was no easy task breaking that one, I'm sure, but break him you did – and Bill; you set him up for auction in New York but then decided he'd be prime resort material.

THE SLAVE FROM CHICAGO:

Our drivers headed us toward the dealer who had arrived before us and had finalized preparations for our sale. He had told us the sale would be in a place exactly like Ancient Rome and we wouldn't be able to tell the difference between THE FIRM's resort and that 2000-year-old society. Sure enough, the slave market looked exactly like something out of a Hollywood epic and at the dealer's there were 16 brick podiums about a foot off the ground for the 16 Category I slaves being offered that day, myself included. At the base of each there were little placards that I just knew had our best features, any defects, and our asking price listed. Even I could make out the Roman numerals listing our prices.

The leg chain was removed, but our ankle and wrist chains remained in place. Our feet were painted white with chalk indicating our foreign origin in abeyance with Roman law and our iron collars were tightened and relocked around our throats so any sores or abrasions caused by the collars over the past few weeks were hidden underneath and we were then each placed on our appropriate podiums with our ankle connecting chain run through a ring set in the bottom of the podium so it would be impossible to leave – even jumping off would trip us and cause a bad fall. It was obvious there would be no escape from our chained positions on the inspection platforms. A last order from the dealer led to the overseers removing all clothing from the sale items so prospective buyers could see what they were getting. Still not used to being totally naked in public outside of my training situations, a real queasy feeling overcame me and I felt more and more like an animal up for auction. Then it hit me! That's exactly what we were. An animal up for auction.

It wasn't long until we got a little customer interest. Although I knew the resort drew people from all over the world, most of the customers were now toga-clad and bristled with fancy jewelry, not unlike our dealer's dress. A few wore pretty fancy tunics which seemed cooler, but most of them were even more adorned with jewelry as if to make up for the lack of a toga. A few, primarily from the Middle East and America, retained their traditional dress for one reason or another. So togas, tunics, robes, and business suits were all in evidence as the customers swarmed around us.

The customers quickly got caught up in the ambience of the open slave market and their inspections were much worse than our dealer doing his preliminary category evaluations, gross as that was. The resort's customers, who had bought many slaves before or they wouldn't have been invited here, knew they had the right to do any damn thing they wanted with the bodies in front of them and that's exactly what they did. No sense of propriety, no sense of shame, no sense of human dignity or decency interfered in the slightest with their inspection of what they were buying. Breasts were squeezed, teeth probed, tits examined and pinched in minute detail, balls were hefted up as if they needed to be weighed, and usually the buyer's began their real inspection asking the grossest questions imaginable to the dealer as they fingered the stock. "How much use has this one had?"; "How long since this one was a virgin?"; "Have you tried to breed this one yet?"; "Where did you find this one?"; "Any problems in training this one?" and on and on and on as if the person they were talking about wasn't even there. Sometimes the slave would be fingered in the most intimate places right there in public and the tears of humiliation, shame and utter defeat streaming down the poor slave's face didn't mean a thing to any of the buyers I noticed. Some of them took notes so if the person wasn't sold before auction time, they'd remember the good and bad points of each slave being offered. Most were sold for the resort's currency at a fixed price long before the auction, however, and their new owners lead them away by neck leashes.

Category I females seemed to be sold at this market with one thing in mind – personal pleasure. In this simulated Roman society, the category I men's appeal was even greater than the females it seemed in that the Roman theme gave the resort's guests license to indulge their wildest fantasies. Our prices certainly reflected this heightened appeal. The twins I had been trained with down in Mexico were placed side by side for maximum effect and they were the first of anyone to be sold. Some man came up in a litter (the first I'd seen in my whole life) carried by four very muscular matched black slaves who had been run at a fast pace to the market, judging by their sweaty torsos and heavy ragged breathing. The bearers were fitted with shiny silver ankle and upper arm and wrist bands, ear and nipple rings, and absolutely nothing else except matching shiny wide silver bands around the base of their genitals. I felt embarrassed for them – hell, I was embarrassed to even look at them – but I supposed somehow they were kind of used to appearing nude in public by now. They gave the impression of a liveried horse which I suppose they were to a large degree. The man got out of the litter, went over languidly to the twins, looked them over casually as he felt their arm and leg muscles, checked their teeth, and then hefted up their ball sac which he roughly massaged. When they started to squirm, he warned them that any resistance to his inspection would lead to a severe beating and even branding. Saying that, he let loose of their balls and proceeded to stroke their shaft until they both had erections. The twins were practically scarlet in embarrassment with such an intimate examination right there in front of everyone but managed to maintain their stance on the podium and, obeying a new command, even spread their legs apart to allow the man easier access to their body. Tears of shame and pure hopelessness spread down their cheeks as the man kept stroking them until finally he got what he wanted: an ample sample of their seed which sprayed out across his palms as the twins shuddered and moaned in abject humiliation. There was no dickering or bargaining over price. The man looked down at the placard, paid the dealer and chained the twins by their neck collars to the back of his litter for transport home. And that was the last we ever saw of the Nordic twins. I don't even want to know what they ended up having to do. Maybe they just ended up as decoration for his parties or something; maybe he wanted some new house servants that were good looking; maybe he was collecting a new stable of litter bearers; but I doubted it. Not after the way they were handled. And that particular handling seemed to be all he was really interested in. More like a 'cupbearer' or a 'personal body slave' or 'bath attendant' or some such other title hiding the truth of the matter. We were a long way from Chicago, I thought, especially recalling the outrageous 'costuming' of his litter bearers.

The weird exotic I first noticed in the marketing barns in New York went next which didn't surprise me in this depraved market. A man with a retinue of about three other men looked him over rather thoroughly arguing about the price all the time with the dealer. When they first wrapped their fists around his rapidly swelling penis, though, all arguing about the price seemed to wither away, and they looked as astonished as I had when I'd first seem him unveiled. They'd barely touched him down there before he had an erection which confirmed what I'd thought all along. This guy was really into this and was clearly a natural whore who, fortunately, was a slave up for sale, so his natural talent could be turned to a profit. There wasn't a bit of shame or humiliation evident showing his monster hard in public and as they continued to stroke it in wonderment (as much as anything), he ejaculated right there on the podium. He looked downright proud of it and looked like he expected everyone to clap or something. Instead, most of us were appalled, wonder-sized as he was. But the potential buyers were mightily impressed, and after hefting up his ringed balls and feeling them after he'd orgasmed for some reason or another (I suppose to see if he felt drained or not), they conferred briefly with each other and queried the dealer with the usual barrage of questions: "Where did the dealer find him?"; "What did he do before?"; "How old was he?"; "Why does he get excited so easily?"; "What sort of training has he had in the area of sex since he performs so easily?"; "Who ringed him and how long has he been fitted?" and on and one.

Finally, they directed a few questions directly to the slave himself, who answered "I was trained since I was a child to give people whatever most brings pleasure to them. When they saw I was going to be exceptional, I was specifically trained to pleasure both women and men expertly with my god-given equipment. I am worth every penny of my price and I will not disappoint you in my duties as a provider of pleasure. It is my destiny and my fate." And with that, he nobly raised his head and arched it proudly while he thrust out his genitals for display once again. I'd heard of male whores who took great pride in what they did, but I never really believed it. Now I did. When they paid for him and ordered him to follow them in his hobble chain to wherever they were going, he didn't even bother to try to cover himself but just followed them naked as the day he was born showing it to one and all rather proudly as he arrogantly walked behind his new owners.

"What a disgusting, sordid person," I thought to myself. "I never dreamed there were people like this in the world, but I suppose with enough training, rotten background, and perverse morality you can produce anything – even a creature like this."

The dealer, well pleased that he'd received top price for this piece of meat, said to his assistants, "He's going to like it where's he going – those buyers own the biggest whorehouse here at the resort. They cater to many women who like well equipped, well-trained, and always compliant stud slaves. But they also cater to rich men who seek out the special pleasures only other men can offer with well-built slaves who are trained to meet any demand no matter what."

Apparently, some customers here at the resort loved playing the role of brothel keepers while others liked the privilege of visiting brothels stocked with such compliant, well-trained slaves. I shivered at the depravity of this resort simulating Ancient Rome – it was worse than my rather frank college course in Roman history had ever even suggested. I think that's because it's hard to imagine how far people will go when you have total and complete control over other people's fate, including their very bodies which tend to turn into meat on the market. THE FIRM specialized in making all of this possible once again, of course, and no doubt profited tremendously in the process.

I think the handsome French slave I'd met only recently while interned in the New York marketing barns got a pretty good home. He lucked out and was bought by a very rich man who was looking for a personal steward who would be big enough and smart enough to control a literal army of household slaves in the huge estate he occupied rather permanently at the resort. His new owner rather casually stroked the slave's large penis to erection, but seemed much more interested in the dealer's report on how he handled being fucked. When the dealer assured him the he had coped with a large thick dildo without much reaction, the man slipped a couple of fingers up the slave's ass to confirm the report. Since that led to only a small grunt of submission, the owner seemed most satisfied and bought him without further ado. My guess is he would end up with a lot of interesting supervisory and organizational duties, avoid heavy chores himself since he was going to be the manager, and lead a very good life – as long as he offered that ass up for a good fucking when his owner was interested.

Finally, I was left with three female slaves as all that was left for sale. Apparently, I wasn't the big draw my dealer thought I was going to be. But maybe I was wrong. Another huge litter arrived carried by eight rather short but very muscular olive-skinned liveried slaves. They were all of the same approximate height and looked Spanish or Sicilian to my unpracticed eye. They were well outfitted: body harnesses (that outlined and "lifted" their pectorals as well as their butt cheeks, confined their shaved genitals in a tight, but totally revealing net pouch, forced a visible butt plug well into their anal tract, and connected to both their thick neck collars and a wide belt around their narrow waists), sandals on their feet, rings through both tits and both ears, and tight ankle and wrist bands. The man being carried, an American judging from his Chino slacks and golf shirt, told the dealer he needed a really big slave as he was forming a new litter bearer team that would feature very tall men who had big muscular physiques as the eye-catcher. As I found out later, only four of them would be needed in that their strength would reduce the numbers needed and a new lightweight gold trimmed litter was being designed specifically for this new team. The idea was to match the team by physique and height, decorate them with arm, wrist, ankle, ear, nipple and neck bands of gold plated brass, dress them in very brief loin clothes of a gold colored silk or, even more spectacularly, have them work totally nude and proceed to bedazzle the public wherever their owner went. It was planned to be theater at its best and the resort was going to be the stage for this man's display of wealth and power. I was the exact height, weight, and frame size needed to complete the team even though I didn't know this, of course, at the time.

I wasn't as lucky as the French slave. After running his practiced hand over my shoulder, arm, thigh, back, and butt muscles, cupping my pecs, "weighing" my testicles, fingering my tits, and checking out my teeth, my large penis seemed to be of greatest interest to him as he engaged in a lively commentary with the dealer as he stroked me to full erection. Despite my extensive training in Mexico, I still felt humiliated and ashamed to have my sexual organs displayed so publicly, especially in front of a total stranger. But my prospective purchaser didn't seem to be embarrassed at all and took his time stoking and squeezing me until I broke out in a sex sweat all over my body and begin twitching as I struggled to control ejaculating right in his hand.

At least I was mortified by the event – in fact at the time I just hoped I'd die on the spot – and when I did ejaculate in the small dish held in front of me, at least I hadn't done so with some look of perverse pride on my face like the slave bought for the brothel. But I was really shamed by this forced exhibit and hoped this fellow countryman wouldn't buy me. But he did, after a lot of haggling and quibbling over the price (which was lowered considerably over what was listed on the placard beneath me), and before I knew it, the dealer threw me a tiny loincloth to "cover myself" and chained me to the back of the American's litter by my neck collar. I'd been sold!

CONTINUING THE TALE OF THE AMERICAN SLAVE:

Once delivered to my new owner's estate there at the resort, his slave overseer led me to the 'stables' where I saw exactly why I was purchased. The stables consisted of four other bearers exactly my height and build. Three were my age or even younger; one looked to be middle aged or so and I was obviously bought to be his replacement. The stables also housed two really beautiful horses used for chariot racing; a couple of huge draft horses used for pulling supply wagons, and a mastiff that was the estate watchdog. The stables were clean and airy and each of us bearers, along with each of the horses, had our own stall with no bars but just some iron rings to secure us when we weren't on duty. The overseer explained when I'd be fed, who to report to in case of severe illness or injury, the names and illustrious background of my new master, and the fact that some days we'd be on duty all day and late into the night while on other days we may never have to leave the stable. It just depended on the needs of our owner that particular day. From now on we'd be in the house livery provided for bearers and we were to always wear that livery when on duty regardless. But fashions change, even here at

THE FIRM's resort, and our owner was always interested in creating the best impression possible, of which we played an important part.

We were to bath daily, keep ourselves as clean as possible throughout the day, and groom ourselves as instructed which in any case meant daily removal of all facial hair except eyebrows and eyelashes and ALL our body hair and he meant all – everywhere – under our arms, around our genitals, even up our ass crack. The hair on our head we would keep, but it would be kept short since our duties led us to be sweaty a lot and sweaty hair hanging down was not pleasing to our owner. Our nails were to be kept neatly trimmed and clean at all times as were our ears and feet. We were to learn to eliminate all bodily wastes first thing in the morning and upon returning to the stable in the evening since urinating while on duty was unseemly, uncouth, and unbecoming to our owner and there was simply no opportunity to eliminate solid wastes except in the stable. If we couldn't learn to manage this, we could expect to receive a complete enema upon awakening each morning.

My God, I thought, wasn't there going to be any privacy at all allowed us? Whoever came up with that idea must have worked at Chicago General Hospital, I figured, long before either of us had ever heard of THE FIRM. At any rate, I decided then and there I'll do something every morning if the strain killed me in the process. If we urinated while on duty, we would be whipped severely upon return to the stables so that we'd quickly learn better manners. Therefore, it was always wise to urinate last thing before leaving the stables even if you didn't feel like it at the time as a precaution. Talk about control!

The overseer, probably in his mid-fifties, himself one of THE FIRM's slaves judging from the brand on his butt prominently displaying THE FIRM's logo, then looked me over pretty carefully and said he'd get me fitted out in the morning after I'd settled in. I quickly looked at the other bearers and saw what was in store for me.

The next morning, I had my high iron collar removed and replaced with a shiny brass collar that was real tight and was so high it forced my head up as much as the one fitted on me at THE FIRM's training school. This one wasn't hinged and was soldered in place around my neck permanently I was told. The steward explained that it had THE FIRM's logo as well as my new owner's name and address engraved right into the collar so I could be easily returned if I got lost or ran away. He added that runaway slaves were invariably returned to their owners very quickly due to the collars and the rewards people automatically got upon returning an errant slave. Runaways could easily be spotted, he added meaningfully, because they always had a big 'Fugitivus' branded on their forehead so people would be doubly sure to keep them secure from then on. He tugged on a ring soldered right into the brass collar and told me that was there for two main functions. I would normally be leashed by the neck to whatever litter I was assigned to that day so I would be part of the litter itself and would take responsibility for the litter since if anything happened to the litter it would also happen to me. He said this made litter bearers pay close attention to avoiding accidents, tipping the litter, or allowing anyone to steal the litter when the owner was on errands since any of those events meant the bearers suffered even more than the valuable litter itself. Secondly, I would be leashed at night to my stable ring so that I would be properly secured when I wasn't on duty, but that chain would be about six feet long so I'd have plenty of movement possible and after a while wouldn't give it a thought.

Next the overseer ran a red hot needle through the non-sensitive part of my ear lobes and installed two brass rings in my ear lobes that didn't hang down far enough to interfere with carrying the poles on my shoulder, let alone rub on my shoulder. They too were soldered in place and he was so skilled at this, I barely felt anything in the process. The hot needle cauterized the wound so there wasn't even any bleeding in the process. I'd heard about cauterization as an effective sterilization process back in the Middle Ages but had never actually seen it myself, let alone experience it. It was not only clean, but the risk of infection from the process was practically nil. Next I was fitted with the brass ankle and wrist bracelets the other bearers all sported and those too were soldered in place to be a permanent fixture of my body from now on. Then I received upper arm brass bands fitted right above my upper arm muscle so there was no way that could ever be removed after the solder had hardened. Then he said he had good news for me: my days of leg and wrist chains were over for now – they would just get in the way and my owner simply wouldn't tolerate all the noise those clanking chains caused and he felt it detracted from our livery.

I couldn't have agreed more and found myself happy as a lark as he removed the constant restrictions. But I dreaded what I knew was coming from looking at the other guys. His only preliminary was that he knew this would hurt a little, but after a day or so, I would have forgotten all about it. There would be no resisting or I'd pay dearly for my lack of cooperation in the matter. After all, it really didn't matter in the long run and if my owner wanted it that way, well, that was just the way it was going to be. As a precaution, he asked two of the other bearers to hold my hands steady behind me and to force my chest out for easy access. He grabbed one nipple, stroked it a bit to get it erect, squeezed it together rather painfully, took a hot needle and zapped me right through the tender flesh with a strong searing sound. I screamed and thought I was going to pass out but the bearers held me steady and then I felt a pain even stronger and looking down saw the unsoldered ring being forced through the newly seared opening in the nipple. As I slumped over, it was quickly through and soldered together just like that. I wasn't aware of the other nipple whatsoever, but when I came to a few minutes later; both nipples felt like they were literally on fire and, as I focused in through teary eyes, both brass rings were clearly 'in place'.

My livery was complete once I was issued the uniform of the day. Today's was a bright red silk cincture and other than being way too revealing by my standards, it was at least a cover so I supposed I should be grateful compared to the stark naked teams of litter bearers I'd seen trotting around the resort the short time I'd been here. After looking at my fellow litter bearers in their tiny cinctures, It was obvious they had been selected with one other similarity other than their height, weight, and musculature – all possessed huge sexual equipment which so strained those tiny cinctures that it automatically drew anyone's attention to that part of their body. I knew I was similarly 'displayed' by the tiny little cloth and, after looking at them, felt considerably more naked than if I'd had nothing on at. With this new perception, I wished I was just kept naked – at least my sexual organs wouldn't be highlighted! But I also realized that my owners could outfit their property anyway they wanted and there wasn't anything I or any of my fellow slaves could do about it.

Overall, the effect of our livery was exotic if not bizarre, but it certainly was showy and that was more of the story here at the resort than any means of transportation. In my eyes, we were about 90% for show and about 10% for locomotion, but this way of getting around wasn't really designed for efficiency to start with. We were fulfilling fantasies of the super-rich – at the very least, it was an impressive display of power and control over others and certainly paraded our handsome bodies and magnificent sexual attributes to anyone who cared to notice us. It seemed that even the other slaves were constantly looking you over – I suppose they knew that if they fell short in the comparisons, they'd soon be shipped off to new owners who would be more interested in the work to be extracted from their body than displaying their beauty at a plush place like THE FIRM's resort.

I, along with all of THE FIRM's slaves, knew as part of our original basic training that THE FIRM operated solely as a business enterprise and that our welfare and comfort didn't fit into this equation. If a greater profit could be made by our toil in a tin mine, being harnessed as a mere draft animal under a constant whip, serving as a short-term amusement for a wealthy sadist 'into' torturing slaves to death, or even harvesting our organs in a slaughter house – so be it. Right now, it seemed, THE FIRM could turn the greatest profit by supplying the best looking, best equipped slaves as stock for the resort.

Although the costume changed from day to day, the metal fittings stayed in place and I quickly got used to the physical demands of the job as well as adjusting to being stared at all the time by those we passed. Our cinctures tended to get smaller and smaller until we were barely covered. But most of the litter bearers that we passed along the street were kept totally naked. Although our genitals were prominently highlighted most of the time in those tiny revealing cinctures, it did offer a little support and kept our huge equipment from swaying around so distractingly as we witnessed in the more common nude bearers.

Since we were forbidden to sexually relieve ourselves in any way, and unable to relieve ourselves when stabled (due to having our wrists manacled directly to the stable ring), with all the many erotic sights we saw around the resort, it was inevitable we were aroused a good deal of the time and those frequent hard-ons were clearly evident to anyone looking at us. There was no way you could hide it in those tight little wisps of cloth. Our American master seemed to enjoy this added display and sometimes fondled us just for the fun of taking us beyond a simple erection to just short of ejaculating while we were standing chained to the litter while the other litter bearers and bystanders smirked at our predicament as we broke out in a sex sweat and began twitching in pre-orgasmic spasms.

Consequentially, after only a few days of this, we were in "constant need" as the overseer put it with obvious delight, and I began to feel like an animal in heat who longed for nothing more than a simple ejaculation. I even found myself evaluating every situation in terms of its potential for 'getting off' – even to the point of rubbing myself against the litter when my owners weren't watching. If someone had ordered me to masturbate right in public, I would have been delighted. My humiliation was complete, I thought dejectedly.

All of us were totally naked when we were chained in our stalls in that the overseer, always looking for ways to save our master money, didn't want us getting our valuable costumes dirty or worn looking when off-duty, and looking at the other guys in their stalls with constant erections didn't help me much when neither I nor they could do anything about those erections. We were very well fed, given decent rest most days, and although waiting for hours and hours in the rain leashed to the litter while my master passed the time at someone's dinner party was not only monotonous with nothing to do and downright unhealthy at times, overall we were fairly well treated. Probably luxuriously pampered by the standards applied to THE FIRM's slaves in mining and construction work, I thought to myself.

I was bored a great deal of the time because there was a lot of waiting many, many days. But other days we got to see a lot of THE FIRM's huge resort and it really fascinated me. Being chained up every day was a real drag, but frankly, I was so tired most nights it really didn't seem to matter – I was too tired to go anywhere anyway.

The other litter bearers were all as young as I was if not younger and overall were a friendly enough lot. But often one of them would not be chained up in the stables at night and I got curious and then envious as why they were allowed freedom and I wasn't. So one day I got up my courage and asked the overseer about it. Due to his age and wisdom, I had come to view this fellow slave as almost a father despite the harsh discipline he maintained at all times, including some severe beatings over the inevitable small mistakes I would make from time to time. His smiled for a brief moment, but then sharply said slaves in his stable didn't need to know everything and perhaps I should be glad I was chained in the stables, but my day would probably come. He reminded me it was out of place for slaves to ask questions and, taking his ever present slave whip, whacked me soundly across the rump to remind me of proper slave manners until my ass was aflame with pain. I never brought the subject up with him again. But I eventually asked one of the guys who seemed to be absent a lot of nights and was always so tired the next morning he sometimes tripped us up in our coordinated lifts and trots and I was getting upset about it.

When I really pressed him about always being so tired, he finally looked me straight in the eye and said it sure as hell wasn't his fault and I should grow up and start doing something around the house other than just carrying that damn litter all over the resort. He and the other guys were getting damn tired of my haughty attitude and not taking on any of the other duties expected of a litter bearer in this day and age.

I stared at him in disbelief and told him I didn't have the faintest idea of what he was talking about. "Get off it," he said and rolled his eyes in disgust.

"No, I really don't know," I pleaded.

"Look," he said, "the master didn't buy that pretty body of yours just to carry his damn gilded litter all over the resort. Litter bearers are supposed to earn their keep in other ways too and so far you've dumped the whole load off on the three of us and acted like you were something special. We're damn tired of it – from now on, you can get in there and hustle like the rest of us and I'll start engaging in little beauty sleeps every night like you've enjoyed ever since you got here."

I still didn't have the foggiest notion of what he was talking about and I guess the look on my face finally convinced him I wasn't putting on an act or something.

"Look," he said, "how much do I have to spell it out for you. The master expects us to pleasure him when that's what he wants and we're supposed to do it just right or we get into real trouble. That's one reason we're never allowed to shoot off – he wants us kept horny all the time so we're eager to serve him at his beck and call. You've never bothered to shoulder your share of that load at all – all you'd done is be the perfect little litter bearer. Well, believe you me; it's how you please your owner in bed that's going to determine your future – not hoisting that stupid litter all over town as a sideshow for the resort's residents."

I just stared at him a long time and it was then that I knew he really did believe I was that naive.

"But no one told me," I shuttered, "and no one ever even hinted I was supposed to do anything like that."

"Look, stupid, and I'm beginning to believe you are really as stupid as you sound half the time, you aren't ordered to bed – that's not what the owners want – you're supposed to volunteer for duty – like it's something you always wanted to do and would take utmost pleasure in doing – sort of like the apex of your life goals so to speak. It flatters them and that's exactly what they want. The master picked your body out very carefully when he bought you, let me remind you if you've already forgotten, stupid, and he wasn't picking you out just to tote his litter around town – no way. He was picking out a boy to service him in bed or, more likely, if your experience is like the rest of us, service his friends when he's in a generous mood, or he wouldn't have bought you to start with. Now, in our owner's eyes, you're supposed to pick him and that means making sure you tell him you're interested and available. Then your turn will come and you can get as little sleep as some of the rest of us," he explained bitterly. "Where in the hell were you trained, anyway? Or did they just pick you up off the streets and ship you here?" he added disgustedly.

With that revelation, I retired for the evening because I felt as absolutely stupid as he had indicated. Jesus, I thought. Just when I thought I could live like this. And here when I was congratulating myself for adjusting so well to slavery! Now I'm supposed to offer my body up for my owner's pleasures, whatever they might have in mind, and volunteer it to boot! And I thought the guy sold at the slave market who was blatantly displaying himself was a perverted whore or whatever I thought at the time. Looks like we had more in common than I thought at the time. Although my Mexican training had certainly included being used sexually over and over until I accepted it as a fact of life, I couldn't remember any specific training on begging a master to use me. Maybe I wasn't paying proper attention at the time, or maybe they didn't cover that part. I knew our bodies were to be exploited sexually a lot and we were expected to response to any and all commands in that area at our owner's whim – but I didn't understand we had to plead for our usage! THE

FIRM could do a better job of training us, I thought. Better training wouldn't have led me to this situation where my fellow slaves were mad at me for being so stupid.

The choice wasn't left up to me, like most things in slavery. My three companions got together after I'll accused the one of being a slacker and volunteered my services for me in their own nasty little ways of giving subtle signals of availability to our master. They did this while they were 'servicing' him by suggesting adventure and variety and hinting I was the best; I was inexhaustible; and that I'd told them I really wanted to be used because I couldn't stand the no-sex situation I was faced with in the stable. Things like that. They even suggested I was really good with them when the master was away from the resort and the overseer allowed them a little relief to keep them in shape. Thanks, fellows!

It wasn't long until the master told me as he alighted from the litter that he'd tell the overseer he was expecting me in late evening. That night I was ushered into his chambers, told to get rid of that silly rag around me and bring him the delight he was sure I could bring him, or he'd personally see I was appropriately whipped in the morning and it would be a whipping I wouldn't forget. With that he reached over and started fondling me until I was erect and then positioned me on my stomach over the edge of his bed and lubricated my asshole thoroughly before plowing into me as he massaged my ringed tits with his hands. But THE FIRM has trained me for just such exploitation and before the night was over, I managed to guarantee I'd escape the threatened whipping, even if I had to use my body like a real experienced whore to do it!

The next morning I had sore tits, a well used asshole, cum dripping out of my rear end, and really felt used and even helpless, but wasn't that the most essential part of being one of THE FIRM's slaves? But the truth is, some of the things done to me had surprisingly produced some of the most erotic feelings I'd ever experienced in my sheltered life to date, and, while I hated being told exactly what to do, I had to admit I looked forward to another round of the sexual arousal, sensuous pleasures, and physical relief I had experienced during the night. Being able to discharge at long last was worth anything at that point – it was pure heaven!

It was good I felt that way about it, because, once started, I got called to my master's room at least twice a week after that.

While I'm confessing, I might as well admit that I got called to the overseer's room almost as often and again, while I never was ashamed or felt dirty about it and certainly not immoral since a slave is not responsible for his actions, I found as much pleasure with him as I did with my master despite the fact he was the one who didn't mind disciplining me frequently with his ever present whip and who made sure I was kept in line at all times. Maybe because of his age and long tenure as a slave himself, he liked to call all the shots and he made it adamantly clear that slaves under his jurisdiction were there for his pleasure, not theirs, and failure to meet his exacting demands would led to severe punishment in the morning. In fact, I liked being called to the overseer's room much better. He remembered when he too had been called to a master's bed repeatedly in his younger days, and often let me ejaculate without seeking his permission and he rarely made me stay hard all night long regardless of how much he had used me already.

Fairly often, my master had some friend of his in the chambers so they could enjoy me jointly. But somehow, even this usage never really bothered me very much – after all, my body was their property to use as they saw fit! I was really learning fast how slaves survive in a world they have absolutely no control over! Three times I got beaten really hard for not satisfying my master or his friends in their use of me. That's all it took because the pain was close to unbearable. After that, I tried my utmost to please him and his friends, no matter what they asked of me. It's amazing how pain teaches a slave his duties so fast. All thoughts of rebellion simply evaporate because a slave always knows that he can be beaten again to an inch of his life at the mere whim of his master. Actually, everything seemed to be working out rather well here at the resort.

THE RESORT'S EMPLOYEE LOUNGE:

Mr. Yamahoma arranged THE FIRM's four employee visitors around the table as he passed out paper and pencil.

"Well, what have we learned after studying THE FIRM's slave from Chicago?" he prompted.

David, Forrest, Bill and Wade all looked at each other to see who was going to start the discussion.

"I can see how I fucked up on his training down in Mexico," Wade blurted out. "That business about not understanding his new owner would expect him to volunteer for bed duty is inexcusable. I'll make sure we take care of that aspect in any future training."

"You're probably right, Wade," Bill said, "but he should of have been reminded of just what's expected of all THE FIRM's slaves when he was being sorted and classified in the New York barns, so it's just as much my fault as yours, Wade. I make sure they're fucked thoroughly at least twice a day by some of our best studs while they're in the barns, but apparently just fucking their brains out doesn't teach them squat about hustling to earn their keep. Any buyers of THE FIRM's stock have a right to expect that level of training at least."

"Maybe it's my fault in selecting this yokel from Chicago almost solely on his physique, good looks, and lack of family," David interjected. "Maybe I shouldn't have ventured so far afield and stuck with the usual -you know, the lifers in prison, incarcerated juvenile delinquents with no family, street people, drug addicts, orphanages, war refugees, children sold by their impoverished parents. Those with a handsome face, a well-built physique, and some heavy equipment between their legs, at least know right off the bat they're going have to hustle to survive. After all, they've been doing it long before we introduced them to slavery. If you select well, they barely notice the difference between their life before we introduced them to slavery and their life as part of THE FIRM's available stock, other than their life is more predictable now and they're certainly better taken care of."

All chuckled at this last observation as its truth was so self-evident.

"A school teacher, for God's sake," David blurted out as he blushed. "What was I thinking of? Slaves are best off not thinking, and that guy was an intellectual if there ever was one. Jesus, when I saw him at the resort, he was still thinking, thinking, thinking away about who and what he was, his situation, how he should react, and all the other bullshit that slaves have no business dabbling around with. It was obvious to me, despite all the training he'd received from you, Wade, and all the treatment he experienced at the barns in New

York, Bill, he still thought it was important what he "thought" about an event or that someone cared about how he "felt" about something. I'm afraid we all screwed up on that one, Mr. Yamahoma," as David looked shamefaced at the ground beneath him. "I'll be a lot more careful in my procuring from now on, believe me, or THE FIRM's headed for real trouble."

"Ah, David, you're too hard on yourself," Forrest broke the silence. "I'm as responsible for this as any of you. No matter what background you snatched him from, David, it was me that was charged with getting him aimed toward the right training and slave assignment anyway. I just naively sent him down to standard training with Wade's operation in Mexico when it's obvious I should have sent him to THE FIRM's breaking school in the Spanish Sahara. Four months in that program and he would have ended up begging a horse to use him if it would ensure him a decent meal. And it certainly would have knocked out any nonsense about one of THE FIRM's slaves thinking and feeling about his present condition. That's why THE FIRM runs the breaking school, anyway, and I was really stupid not to use that facility for that particular slave. I was just trying to save THE FIRM some money I guess by sending him down to Wade's shorter program and it was a bad mistake – a mistake I won't make again, let me assure you."

"You're probably all too hard on yourself," Mr. Yamahoma smiled warmly. "But I can see Mr. Broadley knew exactly what he was doing in inviting you here. We've all learned from our experience already, and the fun's only begun.

Mr. Yamahoma clapped his hands and four breathtakingly beautiful blond boys in their early twenties entered the room and bowed before each of the four visitors, their oiled nude bodies gleaning in the soft light of the room. Each possessed a short, but exceedingly muscular physique and each was very heavy hung, a fact made clearly evident by their rigid erections.

"Enjoy, boys, they're yours for the evening – compliments of THE FIRM."

THE SLAVE FROM CHICAGO (CONTINUED):

While I was on litter duty the next day, I overheard my master speaking to a close friend of his. He was talking about a slave he'd heard of being put up for sale by THE FIRM in New York and from what he'd heard this male slave was more beautiful and striking than any slave, male or female, currently for sale in any of the resort's periodic auctions. All of his friends would be envious if he could buy him for display purposes and he felt it would make a fitting 35th birthday present for himself. He babbled on to his friend about how exotic and unbelievably handsome he'd heard this male slave was and that, in addition, he was a jet black Nubian, a great rarity at the resort in the last few years since THE FIRM was now flooding the slave market with so many farm-bred mulattos.

That night, as luck would have it, I was called to my master's chambers and when I'd sucked and been fucked over and over until he seemed totally satisfied and when I felt it was safe to talk, I whispered to him as humbly as I knew how I'd overheard him asking his friend about the Nubian slave in New York. He was startled I had eavesdropped on the conversation and after being soundly slapped across the mouth for being "too nosy for a slave," he asked me if I knew anything about the Nubian slave. I told him I was caged with the Nubian in New York right before being sent to the resort's auctions and surely it was the same slave since the Nubian I knew was absolutely the most breathtakingly handsome man I had ever seen, but seemingly was fairly untrained in that he didn't seem very interested in men when he was caged with me and was incapable of fucking me with ordered to do so by a potential customer – an event that led to severe beatings for both of us of course.

I suggested he take me along with him to the New York market as his personal body slave and I could find out the extent of his slave training and any weaknesses this slave might have directly from the other slave stock in the barns of New York who had been around him a lot. Not only could I help him avoid a potentially bad purchase, but I could probably find out things that would save the master a lot of money when it came to bargaining over the slave's price. Besides, he could use me to his heart's pleasure on the long flight to New York and back if the Nubian purchase didn't work. I would make every effort to make his journey as comfortable as possible.

He didn't pursue the matter further, but instead rather roughly placed my head between his legs and indicated I should have another go at bringing him pleasure with my humble mouth and nimble tongue, but I knew I had started him thinking about it and proceeded to make him so damn happy I thought he'd forget it was my idea and not his.

Sure enough, the very next day all sorts of preparations were being made for the big shopping trip to New York. Once on board one of THE FIRM's small private jets, I was immediately 'put to work' and by the time the plane landed, my throat and jaw felt paralyzed from constantly being stretched, my asschute was sore and raw from being repeatedly fucked, and one of my nipples was beginning to bleed from my master's constant fondling of the swollen nub. Upon landing, I was told to put on a pair of overalls for the trip to THE FIRM's New York facilities – the first clothes I'd worn in some time, but once in THE FIRM's barn I was ordered to strip immediately so my slave status would be evident to all.

The striking Nubian slave was still for sale at an exorbitant price, but it turned out my information on him was woefully out of date. Apparently, I had been caged with him just days after he'd been procured in the upper Sudan. Now, months later, his training had been completed right there in New York. He was not only better looking than ever, but was literally transformed into a compliant, highly skilled, and eager lover of both men and women – the choice being up to whoever purchased him. Here was living proof of THE FIRM's effective training methods and all of this had been accomplished with an unscarred body, a willing attitude, and an ever present smile on his handsome face. He was even being touted as a potential stud to justify the high asking price. My inquiries among the other caged slaves there in New York only validated everything THE FIRM claimed for the Nubian, especially since many of them had either fucked the Nubian or been fucked by him as part of his rigorous training regime and, although they had been ordered to do so at a time they themselves were tired and worn out in their own training, they still treasured the memory of their time with the Nubian above all others.

Hence, I produced nothing to help my master strike a better bargain and he resented it since even my services in the airplane could have been provided almost as well, maybe even better, by one of the plane's regular stewards. Upon purchase of the prized Nubian, my master would surely be using him in all ways possible on the flight back and I knew my master would put me on the block at the very first opportunity.

But you know what? Slavery had taught me a lot and I could handle it, even with the likelihood that I'd have at least four or five more owners before it was all over, even knowing I would be sexually exploited as long as I was young and attractive, and even knowing I would be worked and worked hard as long as a whip could produce one remaining shiver in my tormented body. Like all other of THE FIRM's slaves, there wasn't a damn thing I could do to change it.

My master delighted in his intimate inspection of the Nubian up for sale and found him as exotic and attractive as had been rumored. When THE FIRM's salesman suggested he try the slave out for himself, my master didn't hesitate and I stood dejectedly at one side while he thoroughly fucked the boy, first while he was on all fours and then with the slave on his back with his long legs drawn up over his shoulders. I could tell he was well-trained by this time – he noticeably clenched his ass at the appropriate times to increase my master's pleasure, and was obviously capable of 'milking' my master with his well-trained ass muscles once my master was deep inside him. There wasn't a hint of resistance at any time – quite the contrary, the Nubian seemed to welcome being fucked as forcefully as possible and profusely thanked my master when he had finished fucking him. Almost as an aside, my master thought he better test the Nubian's fucking abilities and ordered him to fuck me the minute he pulled his long shaft out of the slave's hole.

The black slave motioned for me to get on my back and lift my legs which I did without hesitation of course since it had been ordered by my master. He placed his monstrous erect phallus at my open hole and plunged in to the hilt. Unwittingly, I gasped at the pain and then let out a low moan as he promptly started pumping in and out of me.

"Quiet," my master commanded with some disgust as he looked at my face contorted with pain. "Does you good to get opened up properly and, if it hurts a little, serves you right for babbling out bad information. You, slave boy," he said kicking the Nubian in the butt, "fuck that boy harder. I want to see him screaming for mercy before you shoot your load."

"Yes, master," was the last I heard before I passed out.

When I came to, the Nubian was still fucking me and looked totally exhausted when he was ordered off of me and chained by his neck collar for the trip to THE FIRM's airplane.

Eventually, I too was leashed by my collar and taken to that same airplane but this time tightly caged in the cargo hold, while my replacement was being used in the passenger compartment. Evidently, I had been traded in on the Nubian and would soon be back at the resort's auction block. When I was being unloaded, I saw the Nubian once again. The steward told me the boy had been fucked five times by his new owner, twice by the steward, and three times by the pilot. He looked exhausted as his master led him down the exit ramp by a leash attached to his collar.

I noticed the steward had been thoughtful enough to insert one of THE FIRM's patented medicated butt plugs into the Nubian before he was led away. I knew from personal experience in my training that the special plug, made out of a porous plastic containing all sorts of goodies, would temporarily anesthetize a very sore overworked butt, treat any torn tissue with a mild antibiotic, and soak up most of the cum that had been pumped into him.

I was uncaged, leashed, and taken directly to the holding pens for the upcoming Roman-style auction by THE FIRM's slave dealer at their resort. It was the very slave market where I had first been sold. This time, of course, I sported ear and tit rings, but the gold plated neck, arm, wrist, and ankle bands had been removed in New York – ready and waiting for my replacement, I assumed. The dealer received me chain-leashed to my original hinged iron collar with a naked body freshly shaved and oiled before the New York departure.

The only explanation for this turn of events was from the dealer who said, "Your previous owner has 'tired' of you," but I suspect opening my big mouth about potential future purchases had something to do with it. Especially since the newly purchased Nubian was the same height and weight as the rest of his team of litter bearers and could easily replace me – both carrying the litter, and, as demonstrated right in the airplane on the return trip, in his bed.

Even here affirmative action was affecting my work life, I thought grimly. But I knew slaves were frequently traded by THE FIRM's customers and it was probably one of many changes of ownership I could expect during my lifetime now that my destiny as a slave had been sealed by my recruitment into THE FIRM's inventory of stock.

Once again, a dealer chained me to a sales plinth with legs widespread and placed a sales placard at my feet. This time there was no need to remove a cincture since I was stark naked to start with this time around. Compared to my last visit here, I was considerably more muscular, had tightened in the waist while my chest and hips were even better defined, had greatly increased lung capacity, knew all the appropriate mannerisms of a properly trained slave offered by THE FIRM (like keeping my eyes to the ground when in the presence of non-slaves, never speaking unless asked a direct question, always doing exactly as commanded as quickly as possible, and never flinching or resisting in any way any bodily examination or use of my body), and had long ago abandoned any notions that my body was my own, including its use in an owner's bed.

I was one of about 10 up for sale at that particular auction and most of them seemed as placid and reserved as I was about our pending sale.

AT THE FIRM'S RESORT – EMPLOYEE LOUNGE:

"That slave from Chicago's right back where he started from," Mr. Yamahoma laughed as the four guest employees gathered for an afternoon drink.

"I'm not surprised he got dumped," Wade said. "Although I'm the one that supposedly trained him, I'm sure his owner realized there's a lot better out there."

"Well, his master traded him in on a big black he heard about that was up for auction in our New York barns. The black's about the same size overall so he'll fit into serving as a litter bearer just fine and, from what I understand from our New York sources, is a crackerjack in bed. The FIRM was marketing him as a display slave to justify the huge price they were asking, but I suppose he'll be on display here at the resort anyway, litter bearer or not. That way we can all enjoy the sight!" Mr. Yamahoma laughed as he sipped the drink served by a beautiful slave boy, obviously from some South American country judging by his Incan features.

"Kneel, boy," Mr. Yamahoma commanded, pointing to his side. As the slave boy sunk to his knees with a bowed head, Mr. Yamahoma began playing with the large tit rings highlighting massive pectorals.

"The serving boy is well equipped," Forrest noted as the slave's organ swelled in response to the tit play.

"He fucks well, too," Bill added. "I spotted him here in the bar last night after we were finished with the blonds, and had him sent to my room. He's as eager as a bitch in heat," Bill laughed.

"Mr. Broadley called this morning and thought you four would enjoy watching the slave from Chicago being auctioned off again. Oh, "Mr. Yamahoma continued, "and he added after I'd told him of your comments from our last meeting, that he was glad the little boondoggle at THE FIRM's resort was proving to be so educational."

"Oh, Oh, sounds like we're in trouble," Bill said with a worried look. "I really did goof up when I shipped him over here for immediate sale when I should have sent him for slave adjustment training which we offer right there in New York."

"You're in trouble?" Wade shouted. "What about the guy that was responsible for training him in the first place?"

"Mr. Broadley's been in the business for a long time," Mr. Yamahoma counseled. "He always figures in an error margin – you all know that – and that error margin extends to some of his very best employees. There's no way you can be in this business and expect to be perfect in every case. Let me assure you, you're not in trouble – quite the contrary – Mr. Broadley told me how happy he was you were all enjoying a well deserved rest at the resort. Besides, Mr. Broadley knows as well as I do that the Chicago slave will still work out fine and THE FIRM is going to get a profit off that body for years to come. You'll see! Now, can I interest you in the auction?"

"You know, I never get tired of a good slave auction," Forrest said. "I guess it's because I so seldom have time to go to one anymore. Before, when David and I were just good customers of THE FIRM, we tried to never miss any of the big ones!"

"Come to think of it, none of us here probably get to see the finished product much," Bill added. "We're all so busy getting the stock to market, we never see the market ourselves!"

"The auction is scheduled within the hour," Mr. Yamahoma said. "You better get down to the market now if you want to look any of the offerings over before they're sold."

With that, we quickly finished our drinks and left hurriedly for the market, leaving Mr. Yamahoma still toying with the Incan slave's tits, now a bright maroon color and swollen to double their size. As we turned to say goodbye, the slave boy's face was burrowed between Mr. Yamahoma's thighs and we heard him slurping and gasping as he swallowed the Director's shaft deep into his throat.

"He sucks well, too," Mr. Yamahoma gasped as he began pumping into the boy's mouth. It was typical of the Director to always have the last word.

THE CHICAGO SLAVE UP FOR SALE AGAIN – THE RESORT:

I noticed four rather young men entering the sales arena rather hastily and quickly deduced they were part of the staff here at the resort rather than potential purchasers. I vaguely knew those four: one named David had first procured me into THE FIRM's stock in Chicago, his friend Forrest had then classified me and arranged to have me shipped down to Mexico where the man named Master Wade had been in charge of the slave training procedures, and later I had met the man named Master Bill in New York, who made the final preparations for my initial sale. I wondered what they were doing here at THE FIRM's resort and wondered if they were here, like the paying customers, for fun, or if their visit was for some other reason. Either way, a slave needn't concern himself about it, especially a slave shortly to have his whole destiny decided by a single word "Sold"!

One of the women slaves up for auction was sold early: a plain looking German girl who the dealer claimed had been trained by THE FIRM as a cook "for a noble family" since her enslavement a few years back. A rather stern looking elderly matron became her new owner, but not until she had managed to establish her authority by putting a few stripes across the girl's back with a short whip she seemed to carry at all times.

Next, I was looked over thoroughly by a matron of about 40, including stroking me to erection, hefting my balls, and squeezing my tits before checking out my teeth.

"Not big enough," she complained to the dealer after pistoning my erect shaft with her clenched fist.

She moved on to another stall. I wondered how many male slaves would be stroked to erection and have their balls fondled before she found the freak she was seeking.

As soon as she left, one of the slave handlers snickered as he commented to his co-worker, "That woman has checked out every poor slave boy in this market every time she visits the resort. I wonder when she'll find her dream boy?"

"We get a lot of that here at the resort," the first handler reflected. "You know, people just enjoying themselves handling some pretty attractive meat."

"Window shoppers," snorted his companion. "Goes with the trade, I suppose."

"Well, doesn't hurt anybody," the handler commented.

My balls still ached from being groped so vigorously by the matronly lady, and if everyone stoked my shaft as tightly as she had, my skin would be chafed within the hour, but I knew the handler didn't count slaves in his assessment of who gets hurt. Slaves in any of THE FIRM's facilities were so plentiful none of the customers or staff ever seemed to think of them as human, but merely as talking livestock. Our thorough training insured that attitude would prevail.

"We've got a lot more men window shoppers than women, seems like," the handler added. "Especially looking the big male slaves over – you know, the ones hung like a damn horse."

"Yeah, and I bet most of them are all hung about like a boy of 10 themselves," his colleague snickered. "You know what THE FIRM's sales manager says in that buying guide they give out to all the customers, 'If you don't have it, buy it.' But, for those who can't buy it, he might as well say, 'If you can't buy it; at least feel it!'" and they both broke into a fresh gale of laughter as the first handler came over and roughly groped my balls and fisted my penis as a demonstration.

The next two up for sale were incredibly ugly big brutes in their early twenties who were sold as muscle for some guest's private galley. These too had not been procured and trained by THE FIRM, but had simply been bought up at some wholesale close-out for resale at the resort. Sturdy and muscular, but with few remaining teeth and with hides more whip scars than skin, no one even bothered to shave them anymore. Heavily manacled, they obviously were never allowed any sexual outlets in that their rather smallish sexual organs seemed to be in a state of constant erection which only added to their brutish, animalistic appearance. They went cheap as you'd expect – without THE FIRM's guarantee in back of them, they were merely muscle to row an oar until they were dumped over the ship's side dead after only a few years of hellish toil. When they realized they'd been sold to a galley, they struggled desperately against their chains and wailed in misery until the whip brought them to the ground gasping for breath. They knew this last sale was their death knell.

A young girl was next sold as a serving maid to an Italian countess without incidence. Then a beautiful young blond boy, 18 but still in the growing stages, was sold as a 'coffee' boy to an effete young Arab. He'd have an easy life until his new owner got bored and bought another. If he were smart, he'd make himself indispensable by whatever means it took. But he was probably too young to understand that simple fact and would be right back here for sale by THE FIRM within a few months. I should know, I thought bitterly. Look where I'm at right now!

Within a very short time, another buyer looked me over most thoroughly from head to toe and then checked out my responses to his handling. This included posturing with all my muscles tensed so he could study the definition; feeling me quiver as he stuck two fingers up my ass and pumped them a bit; studying my reaction to inserting those same two fingers into my mouth to check my teeth; and, as I had grown accustomed to when placed on sale, the usual ball massage and then stroking of my penis until erect. This buyer even went a bit further: he pulled on each tit-ring and then twisted them until I groaned and then flinched from the pain, and he stoked my penis long after it was erect until I started leaking pre-cum which seemed to satisfy him for the moment.

"You want to 'test' this boy in the privacy of my office?" the dealer offered. I envisioned being masturbated to orgasm so he could see for himself the quality and quantity of my cum or fucked right then and there and I blushed at the thought of being used so callously, although I knew this happened to a lot of slaves up for auction. THE FIRM was proud of their product and allowed potential customers to conduct any tests they wanted. They realized that, despite their worldwide reputation for quality, few buyers were willing to buy a pig in a poke.

"No," the buyer said. "All I wanted was to see if I could breed him with no difficulties. Having him shoot his stuff won't tell me if his seed's any good or not, but at least I know he's capable of being mated." With that, he let go of my prick and completed the transaction paying the full asking price without even attempting to bargain the price down a bit.

"Want a cincture on him?" the dealer asked as he pointed to the tiny little rag, emblazoned with THE FIRM's logo, dealer's issued free if the buyer was interested.

"Might as well," my new owner laughed. "It'll be one of the last times he'll be all covered up, at least as long as I own him." I blushed in shame and started to sob as I tied the tiny little cincture around my still swollen organ. If he called this "all covered up," I couldn't imagine what he had in mind for me.

"What are you crying about, boy?" the dealer laughed as he smacked me hard across the chest with the whip he always carried. My ringed nipples received the brunt of the whipping and the pain shot like electricity through every nerve in my upper torso. I gasped.

"You modest or what?" as he smacked me again on the nipples, this time even harder. "Slaves can't afford being particular," he shouted rather angrily as he smacked me again, this time right in the genitals, "especially those bringing full price." I doubled over in renewed pain from the new punishment which only made him whip me across my now exposed neck several more times. "You're lucky to get a good owner," the dealer ranted as he continued to rain blows on my open body. "If your owner wants you naked, that's the way it's going to be, and you might as well get used to it right away. Dirt like you don't decide those things, slave!" he screamed as he grabbed my right tit-ring and twisted it until I fell to my knees screaming in agony. "Don't you get uppity with any customer who's good enough to buy you, pig shit. I'll not have my reputation sullied by a slave bastard like you," he added as he smacked me across the face until my face hit the ground. "Who in the hell trained you anyway?"

"Calm down, calm down," my new owner chuckled. "It's only a slave, after all. He'll learn his manners soon enough. The way he's acting, I doubt if he's been a slave all that long. Given a little more experience, he'll learn that being naked all the time is the least of his worries as one of my litter bearers." His droll humor did stop the dealer's whip on my body. "I've never had trouble with any of THE FIRM's slaves before and I don't expect any trouble from this one once he settles in."

Later that day, I was again bathed, body shaved, and refitted with new shiny brass arm, wrist, and ankle bracelets. A new tight-fitting brass collar was welded on, my tit and ear rings were polished and checked that their soldering was tight, and a whole new body accouterment was installed: a broad brass genital ring fitted snugly around my scrotum and the base of my penis. I'd seen it on a number of other male slaves, especially those on public display a lot like litter bearers, dining room and bath attendants, athletes, acrobats, and brothel slaves. It did for me exactly what it did for them: it lifted my sexual apparatus up and out – I was now "displayed" for both sight and feel. But I knew that it also served like a cincture to some extent: it could help prevent hernias as well as a jock strap. Most litter bearers hated and loved the device: they hated being displayed so flagrantly on the whim of their owner; they loved the protection against hernias it offered when lifting those heavy litters. And, despite the vulgar display aspect, it kept their organs pulled up and taut when trotting down the road. All slaves I knew would have preferred wearing a cincture and the covering it afforded. But, if you had to be displayed like this, there were some advantages, at least for a litter-bearer. At any rate, I wasn't asked whether I wanted one installed or not! The installation didn't take long – the soldering burnt a little, but nothing like when my tit rings were fitted.

The next morning, I stared down at my prick so prominently displayed now, especially with the erection I usually experienced in the mornings when I had no relief. It looked twice as big thrust out like this and I felt like a whore. I caught my breath as I began sobbing in utter despair and imagined what I now looked like: an object totally nude, shaved of all body hair, collared like a dog, tit-ringed, and now with banded genitals permanently hefted up for convenient 'handling'.

Just then, the overseer arrived to begin my daily body shave and I quickly tried to control my unauthorized sobs of self-pity.

"Tomorrow, we'll start your flushings," he stated matter-of-factly. "In this household, all litter bearers get flushed every morning. It saves embarrassment for our beloved master, and, of course, you're always clean if someone decides to fuck you. Three every morning, slave, or until they run clean."

Having been 'flushed in my other ownership had prepared me for this, although I could avoid it before if I dumped voluntarily each morning. Not here, apparently, and I'd never considered being fucked "on duty" during the daytime. Obviously, slaves here weren't allowed even a remnant of personal dignity.

After the usual slave gruel for breakfast, I was introduced to the other litter bearers – eight of us altogether – and sized them up. We were closely matched in size, musculature, and sexual equipment. Huge in all three areas and all three areas were prominently displayed. The only thing that differed was our color: two blonds; one other white that was black-haired like me; two blacks with black hair of course; and two brown-skinned boys with brown hair. All were completely body shaved and all were ringed exactly like me, including the wide genital banding, so all protruded obscenely. Three of them had been branded at some point of another – probably born into slavery at one of THE FIRM's breeding farms. The other four had probably been 'broken' as THE FIRM liked to refer to those knowing some other status in life at some point. Standing there stark naked totally submissively with bands forcing our genitals out for 'display', it didn't seem to make much difference at this point who'd been 'born' into it and who hadn't.

The steward then ordered us to bend over, spread our legs as part apart as possible, grab our ankles and spread our cheeks. A metal-tipped whip cracking across one of the black slave's bottom with the accompanying scream hurried our compliance. Next a heavily greased 8x3" leather butt plug was jammed into each of our displayed assholes with a chorus of muted groans, gasps, and grunts as we struggled to accommodate this invasion into our ass chutes. The bulge at the end of each plug was the last to go in; but once the sphincter closed over it, there was no way we could expel it – we were truly plugged. A crack of his whip across the closest slave's legs was accompanied with his order to stand up, get the master's largest litter out, and assemble at the front of the villa for a little trip into town.

The litter was right there in the stable with us, and as we walked toward it, the churning in our bowels caused a few of us to arch back and walk on our tip toes. A few gasped as their butt checks tightened around the anal invader, and some walked splay legged like they were being split in half. But the whip across our backs precluded any adjustment time and we soon had the heavy litter on our shoulders and in place.

When our new master ordered us to a fast trot and backed it up with a metal tipped whip he carried which reached either the front or back of even the most remote bearer, our bowels felt like they were on fire, but the unbearable pace demanded, the constant whip, and the heavy load soon overshadowed our concerns about a fully stuffed ass. Gasping for air, we scarcely had time to consider our bleeding backs, the whip wails on our chests or rumps, and the crushing load on our shoulders. But adjust we did – but only after every single one of us had broken into tears and was openly sobbing between moaning from the incessant whipping. Between my tears, I could make out bystanders richly enjoying the spectacle.

And spectacle it was. Asses churning around the huge dildos stuffed in us; pricks and balls, now stiffly erect from having our prostates continually stimulated, thrust out on full display by our genital banding; and tit rings swinging in perfect coordination with our rapid pace. Our constant gasping added to this scene of total subjugation visitors at the resort so enjoyed. I glanced at our owner, riding so comfortably on our straining shoulders, languidly flicking his whip over our naked bodies, watching our ass cheeks constantly tightening in resistance to the dildos he'd ordered fitted in us, watching the sweat literally flying off our bodies as they steamed in the early morning cool, hearing our constant gasping for air due to the pace he imposed, and seeing our erect swollen phalluses bobbing around in perfect synchronization with our gait. He slowly stroked his own erect phallus as he took in the heady experience. Surely, such total control was the ultimate joy of owning slaves – a fact THE FIRM had understood for years, he thought reflectively.

When we got toward the resort's main downtown square, I felt I was near fainting, and the desperate gasping on all sides told me the other slaves were no better off than I was. But suddenly, he quietly ordered "Halt" and when the litter was smoothly placed on its legs, he walked around us, still chained to the litter bars of course, and inspected his property who were heaving for air, soaked in sweat, and, in two cases at least, bleeding a little in their ass holes.

A small group of weekend vacationers, taking advantage of one of THE FIRM's special offers for those financially unable to be actual customers for their main stock in trade, assembled around the naked slaves and stared at their huge endowments on display. Such visitors, invited by THE FIRM because of their strong interest in owning a slave and their future potential in earnings, could, at this point, barely afford a single well-worn ugly slave, let alone a whole team of these beauties.

"Go ahead," our owner said magnanimously, "feel them all you want. Just make sure they don't shoot," he laughed.

Instantly, hands from all directions grabbed our balls, stroked our shaft, pinched our nipples, stoked our faces, and tried to work the butt plugs back and forth in our chutes. I shuddered in utter despair as the last shred of human dignity melted in my complete humiliation.

"Look at this black slave's tits, Claude," a young man said in amazement as he reached out and rubbed them between his thumb and forefinger. "They're bigger than my wife's."

"Well, I haven't seen your wife's tits, Clint, but they sure as hell are 'well developed' shall we say," his friend answered as he squeezed the same black's balls in his fist. "But feel his balls – you won't find balls like this on most slaves let me tell you," he instructed his friend as if he commonly weighed the slave's balls in his hand. "Go ahead, Claude – you'll need both hands. There – that's right. Now just squeeze them so you can feel how full he is. Now squeeze them hard. See what I mean?" The black slave closed his eyes and quietly groaned as he endured the rough handling.

"Maybe when we get promoted in a year or two, between the two of us, we can afford a slave like this," Claude added as he turned his attention to the black's throbbing prick. After some rapid fisting of the slave's shaft by first Claude and then his friend Clint, the pair proceeded around the litter to handle some of the other slaves' features.

"Why can't you have a rich uncle die, Clint?" Claude said as he hefted the next slave's balls. "At the rate we're going, we'll be too old to enjoy any of this before we can own one." The brown slave shuddered and groaned loudly as Claude roughly squeezed both his huge balls together in his frustration.

One young woman got carried away and rapidly stroked one of the blond slaves until he moaned deeply and sprayed cum over himself and those around him. The girl just giggled and scooped some of his cum up as the slave shuddered from his orgasm.

"I didn't give you permission to cum," our owner said as his whip laced repeatedly over the slave until his back was red with blood. But nothing was said to the young woman who had so enjoyed causing the misdeed.

But our owner's enjoyment of sharing his goods with the public was over, and again we were whipped into a blinding pace home, complete with tears, gasps, groans, and bleeding backs.

That night, our master entertained. In preparation, we had our butt plugs removed, were all bathed, oiled, and 'cleansed' three times before being carefully lubed in our ass chutes. We clumsily waited table, stark nude of course, and the diners could play with our bodies any way they wanted as they dined. But they weren't allowed to bring us to orgasm and I soon understood why. We were the entertainment of the evening. With a clap of our owner's hand, and the overseer's quick instructions, we were to fuck each other until told to change partners or position. We were started by pairs: one black fucking the other; one blond fucking the other, etc. But with another clap of the hand, the fucker became the fucked. With yet another clap of the hand, each fucker became the fucked in a new pairing – this time a black fucking a blond, a brown fucking a black-haired white, etc. Before the evening was over, each of us had fucked every other litter bearer and had been fucked by every other bearer. Since we're been warned we'd be whipped near to death if we 'shot off' during this exercise, we were still ready for the final event hours later: each guest could fuck any of the slaves they wanted.

I was first chosen by a middle aged Syrian who pounded into me unmercifully all the while playing with my tits until they were bright red in irritation. Finally, he emptied into me, only to be replaced by the son of one of his other guests, an Italian millionaire who had something to do with the auto industry there. His son, a striking youth just turned 18, had already pumped big loads into both of the black slaves and thus was able to fuck me for at least an hour before he finally exploded deep within my ass.

That night, chained to my stable post, I fell into one of the deepest sleeps of my life – utter and complete exhaustion. My ass throbbed in pain, my prick was chafed, my tits burned in irritation, my back and butt were black and blue from the whip, and even my jaws ached since I had been commanded to suck off one of the black slaves for a guest's amusement, the very slave who had the biggest prick of any of us. But I had survived.

Each day was similar to that first. The only difference was the nature of our humiliation. Our owner demanded and got total subservience out of every slave he owned. Bearing the litter was always at a full trot, always left us heaving and choking for air, almost always done in total nudity so we could be 'enjoyed' by the populace, and always under the nagging presence of his eager whip which rained its wrath over our shoulders, backs, rump, and legs at every opportunity no matter how hard we tried to please. Occasionally we were fitted in tiny cinctures that revealed everything but added a little color to our 'livery'. Sometimes those cinctures were matched by feathered headdresses that were strapped below our chins for added display. And sometimes those headdresses featured a bit in our mouth so we looked a lot like the horses pulling the Praetorian Guard's chariots in some old Hollywood Roman epic, especially so when we were fitted with long tails attached to our fitted butt plugs. What a show we made each and every day there at the resort!

The evening 'entertainments we provided for our master and his many guests also varied. Usually we were there to play with as we helped served the meal. And after the 'entertainment' part, we were almost always 'given' to the guests to enjoy any way they wanted. But the entertainments themselves varied considerably. We learned to fuck each other in every conceivable position, both anally and orally, both in and out of various wild costumes. Sometimes we fucked the dining room slaves; sometimes the guests 'rode us' fitted with saddles, bits in our mouths, and thoughtfully reined for their control; sometimes they had rough field slaves come in and rape us.

But at least once each week, we were put to stud in our master's breeding program as part of an 'entertainment'. Here, female slaves designated for breeding were brought in off of his various properties there at the resort and ordered to mate with us in full view of the guests. For once, we had full permission to cum and we really looked forward to those evenings. We were expected to have a full ejaculation into at least three of the women slaves – our master didn't care who studded who – all of us were almost perfect physical specimens and any one of us would have produced a well-built, muscular, and probably good looking slave as a result of our unions. Compared to our usual usage, those evenings were a pure delight – even knowing the slightest hesitation would lead to a whipping near death. True, we were force-mated. But we got some relief from our constant sexual tension, the women seemed to enjoy being mated with such well-built good-looking men who were beautifully equipped for the job at hand, and fucking away while people avidly watched and yelled encouragements – even instructions at us – didn't seemed to matter once you got used to it. To amuse themselves, they bet on which stud would shoot first; who would finish servicing all three 'brood mares' first; which woman would react the most to our huge size when we first entered them; which stud got erect first after shooting, and even took to long term betting on which women would get impregnated that night. We pretty well knew who we'd knocked up because we never saw them again for at least a year, but those we didn't were there the very next breeding session eager and waiting. It was the only thing I did as one of THE FIRM's slaves that even remotely reminded me of my previous life in Chicago. I suppose it was fucking a woman since that was the only resemblance.

THE FIRM's slaves had little chance to leave their mark on the world once they became THE FIRM's property. Most just worked until they dropped and were then fed to the pigs, dumped in the ocean, or ground up for fertilizer. But everyone's entitled to a little immortality, even one of THE FIRM's slaves, and when we were force-mated, that was our chance. At least that's the way I looked at it. Fifteen or twenty years from now, you're going to see a whole crop of tall, well-built, good-looking, compliant slave boys at one of THE FIRM's properties – all incredibly heavy hung and probably totally acclimated to their slave status in life – up for sale. They'll be survivors, just like their pappy. And they'll be bred and their sons will be bred, and my lineage will go on! Who says slaves don't have immortality.

———————

This, then, was slavery under THE FIRM's able management. Survival was the theme. Total submission was the goal. I knew I was succeeding as one of their properties. My owner enjoyed my torment, my agony, my humiliation, my shame. The danger was, that with time, I might learn to like it, but that, of course would spoil my master's enjoyment of me. So there would always be new hardships, new agonies, new pains, and new humiliations. And unceasing toil, always for the welfare and pleasure of he who owned me, and, of course, THE FIRM's profit.

BACK AT THE RESORT'S EMPLOYEE LOUNGE:

"Our Chicago boy has got himself a real master, now," David chuckled as he reflected on his observations of the sale, the litter bearer duties, and the dinner parties he had witnessed over the past few days, all involving the Chicago teacher he had 'procured' some time ago for THE FIRM.

"Yeah, Citicus is one cool dude," Bill said. "He runs one tight ship, I'll tell you. No wonder he calls himself Citicus – hell, he might as well be an Ancient Roman the way he makes those boys jump the loops for him."

"THE FIRM should hire him to set up new training programs," Wade chimed in, "except he'd probably kill off too many new slaves in the process. Takes a seasoned slave to keep up that schedule."

"I found it exciting," Forrest said. "And I loved the dinner parties. Reminded me of the good old days when David and I always had a whole stable of well-trained boys around for our amusement. Of course," he added languidly, "we were spending millions then, not making millions."

"Don't feel sorry for Forrest," David countered. "Since he signed up to work for THE FIRM, he hasn't spent a single night without some slave or another warming his bed. And in his position as a classifier, he can pick from hundreds, so the mystery to me is how he can still manage to get it up so easily. You'd think the damn thing would be worn out by now!" David added laughing.

"Use it or lose it, David," Forrest shot back. "But, really, that Citicus is something else again. The control he exerts, the demands he comes up with – all of it just part of his natural being. I really admired him and I'd love to see more of him in action. He's as fascinating to me as all those beautiful litter slaves he owns."

"Exactly, Forrest," Mr. Yamahoma said. "Citicus has a lot to teach all of us working for THE FIRM. That's why Mr. Broadley has arranged another few days of observation at Citicus' estate for all four of you. I'm happy to inform you Citicus himself has invited you to use any of his slaves you find attractive any time you want. He claims its standard protocol in any upstanding Roman estate."

"Great!" all four yelled in exultation. "Back to Citicus' estate!"

A FEW DAYS LATER BACK AT THE EMPLOYEE'S LOUNGE:

"Sorry to tell you this, but your stay here at the resort is over," Mr. Yamahoma smiled. "From the way you all have been going, it's probably just as well – your poor overused bodies need a rest from the looks of you," he smiled as he looked at the four employees of THE FIRM. "THE FIRM's plane to take you back will be here within an hour."

"I did want to add that Mr. Broadley said he thought your visit to the resort was very worthwhile and most instructive. He said whether you're procuring, classifying, training, or marketing – to always keep THE FIRM's resort in mind. At least a few of the slaves you work with will end up here eventually and they should do THE FIRM credit once they're here. The slave from Chicago we've been observing – now owned by Citicus as a litter bearer – is a good example of that and Citicus has informed me all four of you have taken advantage of Citicus' invitation to thoroughly fuck that slave. Oh, I almost forgot to tell you, Citicus will be joining you, Wade, at

THE FIRM's training facility in Mexico in the very near future," Mr. Yamahoma added. "Mr. Broadley invited him to join on as one of THE FIRM's staff, although, Wade, you'll need to watch him carefully until he gets the hang of it – right now, he's a little on the rough side and might injure some of THE FIRM's stock."

"Great," Wade exclaimed. "I sure need some extra help with the increased volume and I can't think of a better person than Citicus. The slaves he had at his villa here in the resort that we were able to watch in action – well, more than watch, especially with that slave from Chicago -are trained to perfection! But I see Mr. Broadley's point about Citicus being a little rough at times," Wade smiled. "So I'll keep an eye on that whip of his. It's good to let new slaves know what slave discipline is all about, but not to the point where the merchandise gets permanently damaged in the process. There's a fine balance in-between, but Citicus will be a great asset down in our Mexican training facility.

"Mr. Yamahoma, I'm sure I speak for all four of us," Forrest began, "when I sincerely thank you for a great visit to THE FIRM's resort. It was informative, instructive, even sobering, but also about as relaxing, refreshing, pleasurable and enjoyable as any vacation I've had. We have a lot to thank you for."

The others quickly added to Forrest's comments. Bill claimed he now knew a great deal more about marketing slaves; Wade said he clearly saw the deficiencies in slave training at the Mexico operation; and David and Forrest both claimed they saw slave procurement and classification in a whole new realm now.

"But I admit I've about had it with sensual pleasures for the time being. I don't think I could get it up if my life depended on it at this point!" David laughed. "Talk about satiation, especially these last few days over at Citicus' estate!"

Mr. Yamahoma whisked us out the door to the large-wheeled carriage drawn by the eight muscular Asian slaves harnessed to the front. We headed toward the airstrip at a fast pace insured by the driver's whip constantly playing over their butt-plugged rumps while rivers of sweat ran down their sleek hairless bodies.

When we got to the plane, there were THE FIRM's 10 selected customers already onboard. They looked as 'satiated' as us, but Mr. Yamahoma stated each had picked out at least one slave to take back with him, purchased for real money at one auction or another during their stay at the resort. Those newly purchased slaves, 19 in all, were already caged for shipment in the cargo compartment. They had cost over $15 million dollars altogether, so THE FIRM had once again turned a tidy profit.

"It's due to your good work that THE FIRM remains so profitable," Mr. Yamahoma said in parting. "Keep it up, and I hope to see you back here again sometime. I never did get to show you some of the resort's more exotic features."

"God almighty!" Bill exclaimed. "You mean there are things more sexy than we saw here?"

"You better believe it," Mr. Yamahoma smiled as the door shut.

CHAPTER IV

THE PUERTO RICAN MARKET

"Forrest, you and David can sniff out promising slave meat better than anyone THE FIRM has ever had," Mr. Broadley started the conversation in his New York Office. "Lord knows you've bought enough of them for THE FIRM from all over the world," Mr. Broadley continued as he leaned back in his comfortable office chair. His current 'chauffeur' was kneeling on all fours between them, his broad muscular back and taut ass serving as a living table for their drinks, his thickly collared neck forcing his handsome head up for display. His huge prick, forced into constant protrusion by his thick silver genital ring, was erect and dripping between his wide spread legs. Both Forrest and David found the beautiful black slave boy a real turn-on and ran their hands through the slave's thick black hair as they felt their own pricks harden.

"Well, we have bought up huge numbers of them for THE FIRM over the years, Mr. Broadley," Forrest replied modestly as he moved his hand down and stroked the slave's butt before returning his drink to the 'table.' "I hope that overall you've been satisfied with our work," David added as he reached under the 'table' and massaged one of the black slave's big tits.

"Most satisfied," Mr. Broadley replied. "Which gets me to why I asked you to join me in my New York office today. When you were last visiting me here, THE FIRM presented you with a couple of what we call 'fun loans' of two of our properties: that muscular black Brazilian that didn't speak a word of English for you, David, and a handsome 25-year-old Latino for you, Forest. I assume the black is working out OK? At least we had trained the brute to respond to four English commands: display, kneel, suck, and 'on all fours'. I take it you have advanced his training somewhat by now, David?" Mr. Broadley chuckled.

"Oh, 'Brazil' worked out fine, Mr. Broadley," David responded. "He was a lot of fun and no matter how much he got used; it never seemed to faze him. One night he got fucked six times, sucked off seven men in a row, fucked four women to their total satisfaction, and got milked dry himself six times on top of that – quite a party. But after 12 hours sleep, he seemed pert and ready to go again."

"You're using the past tense, David," Mr. Broadley commented. "What happened? Did you fuck him to death?" he laughed.

"No," David chuckled. "I returned him to THE FIRM in that I had a friend that wanted to buy him – and at a nice profit to boot, Mr. Broadley."

"I told you the boy had some promise," Mr. Broadley smiled.

"You were right about that, Mr. Broadley. My friend paid THE FIRM a cool one million to personally own him."

"That is a hefty profit, David. Sure beats the stock market," Mr. Broadley reached under the 'table' and began squeezing his black chauffer's swollen balls. "May I ask who the lucky buyer was?"

"He's got a woman owner again, Mr. Broadley," David laughed. "As you may recall, he was owned by a man, then a woman, a man again, then a brothel, then a women, then a man, then THE FIRM bought him and you loaned him out to me – now's he back fucking a woman full time – he's had quite a life for just being 20. I wonder how many owners the boy will have by the time he's 30 at this rate?"

David, noticing Mr. Broadley's play with his personal slave's ballsac, joined him by rubbing and squeezing one of Mr. Broadley's chauffer's huge ringed tits closest to him until he felt it swell to twice its normal size. "Remember, Mr. Broadley, how 'Brazil' had already been cut for a nose ring? Well, his new mistress has him fitted with a big gold nose ring which she uses to fasten her leash to. I don't know why she doesn't just hook her leash to his genital ring like everyone else did."

"You are naive sometimes, David," Mr.Broadley smirked. "Women like nose rings because they can completely control the slave even while he's busy fucking them. A genital leash just gets in the way. The slave isn't fucking them exactly right – a little tug on the nose leash and the slave changes his ways real quick, believe me. Nothing controls quite as well as a nose ring. You should try it sometime. Lord knows you've got enough stock around to experiment."

"Which gets me back to why I asked you over here, David. THE FIRM's procurement division is headed up by two of the most competent men I've ever met, namely you two, David and Forrest. Our warehouse here in New York is kept fully stocked through your efforts – no matter how many we sell – we can always restock with the best flesh on the market. But I've just learned there is an obscure little market north of San Juan, Puerto Rico THE FIRM would like to check out as a possible supply source for Latinos. From what I've been told, that's about all they stock – so selection is very limited – but the price is definitely right. I already have THE FIRM's permission to ask you two to check the place out as soon as possible. Your vast experience in buying slaves will be a real asset and THE FIRM's Board of Directors trusts your judgment explicitly. How about leaving day after tomorrow? THE FIRM will pay all expenses, of course, and will probably throw in a little bonus if all goes well. Interested?"

Forrest and David looked at each other briefly and then nodded their heads positively. "Definitely, Mr. Broadley. We're flattered THE FIRM values our opinion. Sounds like fun anyway. You know both David and I love to look over stock."

"Well, this stock probably isn't up to THE FIRM's standards, so don't be too disappointed in what you two may find. But, on the other hand, you never know. I'll set everything up for day after tomorrow in one of THE FIRM's corporate jets fitted out with appropriate cages and an unusually handsome Sicilian slave whose trained not only to accommodate you two's personal needs in route but who is also a skilled slave handler just in case you find anything worth buying."

– – – – –

The flight went smoothly and, as Mr. Broadley had promised, the Sicilian slave eagerly met all our needs in route, managing to suck beautifully but also take solid fuckings from not only the two agents but the pilot and co-pilot to boot. When he wasn't in full use and when told he could answer questions freely without risk of punishment, the slave related how lucky he was to be owned by THE FIRM, relating some almost humorous tales of being mishandled by various owners prior to being sold to THE FIRM.

Before either Forrest of David realized it, the final helicopter junket was landing in a tropical clearing near a series of shabby tin-roofed warehouses in the jungle. The pilot never turned the engine off as they quickly alighted, but promised to be back promptly at 4 PM. The two men walked the few hundred feet to the compound of warehouses (followed respectfully a few feet back by the naked Sicilian slave) where a large, burly looking black man, dressed in a well tailored linen suit, greeted them.

"Welcome, sirs," the black said in perfect English without a hint of an accent, totally ignoring the Sicilian slave in the background. "THE FIRM faxed me that you two might be interested in some of our wares on behalf of THE FIRM," he added as he extended his hand to greet the two visitors. "Enrico Suarez here. Welcome, both of you, to Puerto Rico. Is this your first time here?"

"No, Mr. Suarez. We've both been to San Juan a number of times, but that's about it. Used to be a small market near the docks there in San Juan but we never actually did business with them. Never could find what we were looking for," David explained

"Yes, well there have been a number of markets here in Puerto Rico that have come and gone. Generally poor quality, so it's little wonder they didn't last long. Usually just some man that had run across a windfall and was trying to turn a quick profit on what he had or a middleman hired to get rid of some undesirable stock."

"That was my impression, Mr. Suarez," Forrest remarked. "THE FIRM was hoping your market here would be considerably more promising. THE FIRM has marketed Latinos for some time now, but the market seems to be rapidly growing."

"THE FIRM has ended up, after several subsequent sales, owning 10 or 15 prime hands over the past decade that once were housed in this very market. That makes THE FIRM a potentially very valuable customer," Mr. Suarez smiled.

"THE FIRM is only interested in prime quality, Mr. Suarez," Forrest explained, 'mainly between the ages of 18 and 25. That way future owners can get some serious use out of them once they're trained. Money isn't an object if the stock is right. THE FIRM limits purchases to boys exceptionally good looking, well muscled with nicely shaped physiques, very heavy hung, and in great health. Of course, THE FIRM also expects smooth, flawless skin, a full set of bright white teeth, sparkling eyes, and a good head of hair. Body hair doesn't matter one way or the other in that THE FIRM keeps all its boys completely body shaved, but THE FIRM is particularly fond of boys with massive pecs topped by large tits. They can be any shade of skin color as long as it's entirely even, and THE FIRM prefers boys cleanly circumcised, although they trim a lot of the boys themselves once they have clear ownership. THE FIRM also purchases a smaller number of female slaves, primarily for sex slaves and as breeders, who are selected mainly on the basis of pure beauty, physique, youth, sexual training and who promise a long string of handsome new slave pups, put to the right stud, for eventual placement at auction themselves."

"Quite a list, sir, although, for male slaves, you didn't mention size and shape of their balls or their sexual abilities," Mr. Suarez said professionally.

"Well," David filled in, "all things being equal, THE FIRM likes big balls close to the body – not hanging down between their legs like an old bull and I'm not quite sure I know what you mean by sexual abilities. Do you train them in that area here?"

"Not really, senor," Mr. Suarez chuckled. "I just meant their ability to get it up when needed. I suppose ability isn't the right word in English. Ability to become sexually aroused is what I meant."

Both Forrest and David broke out in laugh. "If they're in good health and in the age range I mentioned and built like I specified, I would think THE FIRM wouldn't have to worry too much."

"Some are more lethargic than others, it seems. A Latin peculiarity, I suppose. We've had some stock that can't seem to get it up no matter what," Mr. Suarez replied. "It's almost like they are all worn out – and at that tender age yet."

"Well, scratch those," David exclaimed. "You'd be lucky to sell them as rough field slaves, let alone prime stock."

"That's exactly what we do, senor. I dispose of them to the sugar cane plantations here in the Caribbean. A slave there doesn't last long anyway as all his energy is used up by the cane. They bring very little on the block – little more than the transportation costs to get them there."

"Well, Enrico, you got any stock you think THE FIRM might be interested in? By the way, we usually go by our first names. I'm Forrest and this is David," Forrest said rather impatiently. "I know I'd like to look over your stock, just to see what's available this time of year. Just recently, I had been given one of THE FIRM's black Brazilian slaves that proved indefatigable as a bed buck. I don't know if it was THE FIRM's training or his Latino origins that accounted for that. You might have some right here in that league."

"Forrest, I think we have two or three new ones that both of you would enjoy looking over and I would certainly like to get your expert assessment of how our stock compares to some of the other, better known markets. Of course, we generally just stock Latinos due to our supply sources, but, in general, I'd like to know how we stand competitively – including quality and pricing. I know we're weak in variety – but what can you expect in this God-forsaken jungle," he laughed. "Shall we?" he gestured the two men toward a large warehouse to their left. "You can chain your handsome slave to this ring by the front door if you want or you may wish to bring him with you – whatever you want. The property looks Italian – am I right?"

"You've been in this jungle too long, Enrico," David laughed. "He's Sicilian, but you were close," David chuckled as he fastened a leash to the Sicilian's neck collar. "He'll go with us unless the slave's big hard-on bothers you."

As Mr. Suarez unlocked the heavy steel door into the warehouse, both David and Forrest were struck with the constant hum of low groans he could detect as they entered the darkened interior. Mr. Suarez flicked some lights on and the place was suddenly ablaze. The warehouse was large, well ventilated, and divided by two main aisles. Off of each wide aisle were series of small wire-mesh pens, each about 4 x 8 x 6, the sides, top and bottom all covered with the wire mesh; the front of the cage was a large barred door. They were set on a slanted concrete floor with drains running down each side of the building so it was obvious the pens were hosed out periodically to take care of the occupant's wastes. A few of the pens showed fresh droppings on the floor and most showed the results of recent urination, but overall, the place was remarkably odor-free and fresh despite the sweating specimens inside each of the cages. Each pen held one occupant who had his legs hobbled by ankle chains, his arms chained behind him by connecting wrist bands, a wide leather belt locked around his waist which served as both a phallus holder for the dildo jammed up each occupant's butt as well as supported a chain connected to a genital ring which kept the occupant's genitals yanked up unnaturally, obviously to better display them. All wore thick leather collars which forced their heads into a chronic upright position so their handsome faces were best displayed. Some had gags stuffed in their mouths, some were fitted with more elaborate strapped on penis gags, while others were left untouched in that area. All had been completely body shaved which made their nakedness all the more complete, but especially made their genitals loom larger than life without the thick pubic hair surrounding them. There must have been at least 100 in this building alone.

"These boys have been here a while and will be the next up for auction," Mr. Suarez said as we began slowly walking down the first aisle. He flipped another switch and a small gong started sounding. Every pen's occupant leaped to their feet, stretched their legs as far apart as their hobble would allow, went to the front of the cage, and thrust their genitals through the open bars. Their thick collars prevented them from looking down, so they stared straight ahead.

When both of the visitors looked surprised at such a wanton display of their bodies, Mr. Suarez smiled slightly and said, "By this time, they're eager to be sold. It gets boring in that small cage month after month, although we do exercise them twice a day to build up their musculature. And those here over a month are milked twice a day – just to make sure their balls are working properly. Use it or lose it, they say. Of course, we don't milk them for at least a week before auction time so they're fresh and ready."

"If you see anything that interests you, just let me know and we'll get it out for you for a closer inspection," Mr. Suarez said pleasantly. "Of course, we encourage you to try any of the goods out you want or perhaps you might want your Sicilian slave to do that for you. We don't expect anyone to buy a 'pig in a poke' as they say in America," he laughed, "but remember none of them are really trained yet. Still, you could get some idea of what they would be like with some decent training."

The first three cages held very muscular, well-built jet black boys that appeared to be about 20. They were devoid of the usual Negroid features, having straight noses, high cheek bones, thin lips, and bright brown eyes. Their long thick shafts were throbbing in full erection and their balls had been banded to insure prominent display in their hefted, close to the body position. Their skin was silky smooth.

"Nice," Forrest said as he hefted their swollen ballsacs and stroked their long circumcised shafts. "You're claiming these boys are milked twice a day and still show like this?"

"Yep, milked less than three hours ago, Senor Forrest. They're still young, you know, and regular milking actually seems to enhance their semen production rather than just drain them. Works that way in a cow, you know. You'd get a good load out of any one of them if you milked them now, I'd bet. Blacks tend to be good producers as well as hot all the time," he laughed.

"THE FIRM sold a Latino slave to a friend of mine that was bred at some facility here in the Caribbean, Enrico, which specializes in breeding slaves to order. These boys would make good breeding studs, I bet," David commented.

"Among other things, Senor David. But once they're properly trained, I imagine they'd turn into mighty fine bed bucks for some lucky owner, male or female."

The three slaves were interested but humiliated they were being discussed as if they weren't even there. The conversation reminded them once again they were viewed as nothing more than owned property now – no different than the horses and cows routinely sold in their home villages, although they doubted that those horses and cows would have their bodies so thoroughly exploited as they probably would by their new owner.

"Where do you get boys this black?" Forrest asked out of curiosity.

"They're native to the island. Undiluted slave stock dating back to the mid 1800s, probably brought over from the Sudan or Mauritania – one of the northern African groups – as you can see, they're not Negroid. Sort of unusual to get stock not mongrelized one way or another. And I got them already neatly circumcised so

I imagine they're from some Arabic background – they circumcise boys while still very young. My guess is they were sold to some slavers right in their home villages by their parents who needed the money to survive – slavers frequently visit villages in the midst of famine because they know families will part with what's marketable if they're starving and there are always too many mouths to feed. Those sold that way make good slaves. They know their sale has saved their families – sort of a heroic sacrifice, you might say – and they know they'll never see their families again – so they never make an attempt to change their destiny. They also soon realize they're going to get some food and a job to do as a slave – more than they can expect at home where they know they're just a burden. It's getting more and more common since the U.S. companies starting moving out and there's no employment and no money to buy food with. It's about all we've got to sell anymore," he sighed. "The slavers I buy from always seem to have a fresh batch ready."

We moved down the line, but other than skin color and physique size, all of the stock up for sale seemed well-built, muscular, young, reasonably good looking, and in good health. Most were very well endowed, although a few appeared to be just average. Some were strikingly handsome, some were exceptionally well hung, some were almost feminine they were so pretty, and some sported massive physiques coated with layers of well-developed muscle. There seemed to be something for everyone. Most could not speak English, most were totally uneducated, and most had never been anywhere other than their home villages and a few holding pens here and there as they awaited sale. Most had been slaves before and were being resold; a few were raw recruits and faced considerable training before they would be of much worth to their owners; a few had been slaves so long they couldn't remember anything else; and a very few were bred slaves, having been born to mothers who were slaves themselves. Prices varied by age, sex, skin color, amount of training, time in slavery, musculature, and size and shape of their equipment. Young males in their late teens who were well acclimated to slavery, had already had considerable training, were fairly muscular, were exceptionally good looking, and who were well hung were priced at top dollar regardless of skin color. Men in their twenties with the same characteristics cost a little less, with good looking willing-to-serve women coming in behind them. Males older than the prime years brought in considerably less, but nothing as low as the ugly, poorly built, and poorly endowed who were worth little more than their transportation costs to a new work station.

"These are my best stock, David and Forrest," Enrico Suarez said as they continued through the building. "The other buildings are where I keep the other stock that I'm planning to ship down to the Brazilian markets as soon as I get a full truck load. I don't make as much per head on that stock, but there's so much more of it, I suppose that's my cash cow. Actually, that's the biggest market anyway – few people can afford stock like this. But a lot of people can afford just an ordinary looking slave who has a lot of work potential in his bones. These boys here are really 'exotics' when it comes to mass marketing," he continued as we stopped in front of a pen containing a tall, beautiful blond with blue eyes and shiny tan skin glistening with a light coat of sweat.

The blonde's massive well-shaped organ was sticking out between the bars in full arousal.

"This boy doesn't look like he came from around here," David said as he reached down and stroked the dripping shaft. "Where's he from, anyway?"

"Well, Ricky Martin doesn't look Puerto Rican either, does he?" Mr. Suarez joked. "Actually, this boy looks a lot like Ricky Martin did in his heyday, doesn't he? But he is a Latino, David, believe it or not. He's from Martinique and was owned by a French planter there who fathered him off one of his slave girls. He sells all his progeny when they reach an age to bring top dollar on the market. By that time, he's got them pretty well-trained. He's one of my most expensive items because he's almost fully trained as is, and he sure is a beauty, isn't he? Only problem is – he only understands French so far, but a new owner could get him conversant in short order I would think. He's so pretty, I doubt if an owner would be buying him to talk to anyway."

The boy's shaft began to quiver in David's hand as he continued his stroking.

"Watch it or the boy's going to shoot all over you," Mr. Suarez warned.

"Could I try him out, Enrico?" David said as he ran his hands over the boy's muscular chest. "A blond could prove interesting after all those dark haired brutes we've viewed."

"Sure, David," Mr. Suarez said as he opened the cage door and pulled the boy out by his rampant shaft. "How do you want him? On his back or on all fours?"

"I'll like to check out his mouth first, Enrico."

"On your knees, boy, with your mouth open," the slavemaster ordered as he hooked a leash to his neck collar and handled it to David who was hauling his own organ out through an open fly.

The boy swallowed Mr. Simmons's shaft in one quick gulp clear down to its roots and began massaging the embedded organ with his well-trained throat muscles.

"Well, little doubt the boy's experienced in that area," David said as he noticed the boy neither gagged nor choked on the rather large object well down his throat. "I wonder if his ass is as well-trained?"

"We'll soon see," David added as he quickly withdrew his prick from the eager throat and, pushing the boy down on his back, raised his legs up over his shoulders and rammed the huge organ up next to the boy's exposed hole. "Has the boy been lubed, Enrico?" he asked.

"Of course, all our boys are lubed every morning as part of the routine whether it'll ever be put to use or not. Gets them used to it."

Without further ado, David rammed his organ completely up the boy's chute in one long forceful stroke until his pubic hair was scratching the boy's ass cheeks. The blond boy gasped, shuffled his hips around slightly to accommodate the invader, and moaned in pleasure as David began steadily pumping into him. Within minutes, it was obvious he was working his ass muscles around the invading shaft, adding to his user's pleasure immeasurably. The blonde's own organ, trapped between the two bodies, was leaking pre-cum profusely and soon was shooting masses of hot cum on both parties' stomachs as the blond gasped and sighed with each ejaculation. His own eruption didn't interrupt his own ass muscles working on the shaft inside him, however, and, other than the sudden wetness between them, David noticed no decrease in ardor or interest on the boy's part. Nor did the boy's prick ever soften. When David bucked heavily and shot into the boy load after load, the slave beneath him squeezed his ass muscles as tight as he could so his user would extract the last ounce of pleasure from the orgasm. In essence, he milked his user of the last drops and David appreciated this professional added touch as he eventually withdrew his shaft from the boy, completely drained and satisfied.

As soon as his shaft was free from his chute, the blond boy began to lick his own cum off his user's stomach and then completely cleaned his user's shaft before beginning to clean his own body of cum.

"Thank you, master," the blond boy said humbly as he resumed a kneeling position. "How may I serve you next?"

"How much, Enrico?" David gasped out. "How much?"

"Isn't he fabulous, David? Completely trained as you just saw for yourself and by his own father, no less. Ah! The French."

"How much?" David said as he buttoned himself back up and slowly stood up, his knees rather weak in the process.

"Well, as I warned you, he's my most expensive stock, David," Mr. Suarez replied. "I paid dearly for him."

"I don't doubt it and worth every penny. But, I repeat, how much? And, remember, before you answer, the market is limited for a boy of this quality. There aren't too many people you know who could afford such a boy. You run a chance of getting stuck with over-priced goods, my friend."

"I'd thought of that, senor. It's the risk you take when you get into goods of such high caliber. So I'll make it so reasonable you can't refuse," he smiled.

"And make a huge profit to boot, I wager," David smiled back. "How much?"

"In view of the fact you're an agent for THE FIRM, I'll let you have the boy for $180,000 US. He'd cost you at least $250,000 to $300,000 in Toronto or New York and he'd even bring $210,000 in the Mexico City market I'd wager, just because he's blond if nothing else. No telling what I could get for him over in the Persian Gulf or in Africa – probably at least $500,000. They love blonds you know and will pay anything to get them, especially trained boys like this one that aren't going to give them any trouble."

"Sold, Enrico. We'll take him home with me today if you'll get his ass cleaned out and relubed."

"I love doing business with you, senor. You're so…how do I say it…to the point and decisive. Is this typical of THE FIRM? We'll have him cleaned out and polished for the trip home within minutes. Cash or check – we even take credit cards now," he smiled.

"Good – I'll put him on THE FIRM's Visa card," David smiled. "That way THE FIRM won't have to pay for him until he's completely ready to market or he's already been sold in their upcoming Chicago auction."

"VISA it is, Senor David," Mr. Sanchez smiled. "I was hoping that would prove to be more convenient for my customers. Actually, I was hoping they'd spend a little more with the convenience."

"They probably will, Enrico. Probably end up buying two instead of one with all your Latin conveniences," he laughed.

"See anything that interests you so far, Senor Forrest?" Enrico turned to THE FIRM's other agent. "Remember, you can try any of the stock out that you want."

"You've got some decent stock, Mr. Sanchez, and your prices seem to be about right, if that blond boy you just sold to THE FIRM is any example, but your wares are so limited you really don't compete with the big houses at all. As you seem to be aware, you can never ask the prices they demand for similar quality goods, just because they stock most anything anyone could want. The biggest problem though, Mr. Sanchez, is the lack of training. Hardly any major buyer these days buys untrained stock – it's just too much trouble and you never know how the training is going to turn out. Most of the big houses nowadays fully train the stock long before it's ever put on the market and some of them are even guaranteeing their products – some for 90 days, some for 6 months. THE FIRM is extending the warranty up to a year on certain stock where they've done all the training themselves or where they're dealing primarily in bred slaves who've been trained since birth. With your stock here, I don't think you could ever ask more than about 50% of the price for a fully guaranteed trained slave of similar qualifications. Judging from your price on the blond I assume you know all that already, but remember that blond is about as trained as they get around here."

"I appreciate your candor, Senor Forrest. It's obvious you know the market well and I'm grateful you're willing to share your knowledge so openly. I know the limitations of my tiny operation here and am well aware my hope for survival is to offer some potentially quality stock at bargain-basement prices. There's not much I can do about the variety of stock unless I can broaden my sources and that seems most unlikely in this desolate location. Nevertheless, so far I'm making a decent living at it and my reputation is growing."

"And it will continue to grow with such an honest, open attitude," David entered the conversation. "I'll try to swing some of THE FIRM's business down to you, but it'll take a while. THE FIRM's Board of Directors are a most cautious lot and it takes them considerable time to make a major change. But both Forrest and I, who head up THE FIRM's procurement division, are already interested in you as a source of material ready to be trained, I'm sure, or Forrest and I wouldn't be here today. THE FIRM is always on the lookout for fresh stock at good prices and they don't care whether any one trained them or not – they do all the training themselves so they can guarantee all their stock. But, they're mighty expensive," David laughed.

"I'll make sure THE FIRM's Board of Directors gets a full report from the two of us about your market here," Forrest explained, "and, of course, they'll be looking over today's purchase carefully to check out the quality and trainability potential. They could turn this operation upside down – I imagine they buy 3500 to a 6000 head a year from all over the world."

Mr. Sanchez flushed in excitement. "I'd be so grateful, Senor Forrest. Isn't there anything I can do for you in exchange?"

"Well, maybe. David and I were thinking about getting our boss, Mr. Broadley, a small gift in return for all his time and trouble in arranging our visit down to this God-awful spot. Mr. Broadley has quite a stable of handsome slaves for his own enjoyment – but he's never adverse to another one, it seems. Mr. Broadley, who incidentally is CEO of THE FIRM, seems to have a thing for blacks and he just sold his personal chauffeur, a black American, that he thoroughly enjoyed. One of those boys up by the front door might be a good replacement for the slave he just sold – well-built, heavy hung, good looking, and black but not Negroid in their features. I imagine he'd love one of them as a replacement for his chauffeur/houseboy and if anyone could train a slave boy, it would be him. Mr. Broadley manages his own stock and keeps all his own stable of slaves right in line all the time no matter what they're asked to do, and he gets more work out of them than anyone could imagine. Most of his stock is worked 18 hours a day – half in hard labor around his estate to keep their bodies in perfect shape; half in servicing him, his business associates, and his friends. Thanks to good management, Mr. Broadley never has a bit of trouble with them year after year. How about selling me one of those blacks as a surprise gift for him from the two of us? If he doesn't like the slave, he can always sell him off at the next auction."

"Let me give you a slave of your choosing as a small bonus for your time and trouble, senors," Mr. Sanchez said. "It's the least I can do for the CEO of THE FIRM and, hopefully, he will think more favorably toward buying from us in the future."

"Smart thinking, Mr. Sanchez, and one that will hopefully pay off handsomely in the near future," Forest commented.

"Which one did you want?" Mr. Sanchez asked.

"Let's look them over and let Forrest decide," David suggested as all three men walked back to the three blacks' pens followed by the leashed Sicilian whose swollen prick was dripping more than ever. All three of the caged black slaves were still standing with their legs widespread and their genitals poking through the bars. They were obviously excited that the three men were returning to their pens.

"I like the looks of the one in the middle cage best," Forrest said, "but I still think, Enrico, this is a bit much for an out-and-out gift."

"Nonsense, Forrest," Mr. Sanchez countered. "Just accept the generosity and pick one out."

Mr. Sanchez unlocked the cage and, grabbing the slave's shaft, pulled him out into the aisle. "You want him stripped down, Forrest?" he asked as he began to loosen the belt that held the dildo and genital ring in place.

"All but his collar," Forest said as he watched the long, thick dildo, coated with grease, being tugged out of the boy's ass as the slave grunted and groaned. The chain connected to his genital ring quickly turned into a leash handed to his potential new owner.

"He's yours to try out, Senor. He's fairly well-trained – at least enough to do anything you want."

"I'd like to see how he handles being fucked, Mr. Sanchez, since Mr. Broadley would use him primarily as a bed buck if this works out. The other thing we better check out is his sucking abilities. If he's had that monstrous dildo up him for several weeks, as I suspect, I doubt if he's going to object much to being fucked by anything short of a Mack truck. I just hope he's not stretched all out of shape."

"He's still tight, Senor Forrest," Mr. Sanchez said as he stuck one finger up the greased hole. "See for yourself. It's just that the dildo gets them use to being fucked."

Forrest stuck his middle finger as far up the boy's hole as he could reach and wiggled it around a bit. "Yes, he's still tight enough to fuck well, David."

"Go ahead and try him out, Forrest, or have your Sicilian property do it," Mr. Sanchez said enthusiastically. "Or would you like a bit of privacy? I'm afraid we don't have much of that around here."

"I'm not much in the mood right now, Enrico, so I'll let the Sicilian empty a load up his butt All I want to see is how he handles a good fucking and whether he enjoys it or not."

"No problem, Senor." Mr. Sanchez quickly stepped aside so Forrest could place the Sicilian slave in place to properly fuck the black offering, now so excited a constant drip was issuing out of his erect penis.

"Fine," Forrest said as he looked the chiseled body of the new black over, his well developed pectorals sporting huge ringed tits, as erect as his large shaft quivering in excitement.

"Fuck this slave doggie style. You can probably get it in further that way," Forrest commanded the Sicilian slave, still under leash. "And fuck him as hard as you can until I tell you to stop whether you shoot off before that or not."

"On your hands and knees, #630, for a through fucking," Enrico barked at the black slave as his riding crop slashed over #630's butt.

Quickly, the first slave was on his hands and knees with his legs wide spread and his butt poking toward the sky. As soon as he was positioned, the Sicilian slave was entering him and shoving his shaft up its full length before he started a rhythmic pistoning. Both slaves were smiling – the slave on bottom twisted his hips as he groaned in absolute pleasure as the rod pumping him massaged his prostate. The Sicilian slave on top was steadily increasing the tempo as he felt an orgasm rising to the surface. The black slave's daily milking had made him almost forget how enjoyable real sex could be and both slaves wanted to take full advantage of this rare opportunity to cum of their own accord. Within minutes, both of the slaves were caught up in their orgasms – one was spurting a huge load up the ass of the slave beneath him – the other was spurting a sizable load into a large puddle beneath him. For the Sicilian slave, it was the first time in a month he had been allowed to empty his swollen balls.

As soon as the slaves were finished, Mr. Sanchez had the black slave on the bottom lick up the mess he'd made on the concrete floor and then clean the prick of the Sicilian slave fucking him. He then had the Sicilian slave clean out the black slave's ass so all the cum leaking out was sucked into his own mouth. He then pulled on the Sicilian's leash until he resumed his subservient position behind his masters.

"Would you like to try his mouth out before we fit him out for shipment, Forrest?" Mr. Sanchez asked, "Or is it too hot for even that?"

"I better," Forrest answered as he quickly unbuttoned and took his prick out. "On your knees, blackboy, and get that mouth busy on this prick."

The black slave swallowed Forrest's prick in stages, massaging the shaft with his tongue carefully until the entire shaft was well down him and he felt his throat muscles spasm around the intruder. He remembered to run his tongue up and down the shaft while sucking for all he was worth and twisting his head around to rub the shaft against the contracting throat muscles while he bobbed his head back and forth on the shaft to increase the friction in his throat. Soon the slave felt the shaft swell even wider and gobs of cum shot into his throat and was quickly swallowed into his stomach. This master's cum had a somewhat salty, but fresh taste which he enjoyed and he was pleased he had gotten the master to unload so much in this one orgasm, especially when he had seemed uninterested in fucking him. Before he knew it, the shaft was being jerked out of his mouth and he found himself scrambling to clean the shaft thoroughly before he had to be commanded to do so.

"The boy's got a well-trained mouth, Mr. Sanchez," Forrest said as he carefully placed his prick back in his pants and ruffled the slave's hair. "He's obviously had considerable practice."

"He looks good to me," David commented, "but I wouldn't mind being drained by that mouth myself, Enrico, as he once again hauled his large organ out of his pants."

"Of course," Mr. Sanchez promptly replied as he ordered the black slave onto his knees once again.

A few minutes later, the black slave struggled to shallow another huge load down his throat before cleaning his user's organ.

"Mr. Broadley will like that mouth, Forrest," David commented. "Let's just hope he can teach the bastard how to drive that Rolls-Royce of his," David laughed.

"You still comfortable giving this slave away, Enrico?" Forrest asked.

"The boy's been in stock for some time and he's real eager to get a new owner. With blacks as plentiful as they are nowadays, I'll be lucky to get $80,000 for him at a good auction – blacks aren't too popular anymore no matter how well they perform in bed. Makes a nice reasonable gift, don't you think?"

"On behalf of Mr. Broadley as well as ourselves, Enrico, we thank you and want you to know we'll do everything we can to swing some of THE FIRM's purchases your way in the future. Make out the proper papers on this slave, making Mr. Broadley his new owner. Then, if you'll be so kind, I want you to clean that boy inside and out, body shave him completely, get him out of his shackles and leg chains, keep those wrist cuffs on him along with his collar and tit rings, put the dildo and waist belt back on him, and make sure you leave his genital ring in place. He'll be going to New York in our private jet so we don't need to worry about airport security. And package him in some loose clothing and some shoes – nothing fancy – he'll never need it after we get him to Mr. Broadley's estate anyway."

"He'll be buck naked the once he gets to Mr. Broadley's estate, that's for sure," David laughed.

"You wouldn't happen to have a big bow around here, would you, Mr. Sanchez? It would be fun to wrap that around him when I give him to Mr. Broadley once we're back in New York."

"I can do everything but the bow, Senor David. But I think you can buy that at some flower shop on your way to Mr. Broadley's estate."

"Enrico, do exactly the same to the blond slave I bought. Be sure to leave his wrist bands on him. I might need to shackle him after I get him in the car for the trip home from the airport."

"Could we look in the other warehouses before we leave, Enrico, while you're getting the slaves ready for shipment? We don't have to leave for another hour or so," David continued.

"Help yourself. I'm sorry I can't take you around myself, but I really do need to get these two boys ready," Mr. Suarez answered as he tossed the two of them the keys.

The next building wasn't nearly as clean or well ventilated and the many odors emanating were unpleasant. Like the first building, it primarily consisted of small individual pens, but these pens were stacked on top of each other three-fold so that the building held at least 300 cages. The smell of sweat and urine was overpowering. Toward the back was a large open area with shackles and chains fixed into the wall itself. Hanging from the wall were dozens of slaves in various stages of punishment. Most had been whipped raw, others had been burnt with branding irons and electric prods, still others were impaled on huge rough wooden phalluses set into the floor, their feet chained in place so they couldn't move off the phalluses deep within them. About a dozen slave trainers were busily moving the slaves from their cages into the punishment area, their whips constantly lashing out at the bare flesh they were training, while 'trustee slaves' placed a foul smelling soup in bowls attached to the side of each cage and filled the water bowls with a brackish water dripping with worms. Everywhere you could hear moans of real pain, the look of acute suffering, and the smell of blood, sweat, semen, urine and shit. The place reeked of misery and the slaves chained within must have thought they were in Hell itself.

"It takes some time in a place like this to learn you're now a slave," Forrest said philosophically.

"It's absolutely necessary if you ask me, Forrest. How else is a slave to learn his place in the world and begin to appreciate all a master does for them? How long are they kept in here?"

"I have no idea, but I would guess it depends on their background. If they're new to slavery, they're probably kept here until depression takes over and they start to waste away. That's generally when they're broken and can be properly trained. A person can only take so much pain and suffering and, when they just give up, they're broken and you can start seriously training them. About three or four months on the average, I think. Of course, if they've been broken to slavery before or were born into it, this stage is really unnecessary and you can get right on with serious slave training. I least that's what I would imagine happens to all those slaves we ship to THE FIRM's training facility in Mexico."

"THE FIRM schedules plenty of training time. Their trainers spend all the way from one month to a year before they feel a slave is ready for auction," Forrest added. "About a month for a slave born into it or who is being resold – up to a year for a person from a proud, arrogant background that emphasizes personal freedom and decision making – you know, like former lawyers and other professionals. But THE FIRM has found they all break eventually if the trainers know what they're doing – it's just when! Of course, THE FIRM has that special breaking facility for the tough cases over in the North African desert somewhere."

"I've never owned a slave myself that openly rebelled or tried to take his freedom back. Have you, Forrest?" David asked.

"Never, and I don't expect to either," Forrest replied. "As you well know, our own overseer Sergei keeps a firm hand on them all the time – THE FIRM says it's essential to keep a slave adhered to his original slave training and up to their guarantee. That's why that red owner's manual goes out with each purchase on maintenance -you know the procedures recommended by now: frequent beatings, short rations, and extra chores – that sort of thing. It reminds slaves who's in charge at all times. And THE FIRM's owner's manual recommends that all their slaves be collared, ringed, and naked when appropriate. Reminds them they're slaves. Absolutely essential, they claim and I believe them. THE FIRM claims the only time a slave is returned to them for retraining is when the owner hasn't followed the manual – been too soft and lax with the slave or has dressed the slave up like a human. Bad business, THE FIRM says, and leads to nothing but trouble."

"Well, THE FIRM's the expert in this area," David commented, "judging by their merchandise. After all, THE FIRM's offerings are considered about as good as you can get. Whether I bought them from THE FIRM or not, though, as you well know, just like you I keep my own slaves in a constant state of humiliation and shame – I think that keeps them in line as much as anything. Of course, fucking them regularly, whipping them for the slightest hesitation in carrying out your orders, and keeping them chronically hungry and naked also helps. It serves as a constant reminder that you're their master and they're nothing but owned property."

"Well, this is where it all starts," Forrest waved his hand around the stinking room amid the screams of terror and pain, along with the constant moans of suffering, shame, and humiliation that seemed to emanate from all corners.

"What's in the other buildings, Forrest?" David asked.

"Well, let's see," Forrest responded and the two walked through adjoining buildings.

After poking through several of the warehouses and examining them thoroughly, David said, "Looks like it's mainly warehousing of stock for the Brazilian markets – stuff that won't sell here along with those too unattractive to be anything but just raw labor. They're kept healthy, but are all obviously under constant heavy discipline. Makes them more marketable when they do get shipped out. According to the initial report I got from THE FIRM's agent, one of the buildings way in the back is set up just for pure punishment. It's probably where Enrico sends those that rebel or talk back or try to run away. They probably really get disciplined if you know what I mean. The agent's report said it's so bad they'll never try any of that stuff again. The agent said he never actually visited the place, but Enrico told him he wouldn't like what he would see – Enrico told the agent he doesn't even like to go there himself in that it practically makes him sick every time – but it works well so he's not going to change anything. Enrico told that agent he found some sadistic brute in San Juan that runs it for him – claims he gets his jollies that way so he really enjoys his work, so much so Enrico pays him next to nothing. But Enrico says he never has trouble again after a slave is sent there. We might keep the place in mind if we ever have a real problem with any of our own stock."

"Might be good to have my herd tour the place," Forrest smiled. "Sounds like they'd really appreciate my ownership after that."

"Not a bad idea, Forrest," David laughed. "Of course, that black Brazilian you just sold had probably had more than that done to him over the years – remember, he'd been through quite a few owners long before you bought him and some of those owners weren't very nice. Maybe that's why you never had a bit of trouble out of him, no matter what he was told to do."

"He's probably humping his new mistress as we speak," Forrest chuckled. "I can just see those muscular hips pumping up and down with that leash firmly jerking on his nose ring to make sure he keeps the rhythm going to her satisfaction."

"See, all that rough training pays off," David smiled.

It was nearing 4 PM and the two men returned to the main building, picked up their new purchase along with the gift slave, now fully clothed, and, still leading the Sicilian slave by his leash, headed for the landing spot just as the helicopter showed up on the horizon.

"Five going back?" was all the pilot said as he picked up his load.

Once back at the private airport near New York, David led his blonde slave and the Sicilian over to THE FIRM's van, which had been summoned for discrete transit of the two slaves to THE FIRM's holding facility, while Forrest ordered Mr. Broadley's gift slave into his Jaguar.

As they parted in the airport parking lot, Forrest said, "David, when you tire of your new possession, I'll give you 300 grand for him."

"Used?" David shot back. "That's considerably more than I paid for him as you know and when I'm ready to sell him, he'll be well used, believe me."

"Yes, but your training of the boy will only enhance his value."

David thought a while as he languidly ran his hands through the blond slave's hair. "Well, it will probably be a little while, but I just might take you up on that offer rather than place him up for open auction."

"I thought you might. Obviously, you save a lot of money if they don't have to maintain a slave a long period until he or she gets sold on the open market. All that slave chow adds up over a period of time," Forrest chortled.

"Well, in the interim, I'll enjoy him. Like most masters, I do like fresh meat now and then, Forrest. This boy here's going to get a lot of use over the next few weeks what with all the training I'll put him through," David said has he gently toyed with his slave's huge swollen shaft. "But, you're right. By the time I've got him trained just like I want him, I'll probably be tired of him and eager to sell him off – it might as well be to you. And I'll turn quite a profit with your generous offer."

"When I saw the slave shoot off so profusely when you were fucking him, I knew he was a natural for the little harem I keep at our townhouse. That boy actually likes to be fucked and between me, our common business associates the loans out to you now and then, and our friends, he'll be kept mighty busy. They always seem to like blondes, anyway. And, Forrest, the boy's a real beauty whether you realize it or not."

"Oh, I realize it," Forest responded. It's one of the things that really turns me on with him. But just because they're a sight to behold doesn't mean they know how to take a fuck – this boy does and seems to enjoy it in the process. He's certainly worth $300 grand to me."

"Tell you what, Forrest. Sergei, our ever faithful Russian slave overseer, will insist on training him for a few months until he is absolutely sure he will meet any guarantee I want to make when I sell him off. That will also give me a chance to fuck him near to death in his spare time. Eventually, I will then offer you first option on him. But he may not be worth all that money when he's been fucked that hard. Remember, when Sergei trains a boy for us, it's round the clock. He'll have a sore ass and throat the entire time and his tits are going to swell to twice their size before we're all through with him. His body will be pumped up to a beautiful physique and he'll learn to be aroused most of the time by then."

"Fair enough, David. And don't worry about you and Sergei fucking him senseless. A boy like this thrives on heavy usage."

The blond slave being discussed felt his prick began to drip precum in his excitement. Not only was he apparently worth a lot of money which practically guaranteed a good life as a slave, but his new owner apparently planned to thoroughly train him for use on a regular basis. Compared to living in the dismal Puerto Rican warehouse where his only sex life was being milked twice a day, he thought of how fortunate he was and tears welled in his eyes.

David noticed his slave's prick oozing as well as the tears in his eyes. "Don't you want to get sold again, boy, or are you worried about being fucked so hard?"

"I'm just so happy you bought me master," the slave replied as tears began to spill down his cheeks. "And if you want to sell me to the new master, that's fine too, master. You can do anything you want with your new property, master. You fuck me all you want, master, and if you get tired of me, you can sell me to someone else, master. I'm yours now to do with what you want."

"See why I like this new slave, Forrest. He likes to get fucked, he's grateful to be owned, and he wants to be sold when the time comes. What more could any owner want?" he laughed as he reached over and squeezed the slave's readily available tits.

"That's exactly why I want to be his next owner, David," Forrest replied as he reached over and grabbed the blond slave's balls, squeezing them tightly. "David, thanks for the option on this slave and I know you'll let your best friend and business partner use him anytime he wants in the interim. I'll enjoy him too – starting just as soon as I get home and get undressed for a little courtesy fuck."

"Only after I've loosened him up for you first," David laughed.

— — — — —

Forrest smiled as he thought of THE FIRM's van delivering the handsome young black gift slave into the hands of his new owner, Mr. Broadley. As soon as he was delivered, Forrest knew Mr. Broadley wouldn't waste any time in having the slave strip down and sample that ass for himself. Yes, a perfect little gift from THE FIRM's new supply agent in Puerto Rico if all went well.

CHAPTER V

THE FIRM'S APPRECIATION PARTY

Mr. Broadley strode into THE FIRM's luxurious New York World Headquarters. "The quarterly meeting of the Board of Directors of THE FIRM will now come to order. First item on the agenda, 'Approval of the minutes.'"

"Move they be approved," Mr. Ling from Bangkok said flatly.

"Second the motion," Luigi Carposa, THE FIRM's representative from Italy blurted out quickly.

"Next, report of the Treasurer on the blue paper in front of you. I'm happy to report that last quarter we experienced a new record in bottom-line profits. We're up 28%, gentlemen," Mr. Broadley said rather routinely, considering the vast increase.

"Why the big increase, John?" Cyrus Campbell from London inquired.

"Cost of goods took a big dip and THE FIRM took advantage of a depressed market by buying up heavily. Mainly in the Balkans and Middle East, Cyrus. Civil wars there gutted the market and drove prices of stock down to rock-bottom prices. Even the very best quality, which was all THE FIRM was interested in, was selling for a third of what we would of paid a year ago. We've got so many dark-haired in training right now, we're a little out of balance as far as choice is concerned, but the situation will correct itself before too long. Besides, buyers are taking to the new offerings real well – dark haired or not, it's still mighty attractive stock and at a bargain price! We're not experiencing many problems in training, either. Doesn't surprise me – their life here is probably a hell of a lot better than where we bought them up and they know it."

"I move we accept the treasurer's report," Mr. Carposa stated, "with the amendment that our CEO, Mr. Broadley, be commended for his quick response to market conditions."

"I'll second that," Mr. Campbell quickly interjected. "I'd even suggest a bonus for you, John, but you're so damn well-paid now I don't think a bonus would mean much one way or another."

"Hold on to that thought, Cyrus," John Broadley laughed. "I never said I was adverse to the idea of bonuses, you know,"

"I do have a couple of new items of business I would like to discuss with the Board," Mr. Broadley stated rather seriously. "First, a new customer of THE FIRM informed me last week that she had checked out the racial and ethnic categories of THE FIRM's current stock holdings and that they match fairly well the proportionality of the world's population at large. She thought we should be commended on our policy of non-discrimination toward any race or ethnic group."

The Board stared long and hard at Mr. Broadley in an effort to read his face. Then, to a person, they broke out in raucous laughter to the point where some of them had to wipe the tears from their eyes.

"What'd you tell her, John?" Mr. Ling snorted out between his laugher. "I really want to hear that one!"

"Why, Mr. Ling, I told her the truth. THE FIRM adheres 100 percent to a free enterprise capitalist economy and thus rigorously responds to supply and demand. The lady soaked that up, Mr. Ling, stared at me a little bit, and then asked if we would trade exclusively in black Africans or Scandinavian Nordics if that's what people were buying. Without hesitation, I told her that's exactly what we would do. You should have seen her face. It went from bewilderment to anger to embarrassment. But finally, she blurted out 'Good! I'm fortunate enough to own a little stock myself in THE FIRM,' and trounced off to examine some new stock being installed in the room. Within an hour, she had purchased exactly what she had been talking about: a big African stud and a buxom wench from Sweden. Lord knows what she wanted them for," Mr. Broadley chuckled. "Showtime, probably!"

Every member of the Board broke out in hilarious laughter at the well-told story and appreciated Mr. Broadley's dead-pan delivery style.

"Sounds like we should get an award of something," Cyrus Campbell joked, "for being such stalwart defenders of capitalism. Surely someone in the White House or Parliament could come up with something for defending the principles of free enterprise."

"I'd rather get the Baldwin Award of Excellence in Quality," Mr. Broadley quipped back. "If Cadillac can get an award, why can't we? I like to think of us as 'the Cadillac of Specialized Livestock.' Doesn't that have a nice ring to it and to have one of those fancy awards to put into the Board room here – it's so appropriate." The usually staid Mr. Broadley joined the others in their riotous laughter at this point.

After the board members got control of themselves again, Mr. Broadley introduced another topic of new business.

"I think the time is right to show some appreciation to our biggest customers. I've given this some thought and decided a good way to do this would be to throw a little party down at our Key Biscayne estate and invite the big roller customers that really add to that bottom line you just saw. I propose inviting our 100 best customers, defined by total dollar amount of purchases, so that just buying in big volume doesn't necessarily qualify you – that way, we make sure the real connoisseurs that appreciate our quality product and are willing to pay big bucks to back up their good taste don't get overlooked. We could bill it as a costume party and invite our best customers to bring a few of their own slaves with them that are especially interesting or would make a great display or they would just like to show off for whatever reason. What do you think? I was thinking of a two-day event when the weather would be really nice down in Key Biscayne. You would all be invited, of course, as Board members," he concluded with his eyes reflecting his enthusiasm.

"John, we're mighty lucky to have you in charge. That's one of the most creative ideas I've heard in some time. I think it would definitely tell our best customers we appreciate them, the 'show off' idea is great, and, besides, it sounds like fun. I move we approve John's plan," Mr. Austin from Australia blurted out.

"You Aussies just like parties," Mr. Carposa laughed. "I second John's plan, and make sure I'm on the invitation list."

"Outside the costumes and the display slaves they will no doubt drag along with them, what's the entertainment, John?" Cyrus asked.

"Well, I thought we'd send about 200 of our best looking stock down from the New York and Chicago warehouses – those that have finished their training and are waiting for the next big sale. That way everyone could sample the latest wares as the entertainment, and, if we send their managers down with them, we shouldn't have a bit of trouble with them no matter how the party ends up. My guess is some of that stock will be sold before the party's over, which is a little added bonus I suppose."

"Can you handle all of this, John, what with your work load and all?" Mr. Ling asked.

"I'm not going to handle it at all, Mr. Ling," Mr. Broadley smiled. "I'm planning to dump the whole responsibility on the warehouse managers of our New York and Chicago operations. After all, that's where the 'entertainment' will be coming from anyway."

"No wonder you're CEO, John. Count on me being there," Mr. Ling laughed. "I move we approve Mr. Broadley's plan for customer appreciation."

"All in favor say 'aye,'" Mr. Broadley automatically stated.

"Ah, the hell with it," Mr. Austin said, 'let's make it a unanimous approval by acclimation."

"Move for adjournment," Mr. Carposa blurted out.

"All in favor say 'aye,'" Mr. Broadley dutifully said. "I'll see all of you at Key Biscayne."

A chorus of ayes rained down on him and the august assemblage chatted amiably among themselves as they left to their waiting limousines.

———————

"Mr. John Broadley cordially invites you to THE FIRM's estate at Key Biscayne, Florida for buffet and cocktails on Saturday, August 17th starting around 11:30 A.M and ending at your pleasure August 18th. Personal staff, servants, pets, and staff-in-training may be included in your entourage subject to your usual appropriate discretion. Interesting costumes and unique servant displays are encouraged. Please forward the names and/or labels of all members of your entourage who will be attending as soon as possible so that gate clearance can be arranged. Directions and fax number enclosed."

"You got the guest list ready, Mr. Simmons?" John Broadley asked his long time Chicago sales manager and close associate.

"Yes, the invitations are all ready to send out, but I wanted to go over the list once more with our worldwide sales managers before we send them out," Mr. Simmons responded with his usual enthusiasm. "I have a feeling this is going to be an interesting shinding, Mr. Broadley. I know our best customers will show up – who wouldn't when you're providing all that free meat on the hoof – and I have no doubt they're going to be bringing some really interesting "personal staff, servants, pets, or staff-in-training" with them – just to show off if nothing else. But that doesn't mean we shouldn't stock the place with the best of our holdings for their use. My guess is we're going to sell off a great deal of all that we ship down there. Besides, it's always fun to fuck something free for the taking."

"Well, I briefly considered hiring some hustlers widely available in Miami without too much trouble since we would be paying them top dollar, Mr. Simmons. They could service our customers fairly well and there's so damn many hustlers in Miami now we could pick out the best of the lot. But then I thought it would be hard to find ones that looked half as good as anything we have in our own warehouses – let alone hustlers willing to just let anybody do anything they wanted at any time. That's why THE FIRM's doing so well."

"But some of our customers, Mr. Broadley, as you well know, are something else again when it comes to their slaves. I doubt if they go to the bathroom anymore without at least some 'personal staff' accompanying them – at least, that's the idea I get talking to them."

"Well, all of us have a public image to maintain," Mr. Broadley laughed. "Kind of like the Queen's Court or the Secret Service around the U.S. President. Their reputation of unlimited wealth demands some public displays now and then and a really handsome naked slave sure beats a diamond ring or an expensive car for that purpose. My guess is they're used to maintaining a little public spectacle just to maintain their reputations, so to speak. We'll see, Mr. Simmons, we'll see. For all I know, they may turn me down flat. Some of our customers are a strange lot as you well know, Mr. Simmons."

"Naw," Mr. Simmons popped back. "They'll come out of curiosity if nothing else. Hell, that invitation is weird enough to draw them in I would think. Add to that their intrigue with THE FIRM, and your reputation for real money – that alone will do what curiosity won't. They'll come, Mr. Broadley. An invitation from anything connected with THE FIRM, let alone from someone of your social and economic prominence, would be like an invitation to Buckingham Palace or the White House as far as they're concerned. Yeah, they'll come all right."

"Well, we'll soon know. As far as the list goes, all customers who gross over $10 million business a year with THE FIRM should be on the list, along with all members of the Board of Directors. Lesser customers probably wouldn't appreciate the subtle nuisances of the party itself. Oh, and one other thing, Mr. Simmons. Send an invitation to THE FIRM's two main contracted supply agents, David and Forrest c/o my office. They'd appreciate a little break in their busy life and it's always interesting for them to see the finished product in action. There's a huge difference between the raw material David and Forrest furnish us and the finished product you're so familiar with in your Chicago sales outlet. Forrest and David always get a kick out of that. Let's them know all their hard work for THE FIRM pays off! And one more thing. How are the boys being readied for the event?"

"They'll all be exercised, thoroughly flushed, body shaved, lubed, and completely oiled right before the guests arrive and we'll make sure they are all thoroughly rested and fed sparingly the night before. It won't hurt them if they don't get fed again until Sunday night in view of the usage we can expect. Their collars, rings and bands will all be freshly polished and each one will be sporting a fresh white linen bow tie fastened to their collar with THE FIRM's logo on it. That's it for dress, but we're going to make sure no one unloads for at least two weeks before the event to insure they'll all be displaying how interested they are."

"Sounds good, Mr. Simmons. Seems like you've thought of everything."

— — — — —

"Where are we at on the R.S.V.P.'s, Mr. Simmons?" Mr. Broadley asked three days before the party.

"Ninety-five percent of THE FIRM's best customers have already said 'yes, they'll be here' and, Mr. Broadley, every single member of THE FIRM's Board of Directors is coming along with your special guests, David and Forrest. It's THE FIRM's and your reputation, I tell you," Mr. Simmons said admiringly.

"Who else?"

"What do you mean?" Mr. Simmons responded.

"Are some of the customers bringing anyone in tow?" Mr. Broadley asked.

"Oh, that! Well, yes, although they didn't state just what was in tow, just how many!" he laughed.

"Well, how many in tow altogether?" Mr. Broadley pursued the topic.

"Almost 50, Mr. Broadley. Can you believe it?"

"I'm surprised there aren't more," Mr. Broadley replied with a slight smile.

— — — — —

Some of the customers were already at the mansion by 11:15 and were already playing around with a few of the boys who were trying to finish stocking the buffet table. By 11:45, a good half of those invited were already there and a few were already into utilizing some of THE FIRM's slaves for their immediate pleasure. Mr. Simmons saw a large blond originally purchased by THE FIRM from the Texas prison system was already on his knees sucking someone and a hyper-masculine American black with prodigious equipment was bent over a sofa as he was being plowed by one of THE FIRM's newer customers. A very muscular Mexican slave, initially bought by THE FIRM from the prison system there, was vigorously fucking one of THE FIRM's slaves from India under a customer's direct instruction while others were content to just watch the interesting little show. The other staff, supervised by an extraordinarily handsome Russian slave who had been THE FIRM's property for some time, were busily serving drinks and canapés as the party got underway. All of THE FIRM's Board of Directors had already arrived and were busily examining some of THE FIRM's slaves that Mr. Broadley had arranged to be sent down from the Chicago and New York warehouses. It wasn't often they had the time to closely inspect THE FIRM's products and they all agreed it would be a good idea to bed down a few drawn at random to check out the efficacy of THE FIRM's renowned training procedures while they were here.

The very first customer to arrive was driving a plain looking Impala rental car. She was dressed in a simple black cocktail dress, appropriate enough for the occasion, with a single strand of pearls her only decoration.

"I'm so happy to meet the famous Mr. Broadley," she exclaimed to the host of the event who greeted her at the front steps by her car.

"I've been looking forward to meeting some of our customers in person," Mr. Broadley responded smoothly.

"Where shall I park? I didn't see any place."

"Oh, the boys will take it back to one of the parking lots. Do you like THE FIRM's products to date?"

"I can't answer that properly until we get the trunk unloaded, Mr. Broadley, and I'll show you how much I like them," she responded sweetly as she turned back toward the car and unlocked the truck. She drew a small leather whip out of her purse.

As soon as the trunk lid opened, two beautiful male specimens rose from their prone position and climbed out of the truck quickly before kneeling before their mistress, presenting their leashes, attached to their collared necks, to her with both hands in a supplicant's position. They were tall, extremely well-built, and devastatingly handsome. Both wore black leather pants cut low enough to display their muscled abdomens and fitted extremely tight so that their bubble butts, their muscular thighs, and their prodigious genitals were all fully displayed. It was obvious through the thin, stretched leather that both boys' thick, long shafts were fully erect. Mr. Broadley thought to himself that the ultra tight pants made the boys look even sexier than if they were totally naked as THE FIRM's slaves were usually displayed. Above their extremely thin waists rose massive muscular pecs highlighted by big, prominent ringed tits. Their bodies, tanned and oiled, were totally hairless except for their head hair which was jet black and cut short, and both sported unusual green eyes. Most impressively, they were totally alike – identical twins!

Both blushed with embarrassment and shame as Mr. Broadley openly assessed them, not as men but as slaves fully available for their owner's pleasure. Both tried their best to hide their shame, however unsuccessfully, because they had learned it only added to their erotic appeal as helpless slaves.

"Very nice, Madame," Mr. Broadley said admiringly as he quickly assessed the twins kneeling before their mistress, lifting their heads up from their collars to enjoy the shamed look on their faces. "Have you had them long?"

"Call me Tammy and I'll call you John," she practically cooed. "I've had these boys for about four months now and they're working out nicely so far. Perhaps before the day is over, you might find time to enjoy them – you're certainly welcome. I think you'll find them a little unusual compared to what you may be used to." Without changing her stance in any way she suddenly barked "Position!"

The two males leaped to their feet, placed their hands in back of their neck and thrust their chest and pelvis out for full display. She reached down and, with the hand that held the whip, vigorously squeezing first one's genitals through the thin leather and then the other's, massaging both in the process.

"I haven't let them unload for three weeks now," she cooed as she began rubbing their erect shafts through the leather pants. "They should be real interested if this party develops the way I expect it will," she smiled.

"Unusual, er...Tammy? You mean in their looks? They are unusually attractive boys if that's what you mean," Mr. Broadley pursued her earlier comment, openly admiring the exceedingly handsome twins displaying themselves as commanded.

"No, John, although they are uncommonly attractive, I admit," she answered as she continued stroking their erect shafts. "Apparently, a few male slaves are just born 100 percent heterosexual and, no matter how much you train them with the best known conditioning techniques in the world, they just never learn to relax and enjoy being used by another man. These boys here have been trained until I thought they would die in the process. John, we've gone all the way to starvation, beatings, branding, raping, shocking – you name it – and these boys still resent being fucked or ordered into oral service of a another man. Oh, they'll do it quickly enough, no problem with that, but there's a hint of resentment that seems to always flavor their usage that way. For some reason, I really get a kick out of that, especially since they really enjoy being ordered to service a woman in any way you can dream up – but I love to see that resentment in their eyes every time I arrange for another male to use them. I thought you might find it interesting to bed down a male slave who deeply resents what you're doing to them, but will remain compliant enough, knowing what would happen if there was even a hint of rebellion. It's especially interesting when the twins absolutely love all the other aspects of their slavery – having every decision made for them, the total subjection of their will to a mistress, being expensive property responsible only to their owner. To put it bluntly, John, they're addicted to loving every aspect of their slave lives except being fucked up the ass and sucking prick. That's why I think you'll find them unusual in bed – compared to what you're probably used to! I found it's certainly hard to find stock like that at the auctions. Most slaves seem to slide into bisexuality with relative ease. – these boys never did for God knows what reason – genetics, I guess, or maybe they were brought up Southern Baptist," she giggled.

"Where did you get them?" Mr. Broadley said, aware that another car was coming up the driveway.

"At your New York warehouse, John," she giggled, again with a mocking look in her eye. "No, not really, John. Although I've bought a lot of slaves from your facilities, I found these twins at an auction in Toronto. A very small slave training facility there had given up with them because of their little quirk and was willing to give me a substantial discount if I'd take them 'as is.' Turned out 'as is' was just what I was looking for," she said proudly. Before the weekends over, I'll tell you all the details if you're interested."

"Count on it!" John replied.

"You've got other guests to greet so we'll chat later," the beautifully dressed customer said. With that, she issued the command 'Heel' and jerked on the collar leashes for her two slaves to follow her into the mansion. The handsome twins quickly got in step behind her, their hands now at their sides with their heads bowed as low as their collars would allow, their large aroused organs provocatively evident as they pushed against the tight leather confining them.

A couple was walking up the driveway beside the next arriving car. "We took a cab from the airport and left it at the gate. Didn't want to give the cab driver anything to talk about," he laughed.

"Very thoughtful of both of you. We can't have cab drivers spreading tales around town, now can we, although, most of them can't speak English anyway," Mr. Broadley laughed as he shook both of their hands. "Welcome to my home. I'm John Broadley and thanks for honoring me with your presence."

"It's our pleasure, Mr. Broadley. We're not much to participate at these things, but my wife and I both enjoy watching – just dirty old voyeurs, I guess. Both of us just enjoy looking around and enjoying the scenery. Thanks for inviting us. Well, I see you have more guests coming. We're both starving so we'll go in and load up on the food – I'm one who actually goes to these things to eat – can you believe it?" he laughed. "My wife picks around at the food, but swallows everything else up, believe you me – I'll hear every detail for the next year," he roared hilariously. The couple disappeared into the mansion as quickly as they had appeared.

A stretch Lincoln limousine was now in front of the steps and the chauffeur quickly ran around to open the back door. The black was in a skin-tight tailored suit and tall leather boots that exactly matched the car's exterior paint, except for the broad bronze collar around his thick neck. As soon as he opened the door, he dropped flat on his stomach beside the open door.

"I don't believe we've met before, Mr. Broadley," a voice came out of the open door. "I'm Frederick Davis, one of your appreciative customers. Thanks for the invite!" A foot stepped out of the car squarely on the middle of the chauffeur's back as if it was a foot mat. The man quickly emerged from the car pulling two others, chained by their necks, out the same way. The chauffeur grunted from the weight of each person's exit but remained perfectly rigid as he'd been trained.

"And these two beauties?" Mr. Broadley asked as he took in their naked assets, now on full display.

"My personal attendants, Mr. Broadley. Meet Burma and Alabama – I always name my attendants by where they came from," he added brightly. "Helps me keep them all straight."

"Burma and Alabama add a nice touch to your arrival, Mr. Davis. As you seem to know already, I'm Mr. John Broadley, your host."

"Why, thanks, Mr. Broadley. I appreciate that. Some people think these two are a bit tacky stark naked and all, but that's the way I like them. Collared and stark naked," Mr. Davis laughed.

"Well, they look fine to me, Mr. Davis," Mr. Broadley said graciously.

"Wow! You do know how to make a person feel great, Mr. Broadley. Don't be surprised if you have trouble getting rid of me!"

"Are these girls volunteers, rented, or bought and paid for if I may be so bold?"

"The girls here belong to me, John, and have for about six months now. The way I understand it, they've had about five or six owners before I came along despite their youth. People like a change now and then, I guess. Next time I get a chance, I going to trade one of them in on a male slave if I can find one that turns me on. I think it's a little showier when you have a male and female in tow. Where can my chauffeur park the car?"

"The parking lot is in back. Will he be staying with the car or did you prefer him with you, Mr. Davis?" Mr. Broadley answered.

"With me – some of your guests may find him entertaining." The chauffeur was still prone on the pavement since he had not been ordered otherwise. Mr. Davis reached down and jerked the boy's head up by his hair. "Park the car in back, strip, and lock all of your clothes in the trunk. Then find me in the mansion. Is this the only door open, John?"

"Today it is, Mr. Davis. We didn't want anyone snooping around and it makes it easier to keep track of our guest's staff."

"Very well. Use this door here, Asad," Mr. Davis said as he reached down and jerked the black's head even higher until he was staring directly into the boy's unusual blue eyes.

"Yes, master," the chauffeur respectfully responded, a touch of excitement evident in his soft bass voice.

"Looks interesting, Mr. Davis," John commented as the boy gracefully rose to his feet and headed back to the driver's position, his head bowed as low as his thick neck collar would allow.

"He's a handsome lad and well-trained," Mr. Davis replied, "and you'll soon see a body that's developed into a mighty valuable commodity. He's probably hoping to get some use here – I've pretty well limited him to driving the car and looking pretty the past two weeks – in fact, I don't think I've allowed him to unload for about a month now. If someone even touches him, he'll probably lose it and go spurting off," Mr. Davis laughed.

"I thought you said he was well-trained," Mr. Broadley said reprovingly.

"He is, John, but there are limits!" Mr. Davis laughed again. "He's still just a boy – just turned 19 now I think!"

"Where'd you pick him up, Mr. Davis?" John queried.

"He's from Sierra Leone. Orphaned by the civil war there, he had been rounded up with hundreds of others by some local slave catchers who'd pretty well broken him to the realities of slavery before auctioning him off. Some French cartel bought up loads of the best looking ones and, after fattening them up with some decent food, exercising them to full muscular development, and fully training them in what potential owners would expect, sold him off in a private auction in Paris. That's where I bought him about a year ago. So far, it's worked out well!"

"Perhaps we can talk later about that French cartel, Mr. Davis. We're always interested in sources of new stock."

"I've only owned 10 or so of THE FIRM's products so far, but everyone claims they're about as good as they get, John," Mr. Davis responded. "I hope to buy some more with THE FIRM's brand on them soon. Meanwhile, we'll swap notes about that Paris market," he promised as he clasped his host's hand warmly and walked into the mansion, the two slave girls in tow.

A cargo truck roared up the driveway next. A large, muscular, rather rough looking man was driving the truck, alone in the cab. He jumped out and strode purposefully over to Mr. Broadley.

"John Broadley?" he asked. "Alexander Bentley here. Sorry about coming in a truck, but it's about the only way I could get them all here without anyone seeing them."

"Seeing what?" Mr. Broadley looked surprised.

"My personal staff, as you so politely called it in your invitation, Mr. Broadley," Mr. Bentley laughed displaying a beautiful set of white teeth highlighting a craggy, but handsome face.

"Well, let's see this staff of yours, Alexander," Mr. Broadley mused, his eyes reflecting his curiosity.

Mr. Bentley grabbed a huge bull whip from the front seat of the truck before unlocking the back door. A crack of the whip led to an anguished shriek as the lash found a target in solid flesh and the sound of frantic shuffling rocked the truck.

"Get that litter out of the truck and on your miserable shoulders, you bastards," he yelled as the whip cracked out again and found another target with an accompanying scream. Body after body, 10 in all, spilled out of the truck along with a huge gold colored litter complete with a red velvet top and matching cushions. Almost instantly, eight of the men had hoisted the heavy litter to their shoulders and were standing absolutely still with perfect posture, their muscles tense, and with their naked bodies on full display. The remaining two men, obviously relief bearers serving as footmen until needed, had knelt alongside, their knees spread wide to expose their banded erect genitals, their chests thrust out to best display their massive pectoral development highlighted by huge ringed tits. All 10 were fitted with thick, high gold-colored collars that forced their heads upright so you could see their faces. The collars, lined in red velvet, exactly matched the litter.

Mr. Broadley' eyes swept over the sudden display. Every slave was exactly matched for height, weight, physique and skin color. All were about as muscular as men can get, all had their golden tan bodies fully shaved, all featured well trimmed shoulder length straight black hair parted in the middle, all had been banded around the base of their balls and their shaft to insure constant full protrusion of their extra large genitals, and every one of their tits were fitted with 2" rings that matched their collars. All sported a dripping erection even as they stood there silently, strongly suggesting to Mr. Broadley's practiced eye that all were also fitted with large butt plugs stimulating their prostates. Sure enough, a protruding ring of the deeply inserted plugs was evident in each man's tightly clinched ass.

"Very nice, Mr. Bentley. What are they – American Indians?"

"Hung like that, John?" Mr. Bentley laughed. "Hardly. They're Latinos – mainly light-skinned stock from Nicaragua, Mexico, and the Dominican Republic. That stock's so cheap right now you can pick and choose most anything you want," he added. "Of course, boys looking like these cost a little more," reaching out and stroking the massive sculptured chest closest to him and then kneading a swollen ringed tit until the slave softly moaned but never flinched.

"Looks like an old-fashioned Hollywood movie," Mr. Broadley commented, "except," he paused as he again inspected the entourage, "their costuming sure's a lot simpler. Where'd you get them, if you don't mind me asking? Being associated with THE FIRM, I tend to forget all the other markets out there."

"Oh, I picked one or two up as I spotted them in obscure small American markets. But, mainly, John, there's a market way out in the remotest wilds of Nicaragua a good 50 miles in from the coast that can provide most anything you're looking for and at reasonable prices too. Of course, they mainly stock Haitians, Mexicans, Dominicans, and of course lots of Nicaraguans. Hardly any European stock there, let alone Asians or Americans. If you're looking for Latinos, though, it's worth the trip. I can tell you how to make contact if you're interested."

"I'd appreciate it, Mr. Bentley. Latinos seem to be picking up in popularity lately. These boys are really magnificent if I do say so myself."

"They just don't look good, John. Wait 'till you bed one down. I know you're used to the best, but I doubt if you'll be disappointed in any one of them," Alexander Bentley bragged enthusiastically as he began to pump the shaft of the slave boy nearest him. "They fuck as good as they look."

Without further comment, he motioned to his slaves, who promptly knelt in one synchronized movement, lowering the litter to entrance height. Mr. Bentley climbed in, and with another crack of his whip, pointed to the entrance of the mansion. The entire entourage entered the double-door entrance, litter aloft, no doubt to the great amusement of everyone already inside. Mr. Bentley was waving enthusiastically to the guests, cracking his whip over the shoulders and rumps of his straining slaves for an added dramatic effect.

Appearing out of nowhere seemingly, a single lady, dressed in a well-tailored riding outfit, introduced herself to the host.

"Mr. Broadley. We haven't met. I'm Laura Ashley."

"Ah, one of our best customers. Thanks so much for coming, Miss Ashley, but I thought you were bringing a trainer with you," Mr. Broadley said warmly as he clasped her hand.

"Oh, he's coming. But he won't be able to get here for a few hours – he's on a new assignment," she added without further explanation. "I hope that's alright with you. – that is, not arriving together?" she pursed his lips together in a frown.

"Makes no difference at all, Miss Ashley, as long as you're comfortable. I'm sure you'll find some of the other guests interesting to talk to," he suggested.

"I'm sure I will if they primarily customers of THE FIRM," she gushed with sincere enthusiasm.

"Only our best customers, like you, Miss Ashley, so I'm sure you'll have plenty of opportunity to talk as much as you want with them and I'm certain you're going to find some of the staff they brought with them equally interesting," John replied with considerable conviction. "I'm sure your trainer will be more interested in some of the staff than in THE FIRM's customers," he laughed. "Wait until you see what one of the last guests brought along – it took a whole truck simply to move them in," he smiled and then laughed warmly. "You'll appreciate it."

A beautiful black youth, extremely well-built and naked except for a high neck collar and ringed tits, patiently waited to one side until the door was cleared.

"Here's Mr. Davis' chauffeur if I recognize him with his uniform off," Mr. Broadley commented as he reached over and, grabbing the boy's erect prick, hauled the boy over next to the two of them. "A native African, is that right, boy?"

"Sierra Leone, Master," the boy answered as he thrust his pelvis forward into Mr. Broadley' hand for easier handling.

"I've always dealt with Americans," Miss Ashley commented as she stroked the boy's cheek and then squeezed his left nipple between her thumb and forefinger, massaging it until it too became fully erect. "This one's so exotic compared to American stock. And so young too, it seems," as she ran her other hand appraisingly over his well rounded muscular butt checks. "I bet he's a good fuck, don't you think, John?" she asked without a hint of embarrassment. "I'd love to try him out if this Mr. Davis would agree to use of his property like that – you know what I mean, John – we've never met and I'd be just a total stranger as far as he's concerned. Oh, there I go again – prattling away – neither one of us probably knows if this boy even knows how to fuck. Let alone a woman – which way does Mr. Davis swing, anyway, Mr. Broadley? Do you know?"

"No, he had two beautiful women leased by their collars when he entered," John Broadley laughed, "but I imagine this boy here doesn't just drive his car. What about it, boy?" Mr. Broadley asked as he reached down and roughly squeezed the boy's balls with his other hand.

"Ugh," the boy groaned from the ball squeezing but never flinched from his position. "I know how to fuck fine, Master," the boy answered and, glancing over at Miss Ashley, "and Mistress. Never had a complaint. Master Davis has had me fuck lots of his friends, men and women, and lots of his other slaves too for he and his friends' amusement. Course, I've been fucked a whole lot more than I've fucked, but, Master and Mistress, I'm good at that too they tell me."

"Chatty, isn't he?" Miss Ashley commented as her finger slid up the boy's hole.

"I told you he didn't just drive the car," Mr. Broadley chuckled.

"Well, his hole's still good and tight anyway," she added as she wiggled the inserted finger around in him. "Think you could keep from shooting off if I let you pleasure me?" she asked in her straight-forward manner, reaching over and rubbing her hand over the head of his rampant prick, still being vigorously massaged by Mr. Broadley.

"Yes, mistress – I sure can – but I'm going to shoot off if you keep rubbing me like that, I'm afraid."

Miss Ashley's hand shot up and slapped the youth so smartly across the cheek his black skin turned momentarily a reddish mahogany. "You'll not shoot until you're given permission, boy, if you know what's good for you," she stated coldly. "Apparently, your master doesn't handle you much, slave boy."

"No mistress."

Another slap to the other cheek was as swift as the first. "No he doesn't handle you much, or no, I was wrong and he does handle you a lot? Your voice-training is atrocious. Which is it, boy?"

"Sorry, Mistress. He doesn't handle me, Mistress. Just his friends."

"Well, if your master agrees, you'll learn what it's all about once I bed you down, slave boy."

"Yes, mistress."

"With your permission, Mr. Broadley, I'll ask the boy to take me to his owner, now – that is," she laughed and looked down at the boy's genitals – "if you can get your hands off the boy's shaft."

"See you later, Miss Ashley," John Broadley laughed as he released the boy from his grasp. "Good luck if Mr. Davis lets you bed this boy down for the thorough training you promised."

"You're as charming as I'd heard you were," she said leaving, pulling the boy behind her by one of his tit rings.

The next bunch of guests were all eager customers of THE FIRM and were anxious to get their hands on the contingent of THE FIRM's freshly trained slaves they knew awaited them inside. But at the end of that group stood a well dressed Scot, complete with wool kilt, a sport tweed jacket, a sporty tam, and three huge males crawling along behind him on their hands and knees, all chained by their collars to the Scot's waist. Mr. Broadley was bemused by the wanton display of pure power.

"John Broadley," he greeted the Scot.

"Glad to meet you, laddie. Gordon Brown here. And bonnie glad to be here, I tell you."

"Was your flight a problem, Mr. Brown?" Mr. Broadley inquired.

"Pleasant as flights can be, first class or not, Mr. Broadley, but it's a wee long one I tell you," he smiled. "But getting these boys through customs took a while, even though they've all got valid passports and a U.S. visa, they were kind of suspicious – I suppose because of where these boys came from originally," jerking on their neck chains with the harsh order, "Sit" whereupon each one sat on their haunches and let their weight rest on their arms.

"What passports do they carry?" Mr. Broadley asked incredulously as he stared at the naked animals at the Scot's feet. It was hard imagining them riding fully clothed in tourist class sipping a health drink (or whatever their master would allow) just a few hours ago, crowded as they would be due to their immense size.

"Macedonia, Croatia, and Serbia. British and U.S. immigration people are suspicious of those passports to start with, but I suppose these boys' sheer size sort of intimidates them anyway," he stated. "Little do they know they're just slaves. Doesn't seem to me you'd need passports and visas for property – after all they're just a commodity," Mr. Brown complained. "Well, we're here now and these boys are back where they belong – their balls swinging in the breeze, their necks tightly collared, and big, big butt plugs firmly up their assholes."

"Most importantly, you're here now," Mr. Broadley said soothingly. "Doesn't sound like you travel much. I'm honored you made such an effort, Mr. Brown."

"Wouldn't have missed the event, Mr. Broadley. I imagine anything THE FIRM puts on is worth attending," he laughed. "I may pick up new ideas along with some fresh stock. Who knows?"

"Well, Mr. Brown, I hope you enjoy the party enough to warrant the bother of the long trip."

"Wouldn't have come if I didn't think so, laddie. What do you think of these brutes here?" he jerked on their collars once again and the men's heads jerked up. They're as close to my idea of what slaves should be like in terms of size, coloring, musculature, and sexual equipment as I could find. A very long and painful training program has taken them the rest of the way. They're well-trained when you want to get some pleasure out of those big muscular bodies. They're genuine bed bucks by now – the kind that would bring top dollar in one of THE FIRM's auctions I tell you. Lord, listen to me rambling on. Well, Balkans make damn fine slaves anyway, Mr. Broadley, as you well know. You sold them to me," Gordon Brown laughed. "Wait till you try one of the slaves out for yourself. You'll see what I'm talking about." To illustrate, he stuck his finger into the open lips of the slave nearest him and looked pleased as the slave readily slid the finger completely down his throat and started vigorously sucking. "His ass is just as eager," Mr. Brown commended. "We keep them plugged unless we're using them – my trainers insist it takes more than collars and tit rings to remind them of what they are. Frequent use of a good whip, tight genital bands, and the biggest damn plugs you can ram up their ass – all are necessary to get the finished product according to them. That may be to keep them going, but initially, I think fucking them senseless, keeping them constantly naked, strict voice-control, and making sure they're in constant sexual tension without any relief possibilities – that's what produces a really good slave, Balkan or not!"

"A philosopher with a mission," Mr. Broadley smiled. These three slaves were eager to please it seemed, and certainly didn't seem unhappy.

"When I turn one over for your pleasure, Mr. Broadley, you'll think you were in paradise itself," Mr. Brown laughed. "And, by the way, call me Gordon. It's my given name, you know."

"And call me John, Gordon. I think you're one of the last to arrive. Can I escort you and your slaves into the mansion, Gordon?"

Gordon Brown handed the chain leads to Mr. Broadley. The slaves fell on their hands and knees once again and briskly crawled after their owner and his host through the front doors, their massive organs, ever erect, swaying beneath them.

"How do my agents arrange Balkan stock for your purchase, Gordon?" Mr. Broadley queried as the entourage entered the party itself.

"Big market outside of Bucharest, John, according to THE FIRM's salespeople that sold the slaves to me. They explained the whole process to me. Prisoners of war mainly for the older stock; orphans mainly for the teenagers. Some are sold to the dealers by their parents who have too many children to feed anyway. It's sort of a Serbian tradition, so no one thinks much about it. All the surrounding countries love the market – they can get their hands on hard currency by selling off their prisoners and orphans, both groups eating them out of house and home. And the Romanians love it – they get a tax on each sale. Everyone wins and the market's so gutted, the prices are practically giveaway compared to the rest of Europe and Asia."

"I'm not sure the slave wins, Gordon," John chuckled.

"Yes he does, John. What are his options? Starving to death? Being shot at sunrise? Being let loose with no skills in a land filled with 50% unemployment as it is? According to your agents, it's seldom they have anyone seriously object when they're placed up on the auction block. Seemed to me like most of them were looking forward to it. Where else would they be fed, safe, and with a purpose in life? The slave's the real winner," Mr. Brown said in finality.

"Point well made, Gordon. My agent's never share that part with me."

"In my opinion, it seems these Balkans slaves welcome being sold and really don't need much breaking, even when you start fucking them. I suppose they feel that's a small price to pay for all you've done for them. They're so damn grateful, John – it's like nothing they do can ever pay you back for saving them."

"Excuse me, Gordon. I just remembered one of our guests hasn't arrived yet and I need to be out front to welcome him," John said graciously, "but I'm not forgetting your offer of sampling some of that Balkan pleasure you promised. I would like to introduce you to a couple of gentlemen who currently serve on THE FIRM's Board of Directors, Mr. Cyrus Campbell from London and Mr. Luigi Carposa from Rome. They'll be extremely interested in that Balkan market outside Bucharest, especially if really some top-quality stock is available there."

"Indeed we would, Mr. Brown. As you know, THE FIRM is unashamedly trying to corner the market on premium slaves," Cyrus Campbell laughed.

"Mr. Brown, there's a slave inside I'm sure you'd enjoy. Frankly, STUD, that's this slave's name, is the heaviest hung and best looking slave I've ever seen. But, more importantly, he's one of the best fucks I've ever experienced. An American black," Luigi Carposa said brightly. "I thought Italian slaves were the best until I bedded this boy down. I'm sure you'll enjoy him. Now, Gordon, about that market outside Bucharest..." Mr. Carposa guided Mr. Brown back into the mansion away from Mr. Broadley.

"Remember, John, whenever you're ready these boys are yours to use," Mr. Brown smiled as he jerked the slaves collars upward so John could appreciate their handsome faces as he left with Mr. Carposa and Cyrus Campbell. "Where did THE FIRM locate this phenomenal American black, Mr. Campbell?" Gordon Brown turned to his new hosts.

As soon as Mr. Broadley got outside again, he realized his arrival was none too soon. Coming up the driveway was an apparition only Hollywood was capable of: two young, very muscular slaves, one white and one black, outfitted as ancient Roman gladiators, were on either side of a much shorter, white haired gentleman dressed in simple slacks and a golf shirt. Each of the two slaves were enough alike to be twins other than their color. Each had a thick muscular neck, massive shoulders, sculptured hairless protruding pecs highlighted with large dark nipples, waists unnaturally thin for such large bodies giving them a definite V-shaped appearance cinched in by noticeably ridged abdominal muscles, butts that bubbled out from the tiny waists in masses of hairless rounded solid muscle, thick trunk-like thighs with corded muscle clearly viable on the smooth youthful skin, and calves that were all muscle, but perfectly shaped, especially as compared to the thin ankles and high arches of their feet. They were obviously kept body shaved at all times and light oil highlighted the beauty of their skin. Neither of the pair could have been a day over 20 and the similarity of their sexual equipment matched the sameness of their bodies: each had a circumcised shaft that was thick, long, and beautifully shaped without the bulging veins that ruined the appearance of some slave's erect organs. The hole in each slave's gaping crown was clearly visible and each sported a small dollop of white cream to reflect their excitement at being displayed. The large, erect shafts were well positioned atop two large, but tight, balls that hung close to their bodies. Seemingly, no genital rings were necessary to keep the slave's equipment in almost perfect display and to make handling them easier, but close inspection revealed thin rings had been installed behind each slave's balls and over the base of their shafts, no doubt to remind the slaves of their total ownership, to serve as a cosmetic enhancement, or to allow for genital leashing, since a small clip ring installed to the larger genital band allowed for a lead chain to be used when necessary, convenient, or simply to add to the total appearance in public.

The slaves each wore full bronze helmets with uplifted visors, thick bronze slave collars with their names "Brutus" and "Rufus" noticeably engraved on each one, thick bronze wrist and ankle bands welded in place, upper arm bands welded above each of their biceps, and a large brand of ownership ("EC" surrounded by a circle) prominently displayed on each of their right pectorals and on each of their left rumps. Both slave's ankle bands were linked together by a chain which was long enough to clatter as it was dragged along the pavement, but short enough to prevent them running.

John extended a hand of welcome to the clothed man between the two strikingly handsome slaves.

"Edward Celonius, welcome. John Broadley here."

"How did you know it was me?" the silver haired gentleman said with a bemused curiosity.

"You're a legend when it comes to handsome display slaves, Mr. Celonius," John Broadley replied with a smile, reaching out and running his hand across the raised scar of the prominent ownership brand on the chest of the slave right in front of him. "Complete even to the owner's mark," he smiled again as he circled the brand 'EC' with his finger.

"I thought they'd add a little color to the festivities, Mr. Broadley," Edward Celonius smiled as he reached down and wrapped his hand around the massive swollen shaft of the white slave on one side of him and began gently massaging it. "They're so damn big that when I order them to fuck each other, it's quite a show."

"I'm sure it is and one our guests will no doubt enjoy," John Broadley smiled warmly. "It's not every day you get to see boys fucking wearing bronze helmets," he laughed. "I love the way you have the boys decorated."

"Just a touch here and there," Mr. Celonius winked. Everything, even the helmets, are either welded or locked on. That way, nothing gets lost and they're always the same," he added with a tingle in his voice.

"How do you cut their hair?" Mr. Broadley asked.

"Oh, that. Well, we do unlock the helmets every third month and harvest their hair. Sell it to a wig maker in Frisco who's eager to get it. Sell their sperm to a slave breeder in Saudi and lease the boys out as decorations for some of my friends' parties where I can count on them being discrete about the boys being slaves. Rent them out as models for some of the bolder magazines and to ad agencies when they need Roman gladiators and I contract them out to a whore house in Frisco at least three days a week where they get a good working over."

"Aren't you concerned about renting out slaves to non-slaveholders, Edward?" Mr. Broadley asked with some concern.

"Mr. Broadley, I've found most of those types of enterprises don't give a damn whether they're slaves or not – in fact they tell me they prefer them being slaves because it's so much less hassle. At any rate, they're never going to turn the boys over to the police or anything stupid like that. After all, when they buy a slave's services, they're as guilty in breaking any antiquated anti-slavery laws as the owner and they know it. There's so many 'underground' slaves floating around anymore, I'm not sure anyone's objecting anymore. If so, their objections aren't amounting to much. Slavery just keeps growing and growing each year if you ask me. There's just too many people profiting to ever stop the growth. But, hell, why am I telling you all this?" Mr. Celonius laughed. "What with you heading up one of the biggest outfits in the world?" he laughed again.

"Not the biggest yet, Edward, but certainly the best," Mr. Broadley laughed.

"No argument there. Everyone I know claims you're top quality. But let me get back to what I was talking about leasing out these boys. Oh, yeah. All in all, under careful management, I got what I paid for them back and then some before I'd had them a year, even taking out the cost of their training, feed, and fittings – not too shabby, do you think, John?"

"The financial advantages inherent in slave ownership has always been underrated, Mr. Celonius," Mr. Broadley replied. "As you say, good management is the key element to success in this area. I'm afraid so many of our colleagues are so wrapped up in just the thrill of owning another person and being able to order them to do absolutely anything they ever fantasized about, that the profit potential is completely overlooked. It's refreshing to meet someone who realizes that all a person's fantasies can be fulfilled without question, but tremendous profits can be made simultaneously. Takes a good businessman to have a plan. That's how THE FIRM has been able to make a little money, Mr. Celonius."

"More than a little, Mr. Broadley, from what I've heard. I'm not in your league, but I'm working on it," Edward Celonius chuckled. "Right now, I'm planning on buying and then training five more teams just like this one, Mr. Broadley. There's always a market for them – got three teams working the circuits right now. Damn good investments."

"Beats the stock market hands down," Mr. Broadley laughed as he reached down and hefted the heavy ball sac of the black slave, weighing it in his hand. A strong shudder ran down the slave's legs as he did so, although the black didn't move.

"A little skittish aren't they, Edward?" Mr. Broadley commented as he began massaging the balls in his hands. The slave's tremors did not stop and a look of absolute terror seemed to peer out from under the helmet's brim.

"A little, Mr. Broadley. They have reason to be. You see, John, I've trained them to such a high degree of absolute obedience that they run scared most of the time."

Mr. Broadley quickly looked into the white slave's eyes.

"Slaves should know what's expected of them at all times, Edward, but both of these boys look absolutely terrified all of the time. I'm curious. How'd you train them to that level?"

"The secret's in the helmet, Mr. Broadley. See this little bulge in the back of the helmet," Mr. Celonius said as he patted on a prominent bulge in the back of the black's helmet. "That's the power source for the electrodes. You see, John, the electrodes to the pain center of the brain are spring-loaded inside the helmet so they always rest right on the appropriate spot on the cranium no matter how much their heads get knocked around. Once I press this button on my transmitter, they feel pain like you can't imagine – it's direct from their own brain's pain center. The harder I press the button, the more pain they feel. Let me show you," Mr. Celonius said as he pressed lightly on the small black transmitter clipped to his belt.

Instantly, both slaves crumpled onto the floor screaming in torment as their muscles forced each of them into a fetal position and their muscles froze in constricted anguish. The pain was so intense their screams melted into a horrid gasp of pure, unadulterated agony. Tears sprang out of their eyes but their misery didn't allow them to sob, cry, groan or do anything other than their eyes revealed the stark horror of their situation.

"See, Mr. Broadley," Mr. Celonius commented as he released the button and the two slaves gasped for air. "Quick and instant discipline. They learn quickly once the helmets are on them."

"I can imagine, Edward. I'm surprised they haven't made some attempt to damage or remove the helmets."

Mr. Celonius laughed heartedly. "Oh! They've tried alright. We've had to redesign the helmets three times before we got these tamper proof models. First, we have to weld the helmets on or they would break the locks we had on the helmets originally, even when they broke their jaws in the process. Then they tried to bang their heads into walls to loosen the batteries, but they can't do that anymore because the batteries are part of the helmet. The white boy here repeatedly knocked himself unconscious trying to loosen the batteries when it was just a battery pack. And the black tried to stick his head in water to short it out – even when he passed out from lack of oxygen. Can't do that anymore – it's entirely waterproof now. You can knock it to hell and back, drown yourself in it, and the shock goes on. Totally slave proof now!" he said with a note of pride. "They don't even try anymore. It's easier to just obey instantly, or just take the pain like they did right now when I gave you this little demonstration. John, even if they went totally berserk, there's no need to worry. Push all the way down on the button and the slave is totally unconscious for at least an hour or so. You can even kill the bastards with it if you want, but you'd have to hold the button all the way down for at least 30 seconds to do that. I didn't realize it before, but pain alone can kill a slave if it's strong enough. No need to worry about rogue slaves fitted with this helmet," he laughed.

"I take it you've had some slaves go mad or try to kill themselves with this type of training, Edward, or you wouldn't have gone to such measures to design such a foolproof training helmet."

"John, I can see you've had some training experience yourself to ask such a good question. Of course, we lost a few in the original training program until we got the helmet just right. Now, we're training slaves routinely to our standards of exact obedience with no troubles whatsoever, as these two so clearly demonstrate. They'll do anything you want instantly and without questioning and thank you for it," Mr. Celonius said proudly.

"I kind of like that look of abject terror the slaves seem to have, Edward," John commented. "Is that a side effect of the helmet training? Or does that take additional training?"

"Nope, it's part of the package. Once those electrodes fly into use, the 'look' emerges in just a few days. It is sort of a nice touch – you don't see that all that often in slaves anymore it seems."

"No you don't. It gives your slaves a novel and unique look that becomes them in their role as your property. I imagine it will up the price considerably. How many teams are you going to put on the market trained like this, Edward?"

"Just as many as I can buy up and get fitted out with the helmets. It only takes a few weeks to train them once they're fitted properly. The problem is finding boys on the open markets that are closely matched as a team, built like a gladiator would be, but with those thin, thin waists and bubble butts, and young enough to offer a lifetime of service. And, of course, I like them hung heavy and pretty!"

"Who doesn't?" Mr. Broadley interjected.

"No, really hung heavy, like these boys here," Mr. Celonius continued. "I have to look over thousands and thousands of slaves, probably over ten thousand, before I can find two boys meeting all the specifications I'm looking for."

Mr. Broadley couldn't help but reflect on how extensive slave marketing had become over the years and how THE FIRM occupied only a tiny segment of that market, hopefully at the very top.

"I don't doubt it. Lookers like these two only come along once in a while. Ever thought about breeding them and saving yourself a lot of trouble."

"I'm going to, but it'll be 16 or 17 years before that'll pay off. In the interim, I'll just keep searching the markets both here in the United States and throughout the whole world. But, you're dead right, Mr. Broadley, the only real solution is to breed the bastards. Then we can get exactly what we want without hunting all over God's green earth!"

Mr. Broadley again reflected how wise THE FIRM had been to set up its own extensive slave breeding operations years ago.

The two slaves had recovered enough to get back on their feet and assume display position. Despite their use in the recent demonstration of the embedded electrodes, their shafts were once again erect and prominently displayed. But the look of sheer terror emanated from their eyes.

"Take your gladiators inside, Mr. Celonius, and join the party. The guests are going to get a real hoot when they see what you've brought with you."

"I hear some of your own stock is well worth a visit, Mr. Broadley."

"I hope they meet your expectations, Edward. Feel free to use any of them that interest you. That's why I've got them here. More important, they understand completely that's why they're here – to satisfy the slightest whim of any guest. Enjoy!"

"There's an offer I can't refuse," Mr. Celonius responded with a deep laugh, grabbing both of his slave gladiators by their salient pricks and leading them into the main hall.

CHAPTER VI

MEETING DEMAND IN THE WORLD MARKETS

Mr. Broadley was in Rome to inspect one of THE FIRM's monthly venues there. Rome had turned out to be a huge market for their products and what had once started as annual auctions were now monthly due to the huge demand. Rome, along with Rio, New York, Hong Kong, and Chicago was now one of THE FIRM's top five markets. The super wealthy from all over the world made it a point to attend at least one of the monthly sales each year, impressed by both the variety and quality of offerings available.

On this visit, Mr. Broadley was the personal guest of Count Luigi Farentina, one of Europe's leading industrialists, a direct descendent of Italian aristocracy, and one of THE FIRM's frequent customers. From the very beginning, Mr. Broadley and Count Farentina had enjoyed each other's company and had remained close friends over the years. Being a guest of the Count was always a treat. Not only was Count Farentina's remote villa outside Rome totally private, but it was also luxurious in the Baroque style so rare nowadays. The Count was particularly proud of the villa's large staff, most acquired at one or another of THE FIRM's auctions, who always seemed eager to meet the desires of any and all guests.

This morning, the Count and Mr. Broadley were having coffee on one of the villa's many outdoor verandas since the weather was superb. Three of the Count's staff were in attendance.

Standing beside them with coffee pots in hand were two beautiful Italian boys no more than 20-years-old. Identical twins, they were absolutely startling in their handsomeness. Although relatively short, they were superbly muscled, heavily hung with beautifully shaped organs, and each had large sparkling blue eyes, long thick dark eyelashes and eye brows, and flowing black hair kept shoulder length. Their most unusual trait was their hairless skin, however. It was the skin of a young teenager – tanned to perfection – so smooth it seemed pore-less – and perfectly flawless throughout their body. The third staff, a huge muscular black man, was on his hands and knees serving as a living table between the two gentlemen. All three men were outfitted as the Count prescribed for all his slaves: totally nude with shaved bodies, locked green leather 3" collars fitted tightly around their necks complete with the Count's court-of-arms embossed in gold on them; broad green leather genital bands encircling both the scrotum and shaft forcing their large manhood into blatant display; and a miniaturized version of the Count's coat-or-arms branded prominently onto their left rump and right pectoral. All three had been purchased from THE FIRM – the twins about a year ago right here in Rome and the black at THE FIRM's Mauritanian warehouse in Nouakchott almost five years ago when the black was a mere teenager and relatively cheap.

"Did you notice this item buried in the back pages of Il Figaro, John?" the Count asked as he folded Rome's largest newspaper back to the page he was referring to while idly stroking the erect penis of the Italian twin standing next to him, coffee pot in hand.

"Not unless you have an English-language edition sitting around here somewhere that I didn't notice, Luigi," Mr. Broadley chuckled as he studied the handsome face of the Italian slave being fondled while sitting his cup down on the quivering back of the black slave serving as their table. Rid of his cup, he casually reached down and began massaging the black's large ballsac swinging between his wide-spread legs. "Lord, Luigi, don't you ever let this boy unload? His balls feel about as full as they get," he chuckled as he continued his vigorous massage.

"To answer your immediate question, no," the Count laughed, "I don't allow slaves to unload unless I command it and it's been a while for these three, I suppose. We Italians think slaves should be kept in a state of constant need," he laughed again as he increased his stroking of the Italian slave. "Keeps them on their toes and reminds them it's our body, not theirs." Looking at the young Italian slave rather sternly, he said, "Don't you shoot, boy, or you'll get a whipping you won't soon forget."

"Yes, master," was all the response the slave could safely make as he renewed his efforts not to orgasm as a result of his master's play.

"Well, let me read this interesting little article to you in English, John," the count said as he continued stroking the slave.

"Oct. 23, 2010 (AP) – Washington. The Attorney General approved new rules yesterday creating special immigration visas for people smuggled into the United States and forced into prostitution, domestic service or farm labor. These 'T-visas,' created under a federal law passed in 2000, will allow victims to remain in the United States if they can persuade immigration authorities they would face "extreme hardship involving unusual and severe harm" if returned to their native countries. After three years, victims can apply to remain in American permanently."

"Think that will affect THE FIRM's operation in the States, John?" Count Farentina frowned. "You must have a least a thousand or so locked up in your U.S. warehouses awaiting sale right now for just what he's talking about."

"Probably, Luigi. But that legislation isn't going to affect them one iota now or in the future. The good U.S. Attorney General is just mouthing off to the press again. After all, that law was passed in 2000 and nothing has really happened to change anything. He's not into doing much about it actually. I'm not claiming he's pro-slavery – I'm just saying the times aren't politically right for defending civil rights – especially for those who never had any to start with, like our imports into the U.S. Besides, THE FIRM is a regular campaign contributor, you know, to insure that no one in Washington ever gets overzealous in their investigations."

"Well, you seem to operate here in Rome unabated. Is a lot of money crossing politician's palms here?" Luigi asked non-judgmentally.

"No. Don't need to here. Whatever party is in power here is happy there's an easy way to get rid of society's problems without costing them anything. In fact, it's the opposite here – we pay them for their excess prisoners and social burdens with no family to support them – THE FIRM pays corporation taxes like all other sales organizations – we even pay a value-added tax on each sale. We've become a significant item in their national income and they know it. Luigi, it's that way in most places of the world anymore. Only a few countries, like Great Britain and the U.S., make us operate deeply underground so to speak. But they're losing out on all those taxes. Take that handsome Italian boy whose sweating bullets now trying to avoid shooting off in your hand. He and his twin here were chronic burdens on Italian government services until THE FIRM took them off everyone's hands. Orphans and raised at government expense, they were so untrained and unskilled as adults they quickly joined the ranks of the chronically unemployed until the government got tired of paying them unemployment compensation month after month and, through the good efforts of their secret police, eventually secretly sold them to THE FIRM for training and eventual sale. It wasn't a year until you had them here serving you. The government has solved their problem and made some money in the process; THE FIRM made some money when they sold them to you; and you seem to be happy or you would have sold them off for a profit by now. Everyone's happy, so who's going to rock the boat, Luigi?"

"Point well made, John." the Count replied. "Even this slave would be happy if I let him unload. I would like a little fresh protein with my breakfast anyway. OK, boy, shoot into the juice cup here and then assume display position."

"Thank you, master," the Italian boy gasped as he quickly aimed his throbbing prick at the juice cup and let loose the first of five prolonged streams of steaming cum until the cup was almost full.

"Master, thank you," the slave reiterated after his balls had completely emptied. He quickly assumed the correct commanded 'display' position for a slave: head straight ahead with eyes lowered, feet wide apart, muscles tensed with arms behind his neck, and pelvis thrust out.

The black 'table' slave's prick was dripping pre-cum copiously onto the floor beneath him as Mr. Broadley's ball massage continued, but he dared not move or the items balanced on his broad back might tip. Mr. Broadley looked over at the other twin, still holding the hot coffee pot. He thought he looked envious as the slave's erect prick twitched, reflecting his own need.

"When you get bored with these three," Mr. Broadley said without interrupting his ball massage of the black, "I've got a customer who would pay top price, Count. They'll take all three of them without any negotiations, I'd wager."

"Who's that, John?" the Count said as he mixed the slave's fresh cum with his juice and drank it down in one gulp. "Refreshing," he commented as he swirled the solidified cum around in his mouth before a final swallow. "The boy's cum is still sweet despite being kept in storage so long," he chuckled. "I try to drink at least one load down a day – keeps you young according to the latest research. Better than just vitamins. Do you partake of youth's nectar, John?"

"I'll answer the last question first, Luigi. I'm probably too old to turn the clock back now, Luigi, so, no, I don't swill down the 'nectar' as you call it. But a lot of my customers, especially those facing a mid-life crisis, certainly do," Mr. Broadley answered with a laugh. "Good milk studs are bringing top prices these days as demand is going up. Drinking a few stud milk cocktails sure as hell couldn't hurt you and, as the research says, it probably helps. But I still prefer the taste of a good cup of cocoa. I guess I'll just age naturally," he laughed. As to your other question, the answer is "MaleServe."

"I've heard of them, John. Aren't they the ones who lease out slaves, mainly as temporary waiters, entertainers, house cleaners, gardeners, and whores?"

"That's the one, Luigi, but they're been so successful they're branching out. They're opening their own resorts now for the lower and middle classes that can't afford specialized slaves – you know, the places that cater to your every need – like here," he chuckled, "but it's only a temporary vacation – not a life style like you have here at the villa."

"I thoroughly enjoyed my stay at THE FIRM's own resort out in the Pacific, John. If you're selling to MaleServe so they can open their own resorts, aren't you scared they're cutting into your territory?"

"No way, Luigi. THE FIRM's resort is aimed at people like you and me – those who generally have whole stables of slaves available to them anyway. THE FIRM's resort offers fantasized stage shows, highly specialized and exotic slaves available nowhere else, and slaves trained to incredible levels of sexual skills – levels that take years to obtain. THE FIRM offers the rich and famous something different, unobtainable anywhere else, and quite novel from what's available within their own property. MaleServe is aimed at those who, under current market conditions, can never afford a slave of their own and are willing to save up for years to be a "master," no matter how briefly. MaleServe is offering a heady experience – one they'll never forget – for a fraction of the cost of actually owning a slave. After that experience, they'll forever want to own a slave, and if fortune turns their way, they'll be in the market for a slave. Now, Luigi, guess who's most likely to supply that slave? THE FIRM. Let's just say THE FIRM doesn't view it as competition, but as generating a future as well as an immediate market for us. The immediate market is MaleServe's huge buying of our stock right now; the future market is all those who buy into MaleServe's vacation package and develop a taste for something more permanent."

"John, you're a genius. No wonder THE FIRM stays on top," Luigi exclaimed as he drank another sip of coffee and motioned the undrained Italian twin over to him, pointed to the floor between his legs, and watched the handsome slave sink to his knees and open his mouth as he leaned forward into his master's crotch. Without another word, Luigi Farentina thrust his own organ completely down the boy's throat as the slave struggled to accommodate the invasion without gagging. "Feel free to use either of the slaves to relieve yourself, John, if you're in the mood. They're both well-trained – but the black's really fun – he's got a mouth like velvet."

"Thanks, Luigi, but I can't linger – I've got to get to the auction barns right away before the sales start."

"You're really something, John. Always work before pleasure. But, just a moment and I'll go with you if you don't mind. Get that mouth, going, slave, and squeeze down with your throat muscles. I haven't got all day."

The slave on his knees tried to respond despite his stuffed mouth, but it was obvious from his hollowed cheeks, his stretched throat muscles, and his lips working their way up and down his master's shaft in a firm grip, that he was responding to his master's command.

Within seconds, Count Farentina was shooting load after load down into the boy's stomach as the slave struggled to swallow every drop. Mr. Broadley watched as the eager slave then cleaned off his master's shaft as he'd been carefully taught and then reinserted the now limp shaft back into the Count's trousers before lowering his head in subservience once again.

Both men quickly left the veranda and headed for the waiting limousine to take them to THE FIRM's Rome operations. The three slaves remained in place exactly as the masters had left them: one standing in display position; one sitting on his knees with head bowed, licking excess cum off his lips; and one on his hands and knees still dripping pre-cum from his still erect prick. They would stay that way until the steward reassigned them to other duties when he next checked the breakfast veranda.

As the men were speeding to THE FIRM's warehouse close to Rome's airport, Count Farentina casually mentioned, "I am getting bored with the Italian twins and that huge black, John. Not that they are unsatisfactory in any way, but I do like fresh meat occasionally. What did you mean when you said you thought this MaleServe would give me top price on the goods?"

"Well, Luigi, they're exactly the type of slave that works out well for them in their resorts: experienced, well-trained, totally accepting of their slave status, easy to manage, and, since they've been used pretty heavily up to now by their current owner, unlikely to rebel to heavy usage by their customers. I imagine you could unload all three of them at over twice what you paid THE FIRM for them. Not a bad profit! And I assume you've enjoyed them in the interim?"

"John, act as my agent if you will. If you can get twice what I paid for them, you can keep anything above that you can wangle out of them, and deduct 10 percent agent's fee from the price I've agreed upon. They can have them today at that price!"

"Luigi, I can guarantee it now. If not, I'll buy them myself. Call your villa and have your steward clean them up inside and out – remember three enemas each since they're going to be transported – a full body shave and no food intake of any kind. Have him put each of them into a shipment cage and delivered here to THE FIRM's warehouse. We'll just leave them caged until MaleServe decides where they want them shipped. As soon as we get to THE FIRM's office here, I can check to see what you paid for them, double it, deduct my 10 percent and make out a check on the spot while you're signing over the ownership papers. It won't take more than two or three minutes once THE FIRM's sales agent takes over."

"John, you're so damn efficient. Now I'll have to look around for some replacement stock at THE FIRM's sales this afternoon. It will give me something to do this afternoon that I always find interesting and engaging. Where do you think those slaves will be going, anyway?"

"Luigi, my guess is all three of them will be shipped to the Caribbean. MaleServe has a huge resort on an island they totally own there. It's relatively isolated from prying eyes yet easy enough for their customers to get to. From what I hear, that place is simply eating up slaves so they have to keep sending fresh stock over on a regular basis."

"You mean they kill the slaves off, John? Sounds mighty expensive," Luigi responded without undue emotion.

"No. I overstated it. It's just that MaleServe makes sure everything is always profitable. I simply meant that the place is growing so rapidly they need more and more stock for all the customers they're getting. But, over and above that, there is still a rapid turnover. Slaves there get so much use they found they were literally wearing their slaves out over a long period of time, so much so they don't bring much on the resale circuit. So MaleServe works them hard – very hard – for only about three or four years and then packs them up and sends them back to their own sales outlets for re-sale. They still get a decent price out of them – of course, nothing like they pay us when they're fresh – but they're sold readily enough to those looking for a bargain in used slaves. But used they are by that time, Luigi," John laughed. "They're no longer in the condition you or I are used to or anything you'll see for sale this afternoon at THE FIRM's auction."

—————

The sale had been most successful and gave Mr. Broadley a good opportunity to study THE FIRM's Rome operation. His good friend, Count Farentina had found three replacement slaves to his liking and Mr. Broadley was sure he was now back at his villa sampling his new purchases. Although he was beginning to feel a little tired from the day's activities, he looked forward to the dinner at a renowned Roman restaurant with his two longtime colleagues, Forrest and David, who headed up THE FIRM's procurement operations. He could wait until tomorrow to start dictating his report on THE FIRM's operation in Rome for the Board of Directors. Tonight, he wanted to share his news with his trusted cohorts.

— — — — —

"Forrest, and David," Mr. Broadley said pleasantly as he shook their hands in the lobby of the palazzo now turned into a plush restaurant. "It's great to see you again. Sorry to drag you all the way to Rome just to talk to you, but what I have to say is important and I wanted to share it with you both personally."

The maître d' led the three men to their reserved table. Mr. Broadley started, "I'll get right to the point. THE FIRM's Board of Directors has just signed a new contract that should really up our profits but will involve both of you, Forrest and David, almost immediately. We're all pretty excited about it, because the potential is so big over the long haul."

"Thanks for inviting us to meet with you, Mr. Broadley. David and I are always interested in any new developments with THE FIRM. After all, THE FIRM is practically our life anymore."

"Yes, THE FIRM does sort of take over your life, doesn't it, Forrest? The work is so time-consuming I guess it just can't be helped, but..." he sighed, "the compensations are hard to beat."

"Can't complain, Mr. Broadley. You said when we first signed on we could make up to 10 million a year. Last year, both David and I were each clearing over forty million. It seems almost unbelievable, especially when I have to admit we so enjoy our work it's hard to imagine doing anything other than what we do."

"And do it so well," Mr. Broadley responded. "But the new contract will put you to the challenge," he chuckled, "but forty million a year for you may seem paltry after we get up and running on this new venture."

"I like it already, Mr. Broadley, and I don't have the vaguest idea of what you're talking about with the new contract. Doesn't matter – I'm game and I'm sure David will feel the same way about it."

"I knew THE FIRM could count on you two," Mr. Broadley replied. "Procurement will be the key element, I'm sure."

"Mr. Broadley, you've kept me in suspense long enough! What is the new contract?"

"Ten years – one thousand head a year – each head bringing in $700,000 once they're completely trained and guaranteed – with THE FIRM offering to take any stock back that doesn't work out in field operations. David, that's 70 million a year income for 10 years or, if you prefer, .7 billion dollars coming in over the next decade on just this one contract. That's NOT small potatoes."

"God Almighty!" Forrest whistled softly as he caught his breath. "Who in the hell wants that much stock and what in God's name are they going to do with it? DeBeers diamonds switching over to slave labor completely? Toyoto Motors abandoning paid laborers? The cruise industry going over to slave crews entirely?" That's one hell of a contract!"

"Indeed it is, Forrest. But you'll never guess what the stock's for – nothing as pedantic as your rather logical suggestions," Mr. Broadley laughed.

"Mr. Broadley, I'm dying of suspense," Forrest pleaded.

"Oh, OK. It's for a new international service cartel. 'MaleServe' they call it, with operations being set up initially in London, New York, Vegas, and Hong Kong. Within a year, they'll be opening salons in Chicago, Mexico City, Rio, Tokyo, Sydney, and Berlin. Each salon, as they call their, well, what we used to vulgarly call a whorehouse, are upscale, luxurious, antiseptically clean, and HUGE – up to 400 'choices' – any damn thing anyone could possibly want – available in each salon once they're fully stocked. And all that stock will be exclusively supplied and trained by THE FIRM."

"Perfect!" Forrest exclaimed. "Absolutely perfect! It's an area where THE FIRM is perfectly positioned. Slaves are the only sensible way to stock a pleasure house – and THE FIRM's reputation for top quality slaves along with their superb training expertise makes it the best choice for supply."

"There's only one problem," Mr. Broadley interjected.

"Yes, I've already thought of it," David responded briskly. "Why buy a slave when you can rent one so cheaply?"

"Your keen mind always goes right to the core of the problem, David," Mr. Broadley said with sincere admiration. "But, you know, I don't think it will be the problem we think it might – getting pleasure from a rented body isn't anything like the joys of actually owning a slave – where you can control their whole life, determine their destiny, make all the decisions, – renting a body for the night just isn't in the same league as slave ownership."

"You're right as usual, Mr. Broadley. It's the power trip that's intoxicating and addictive. THE FIRM will be selling slaves as long as we can supply them – no matter how many bed bucks are being rented out right and left."

"Nevertheless, it will be a nice service for those who couldn't dream of slave ownership themselves. Sort of a sampler of what life might have been like if you had real money," Mr. Broadley summarized. "I think MaleServe will have all the business it can handle no matter how much it charges. It's still a lot cheaper than buying a slave – even a ugly, old worn out slave would cost a lot more than a night at MaleServe with a handsome well-trained slave supplied by THE FIRM."

– – – – –

After a delightful dinner, Forrest and David saw Mr. Broadley off for New York in his personal jet at a private airstrip north of Rome. They were exuberant over THE FIRM's new contract with MaleServe but realized it would be a little more work on their part. It would be well worth the effort in view of the huge profits involved for everyone, including themselves, connected with THE FIRM. Now the two realized it was time to examine minutely the situation from their end of the business.

"David," Forrest started, being the more analytical of the two, "1000 head a year increase isn't too bad, except MaleServe will demand good looking, appealing, and very well-trained stock. THE FIRM's guarantee is going to be put to the test what with the demands MaleServe will be placing on their new purchases. Sounds to me like those poor boys are going to be fucked day and night, but meeting the guarantee really isn't our problem – that's up to THE FIRM's training division. But getting stock that can be trained to that level and can hold up to all that usage year after year certainly falls in our bailiwick."

"You're right, Forrest. The training division does have their work cut out for them. A lot of the stock we're going to be able to acquire will be anything but willing at first," David chuckled. "Still, both you and I have certainly had our share of THE FIRM's slaves at our beck and call who were hardly willing when we first got our hands on them and yet, after we got them back from their training, we both fucked them day and night when we had them and they seemed to work out all right," he added with his eyes twinkling. "THE FIRM's trainers certainly seem to know what they're doing. I doubt if we can send them much they can't train by now."

"Yeah, David. Their initial attitude toward a life of sexual slavery doesn't seem to have a thing to do with how they work out in the field once their training is complete. Hell, sometimes I think the more resistant there are originally, the better they turn out in the marketplace and the more they seem to enjoy their new life. At any rate, I figure the increased productivity of THE FIRM's breeding farms will take care of about 100 to 150 of the increase. The fact THE FIRM has very wisely already doubled their breeding farms isn't going to help us for at least a couple of decades until all that stock reaches market age, but it shows THE FIRM is thinking ahead and right on top of the situation. But they have substantially increased productivity at the farms they've had going for awhile and that's going to help us out. A lot of that stock is almost market-age now – 18 to 20 – dependent on their maturation rate." Forrest spread his hands about a foot apart to illustrate what he meant by maturation rate.

"THE FIRM never sells stock off before it's fully ripe – only sensible way to do it in my opinion," David interjected. "By just waiting until the stock's in peak condition and then marketing it not only gives THE FIRM top dollar for its product but insures training up to the guarantee level. The only way to do it," David said with finality.

"Any ideas where the rest will be coming from?" Forrest queried.

"As a matter of fact, yes," David laughed. "We need to check out the Australian refugee camps right away. I understand the Aussies have had it up to here with the flood of Asian refugees pouring in on them and they are even more tired of feeding and clothing all of them year after year. Some of the newspapers are screaming about the terrible, inhuman conditions in a lot of the camps but nobody seems to care. Some of those refugees will be without family, around 18-25 years old, basically good looking and well-hung, and, once they're fed and exercised properly, can be molded into the handsome, muscular boys we're looking for. I understand they are treated so badly in the camps that anything looks good to them now, so I doubt they'll mind very much being sold to us even if they do find out about it before the fact."

"Sounds promising, David," Forrest replied. "The camp managers will be most eager to turn a quick profit by selling some of the best off to us. It will give them that many less to feed and clothe, and I've noticed in other countries they always claim sales to us as 'successful placements' to the World Health Organization and the U.N. investigators. Makes them look good to the world at large. We can easily buy up their unclaimed stock that has exceptionally good looking bodies and are heavily hung. You know we'll get them dirt cheap and have them shipped out to THE FIRM's training centers before they have even realized what has happened to them. Training will give them plenty of nourishing food to fill out those bodies, exercise them to muscular perfection, and give them a real purpose in life – something that most of them have never had anyway. They'll probably take to training like a duck takes to water. Most of those refugees that are young and good-looking are usually fucked half to death in the camps anyway by all the guards and wardens, so that part of their training should go fast – nothing new to those boys usually. Of course, they're going to be primarily Asian stock and we need more variety than that."

"Well, Forrest, we can balance it with buying up more stock at the Macedonian markets in the Balkans which will give us a good batch of blue-eyed Greeks and Slavs. You know a lot of those put up on the block there will be exactly what MaleServe is looking for: well-built, handsome, heavy hung, and well muscled. And they tell me they take to THE FIRM's training strategies very well – no trouble at all with them after a few months of teaching them their new place in society.

"And we can probably double our purchases at that new Puerto Rican market out there in that God-forsaken jungle. Our friend Wade over in training tells me that by training with a heavy whip constantly on them and being fucked four or five times a day, those Hispanic boys are ready for market in just four to five months. He's real pleased with them. Of course, they'll all be Hispanic, but we'll try to buy as many blue-eyed and brown-haired as we can to make it a little more varied."

"I can see where Wade is pleased with those from the Puerto Rican market, David," Forrest replied. "The ones I seen sold at THE

FIRM's auctions fully trained sure seem to know their place in the world and always seem very eager to please their new masters. But you can tell they've been whip-trained, David. If you feel their backs and rumps carefully, you can feel the lesions deep down – nothing to mar their hides mind you – but deeper down there are some scars you can feel. I imagine it's those scars that make them such damn good slaves – really better for them in the long run – a constant fear of punishment ingrained into them one way or another makes for a much better slave – keeps them out of trouble – and, in the long haul, allows them to be a lot happier in their new life."

"Good thing you're not in training, Forrest," David laughed. "You'd spend half your time philosophizing."

"David, I think we should check out the California juvenile correctional facilities. I've been reading in the newspapers that almost every inmate in the system that's half decent in the looks department has been sexually exploited on a regular basis once they're in the system. Almost all the boys are under conditions of constant humiliation, inadequate food, and really harsh physical punishment for the slightest violation of their rules. According to the newspaper reports, some of the boys are so desperate the suicide rate is really getting embarrassing for the state. I'm sure the superintendents of those facilities will be more than happy to sell off a lot of their inmates that are impossible to place because they either don't have any family or their family has abandoned them. If we promise to take the really good looking ones off their hands that are heavy hung and already have been fucked regularly for a half-way decent price, I'm sure we can pick up quite a few that would be perfect for the MaleServe market. Those we buy up will probably find slavery easier than their life before. At least, THE FIRM will feed them well, give them an environment that's easy to predict with clear expectations and a real feeling of worth. Their purchase price alone will give them a feeling of self-worth they may have never had in their life, let alone in the state's correctional facilities. Hell, they'll be half-trained before we ever buy them up! And, David, I hear Arizona is just as bad, or should I say good from our perspective. They say either state is almost as bad as Texas and Mississippi. You and I both know that's been one of our best sources for many a year now. Since we've harvested stock in Texas, Mississippi, and Alabama for years now, we sure know how to go about doing it – I'm sure the superintendents in California are just as underpaid and greedy as they are in the states we're more familiar with. Should be able to get some really good stock at bargain prices."

"Great idea, Forrest. There's one other source we should investigate," David added.

"I bet I can guess. Afghanistan?" Forrest laughed.

"You bet. With all the orphans and unwanted and hungry there and no hope for much of a meaningful life – it should be an easy market. We just need to tie in to some operating slavers there. I suppose they're as active now as they have been in the more remote regions of Pakistan for years. Lord knows we've bought up enough Pakistanis to fill a warehouse or two over the years," David said with considerable enthusiasm. "You know, those Pakistani slavers we deal with can deliver most anything you want given a little time. They're especially good with just the type MaleServe will want. That type of stock is just like the ones they catch to use themselves before selling them off. When you buy from those rural slavers, the stock is already pre-selected to be handsome, hung, and muscular. And by the time they hand them over to us, they're also at least 75% trained to full slave status and at least 50% trained for full sexual service. Makes for a good buy! I imagine we can buy up at least 500 – 600 a year from Afghanistan alone exactly as we want them. If not, the Pakistani dealers can fill out the ranks for us."

"Well, David," Forrest announced with a satisfied look on his face. "In theory at least, we've got our additional stock and it's varied: Asians, Hispanics, Greeks and Slavs, Arabs, and Americans from California, Arizona and, of course, the usual Texas and Mississippi stock. We may be a little weak on blacks, but I imagine we could take care of that with some careful selection in both Puerto Rico and from the U.S. correctional system. The demand for American blacks has held steady over the years and they still bring a premium on the auction block."

"Forrest, you and I both know that premium is in large part because THE FIRM has always taken pride in stocking black 'pretty boys': beautiful creamy skin, long thick eyelashes, hairless muscular bodies, and hung like horses. Everyone seems to want at least one black or so in their collection, especially when they look like that," David laughed. "Me, I'll take an Italian boy any day."

"That's because you have a thing for Mediterranean types and you pick them for size on top of that. If big dicks are your thing, those Slavs in the Macedonian market were pretty remarkable if you'll recall."

"Got me there, Forrest," David laughed. "My Italian boys are hung about as heavy as they get, but I admit the Slavs were something else again."

Forrest chucked. "David, we've both seen some unbelievably hung boys in the Brazilian markets if you don't mind them being ugly. Practically freaks if you ask me…but could we get back to the topic at hand. David, I see at least 1000 more stock a year without even sweating hard that would be the exact type MaleServe would want. You take Australia and Puerto Rico – I'll check out Afghanistan, Pakistan and Macedonia – and we'll both take on the U.S. correctional system. We'll probably end up with so damn much stock Mr. Broadley won't know where to put it all!"

CHAPTER VII

MISSION COMPLETED

"David?" Forrest asked as he phoned his friend, settling back into the airplane seat.

"Yo, buddy," David replied. "Where are you at, anyway?"

"I'm on a plane heading back to Rome. Finally finished up in Macedonia. Where are you at?" Forrest queried.

"Well, right now at a hotel in Canberra," David laughed. "Just got back from my last trip out to the refugee camp. How did you fare in the Macedonian markets, Forrest?"

"Two-hundred-fifty-two big ones, David. All collared, cleaned inside and out, body shaved, and caged with a big plug up their backsides. They're on their way to THE FIRM's European training center outside of Rome as we speak. I'm shipping them by a chartered yacht with high security so it'll only take a couple of days for them to get to that small secluded port near the training center we use. The security staff will hose them down every 12 hours so they shouldn't smell too bad once they get there and they'll feed them the usual dry food after they hose them down so they'll be OK – a little stiff and sore up their ass from those huge butt plugs, but otherwise fit as a fiddle."

"Jesus, quite a haul, Forrest. You just lucked out or was the market gutted?"

"Well, there seems to be no end to the war prisoners they want to get rid of fast as they're eating their captors out of house and home. Add to that all the refugees the local slave catchers haul to market. I did luck out in arriving there just when their pens were so full they were chaining up people to the bars on the outsides of the cages. So they were most eager to sell! But when I said big ones, that's just what I meant, David. I don't think there's a single one under six feet and weighing in at less than 200 pounds. And hung to match – none less than 8" flaccid and I bet they average 10" before they're even played with. A few of them are just phenomenal. I bet it's the lowest price THE FIRM has ever had to pay per pound of prime manflesh, especially for boys hung that well. I just hope you were able to find some smaller stock for our customers. Not everyone likes boys as big as I bought. Sort of scares them off, I guess," Forrest laughed.

"Well, it is sort of like fucking an ox," David chuckled, "no matter how well they're trained. Don't worry; I was able to get some small ones specifically for the MaleServe contract, Forrest. Small, that is, in physique but still big where it counts."

"How many? Forrest asked.

"One-hundred-forty at last count. Ninety-eight from the main refugee camp, and 44 from a smaller camp further out in the desert. That's 142 I know, but we lost two of them in initial training. Stupid handlers!" David spit out. "Their cost is coming out of their pay."

"Unusual." Forrest said. "What happened?"

"Well, those two were really small, even for Cambodians. Couldn't have weighed over 80 pounds wet. Like most new stock, they were already in shock when the handlers forced 12 x 5 dildos up them all the way, harnessed them in, and when they passed out, didn't notice they were hemorrhaging like crazy. Next morning, when they went down to whip them out of their pens, they didn't move no matter how hard they laced into them. All I could do was string them up as an object lesson for the other new stock before they started stinking and then we turned them back to the camp commander for burial. He didn't mind as long as we didn't ask for our money back."

"Did you get rid of the handlers," Forrest asked.

"No, it was the first big mistake they'd made and they've been with THE FIRM for a couple of years now. But we're deducting the cost of those two from their wages over the next few months. I think they've learned their lesson now. Forrest, we've got to have handlers that push to the limits – it's just these two went too far this time. They won't do it again. My only worry is they'll play it too cautious in the future so as to not risk any salary deductions and end up being too easy on the new stock. Slaves, especially those newly enslaved, have got to realize immediately that their very life is up to the handlers, or training will be slowed down."

"You don't need to lecture me on that point, buddy. How would you like to be dealing with 250 new stock, all a hell of a lot bigger and stronger than you are?" Forrest laughed. "But mine can handle the 12 x 5's up their butt just fine – just a little reminder of who's running the show. You probably should just stock 10 x 4's with Asian stock, David."

"Possibly, to play it safe, Forrest. But not all Asian stock out of the refugee camps are small. We could have bought up some boys as big as your Macedonian slaves if we'd wanted. Some Malaysians and Sri Lankans in the camps are over 250 pounds, built like bulls, and hung like elephants. It's just I was deliberately buying up smaller boys because that's what we need to round out the MaleServe contract."

"One forty – two fifty. That's 390 this week alone. Let's see. We got 210 out of the California correctional facilities – about half of them black, the other white; 90 more out of the Arizona prisons – most of it white or white and Indian; and 240 out of the Puerto Rican warehouse – most of them blacks or mestizos. With this week's purchases, we're up to 930 prime stock with a good mix of color, overall size, and race. We'll easily pick up 70 more in the Roman market next week and that will meet the MaleServe contract of 1000 prime studs ready for their salons once they're properly trained. Not bad considering it's just taken us a little over a month to round them up, David."

"Not bad at all, Forrest. Of course, we still have to worry about fulfilling THE FIRM's own needs and you know as well as I do that they'll lose a few in training, so we better plan on at least 1030 going into training to be sure they deliver 1000 to MaleServe fully guaranteed. Even THE FIRM's training doesn't succeed with all stock. Three percent failure rate isn't bad though. A few just die, but most of them just don't reach guarantee standards no matter what they do to them, so they sell them off to the Brazilian meat markets where training isn't so important – hell, those Brazilian buyers keep them chained all the time anyway with a whip over their heads, so who needs training?" David laughed. "Anyone can be fucked endlessly if they're chained over a sawhorse and whipped with a steel-tipped whip if they don't cooperate in their own fucking. Me – I like a well-trained boy from THE FIRM's training program that likes nothing better than pleasing his master no matter what's asked year after year. It's worth that little extra THE FIRM charges for their guaranteed goods."

"Still, all in all, THE FIRM's training program is rather remarkable," Forrest commented. "Take this last batch I bought. Just a few weeks ago most of them were in either the Serbian or Bosnian army. Now they're crammed into those tiny shipping cages with a huge dildo up their butt knowing they're now just slaves sold on an auction block to the highest bidder. From the time they were captured, they've been repeatedly raped, milked regularly, and handled until they were raw so they surely have some idea their bodies are going to be used one way or another by their new owners, whoever they are. With a good six months of intensive training under their belts by THE FIRM, they'll be full-time whores working in MaleServe's brothels without a murmur or protest. Probably enjoying it, if THE FIRM's training holds up as it has in the past. THE FIRM's training program is probably its greatest strength," Forrest concluded with a satisfied look on his face.

"Well, Forrest, don't underrate THE FIRM's two chief procurers," David laughed. "After all, the trainers couldn't do much if the stock wasn't trainable. It's proper selection that makes all the difference in the world. Forrest, you know yourself, when you looked those boys over in the Macedonian markets; you intuitively knew who'd take to slavery well and who would cause more trouble than they were worth. After all, Forrest, between the two of us, we must have bought up at least 30,000 stock by now over the years. Experience pays off," David concluded.

"I suppose you're right. I remember one of the last slaves I bought yesterday. When I hefted up his balls and massaged them in my hand, I heard the handsome bastard almost purr in contentment despite the contemptuous look he was giving me. When I started stroking him, he was hard as a rock in seconds and I could see he was embarrassed at getting hard so easily in front of his fellow captives.

When a drop of pre-cum appeared after only the first two strokes, I knew we had a natural slave on our hand that would do anything to get off – anything a master would want. I told that slave his fate was determined the minute God gave him such a beautiful body and such large eager organs that just begged to be played with. One way or another, now that he was a slave, he would end up using that body to bring others enjoyment. He wanted to get off so badly as I continued stroking him, I'm sure he believed every word I said. MaleServe will love him," Forrest laughed.

"When can you be in Rome, David? It's no fun shopping without you at the Roman open auctions. They're scheduled for this coming weekend."

"I'll be there, buddy. Should be able to make it by Thursday night. That will give us a chance to look over the stock all day Friday and buy like crazy on Saturday. Sunday we can sample some of what we've bought."

"Sounds good. Let me know when you'll arrive and I'll pick you up. You can get a hold of me at THE FIRM's suite in Rome since no one else was using it this week. Incidentally, David, THE FIRM has arranged for a few of the dealers we've bought from before at the Roman auction to send three boys over to the suite as soon as I arrive – "sample goods" they're interested in selling to THE FIRM. I understand they're loaning us a 'sample' black from a new lot of Nigerians they have up on the block, an American blond boy shipped over by the Mafia for sale, and a Kurd they bought in Turkey whose supposed to be phenomenal. They told THE FIRM they were all thoroughly trained to full usage and all three of them were eager to be sold. But you know that doesn't necessarily mean squat by THE FIRM's standards. But they might be fun. Did you want me to bring them to the airport with me so you could start playing around on the trip back from the airport?"

"You're going to be in Rome three days before I arrive, Forrest. By then you will have fucked all three senseless if I know you. But I haven't had a blond since I hit the refugee camp markets, Forrest, and I'm sick of black hair. Bring the blond American if he can still walk by then and I suppose you'll bring the Nigerian for yourself, knowing how well you enjoy black slaves. But the Kurd sounds different. Oh, hell. Bring all three if they'll fit in the trunk. I can pick and choose once I get there and see what they look like. The ride will be good for them."

— — — — —

David was using THE FIRM's main transport plane for his flight from Australia to THE FIRM's well-camouflaged airstrip at their European training center discretely hidden in a remote area a short distance from Rome. The plane was primarily set up for cargo with space for 400 separate slave cages in the fuselage. Near the cages were pleasant quarters for the ever-present slave handlers, complete with comfortable beds, a galley, showers, a TV lounge, as well as a full supply of 'correctional equipment of penis gags, dildos, tit clamps, whips, truncheons, electrical shock prods, and restraint chains ready to be utilized as needed. Between these quarters and the pilot's compartment was a super-luxurious apartment for any of THE FIRM's executive staff on board.

David found this 'executive cabin' most comfortable on long trips like this. Especially since he usually sampled some of THE FIRM's newly procured stock between stretches of sleep. This time, he had had three slaves moved from the cages in the rear to his cabin: an absolutely beautiful Australian boy of 19 he had bought at the very last minute out of a provincial Australian prison near the Canberran refugee camps; a small Cambodian boy of 18 with an exceptionally muscular physique and unusually handsome facial features; and a large handsome Sri Lankan lad with beautiful green eyes, a naturally hairless body, and exceptionally large genitalia. All three seemed resigned to their fate and offered no resistance as he mounted each of them in turn. It would be hard to pick which of the three performed best for their master's benefit in that all three sucked just as well as they took to be fucked. MaleServe would love them.

— — — — —

Forrest met David at the airport as planned with the three loan slaves stuffed in the trunk of his limousine. Prior to landing, David had showered and freshened up while one of the slave handlers moved the three slaves he had been using in his luxurious quarters on THE FIRM's plane back to transit cages in the hold with all the others.

"I lied," David greeted Forrest. "I told you I hadn't had a blond in weeks and I bought one from an Australian prison just hours before I took off. A gorgeous 19-year-old Australian orphan hung like a horse that's fully trained and I picked up dirt cheap and...."

"Let me finish your sentence, you bastard. You fucked him the whole way here," Forrest laughed.

"Well, not the whole way, Forrest. I did sleep off and on."

"I would guess the Australian blond boy wasn't alone in your compartment," Forrest smiled. "How many, David?"

"Two others, Forrest, if I must confess to my best friend," David laughed. "A tiny but absolutely beautiful Cambodian boy who sold himself into slavery and a huge Sri Lankan who'd been a slave since he could remember. Ever had a Sri Lankan, Forrest?"

"Not that I can recall, David, but who knows? I don't always interview slaves before I bed them down," Forrest laughed. "How was he?"

"Great and he's practically fully trained already. Did you bring that fresh meat you promised with you?" David prompted, looking pointedly at the limousine's trunk.

"You're insatiable, David," Forrest said affectionately as he hugged his long time best friend and fellow chief procurer for THE FIRM. "Yes, all three are crammed in there and I suppose ready for action."

"What do you mean, suppose?" David shot back.

"Well, it's been three days and I didn't have much to do, so... I suppose you could say they're a little used by now," Forrest smirked.

"Fucked half to death is more the truth of it, I imagine. Can they even walk anymore?"

"They're probably a little sore, but a light whipping will take care of that," Forrest laughed. "I don't think these three slaves expected as much use as they got. I had them fucking each other a lot to pass the time when I couldn't get it up anymore."

"You're something else, Forrest. Have you completely used them up or can I at least fuck them once just so I know what I missed?"

"Oh, they're good for that and, out of complete consideration for you; I haven't let them shoot off themselves for the past 12 hours. They're still interested – just sore."

After the limousine had maneuvered into an isolated parking spot where naked chained slaves would not be noticed, David said, "Well, let's get them out and I'll take a look."

Forrest popped the trunk lid and the three slaves were indeed jammed into the trunk where they could hardly move, pressed firmly together spoon fashion. Forrest swung the first slave's legs over the lip of the trunk and the slave struggled out the best he could considering his wrists and ankles were both closely manacled. The other two slaves quickly struggled out on their own and assumed the standard slave's position: legs apart as far as their chains would allow; their shackled wrists placed in back of their head, their muscles tense with their pelvis thrust out as far as possible so their sex was on full display.

"Those dealers knew what would sell," David said as he reached out and hefted the American blonde's large semi-erect prick and began to slowly stroke the boy. The organ instantly hardened and a drop of pre-cum formed on the head. "Is this the boy the Mafia's selling?"

"Yep. He'll bring a good price, but, I'll warn you, he's been well used," Forrest commented, "long before I got a hold of him. Still, I think you'll enjoy him. He's cooperative enough."

David kept stroking the swollen staff while he roughly massaged the boy's ball sac with his other hand and noticed the boy held posture despite flinching just a little. It was obvious his balls had been handled quite a bit over the past few days and were still sore. He shifted his hand up to the boy's pecs and admired the neat brand mark the Mafia had burnt into him somewhere along the line. David knew all Mafia's slaves were branded early in their original ownership by the Mafia. It actually added to their slaves' values in that subsequent owners knew the Mafia would always trace them down if they tried to run away and would return them to their current owner no matter how much the trouble. It just made a Mafia-processed slave a little more valuable on the world market as well as let the slave know he was a slave for life, no matter who owned him at the time. Every time the slave felt that brand, he knew his fate had been decided for him and the best course of action was simply to please his owners, no matter who they were or what they asked of him. David also noticed the numerous whip scars buried deep beneath the boy's skin, especially across his back and butt. David knew slaves who had experienced tremendous pain in their initial training were thereafter ruled by fear of pain. As David prodded deep into the boy's butt checks and felt the scar tissue, the familiar look of raw fear crossed the boy's face and he shuddered in remembrance of his training. Such training, David knew, never faded and lasted a lifetime, ensuring a hard-working, ever compliant slave no matter how hard they were worked or what they were asked to do. The boy would bring a good price at the upcoming auction.

David next looked at the Nigerian black who was hugely muscular with a shiny jet black skin. By now, he too was fully erect just watching the white boy get handled and smiled brightly when David clasped his ball sac and started squeezing. A beautiful set of dazzling white teeth highlighted his face as he obviously enjoyed having someone play with his balls. His long, thick shaft shuddered as the first few drops of pre-cum displayed themselves on the erect tip. "How is he to fuck?" David asked.

"Good and tight and he seems to really enjoy it judging from all the moaning and sighs coming out of him while you're plunging into him. He shoots off every time you fuck him if you don't order him to control himself – shows how much he likes it," Forrest said. "He's better trained than the Mafia slave – he can pump you dry with his ass muscles once you're in him without any effort on your part. Buyers are going to love that," Forrest explained.

"Beautiful skin," David commented as he ran his hands over the well rounded buttocks of the Nigerian slave noticing he too had been thoroughly whip trained judging from the numerous weals buried deep in his flesh. He ran his hand over the shoulders and felt even thicker scars. It wasn't unusual for African slaves, David knew, in that the huge lots gathered up had to be broken into accepting their slavery fast. Severe whip training squelched all rebellion, quickly informed the slave he was no longer in charge of any aspect of his life, usually guaranteed quick and complete compliance to anything that was demanded of the slave, and was long lasting in that it instilled fear of pain as one of the slave's main motives until he was fully acclimated to his new life. David shifted to the front of the slave's body and began massaging his large distended tits. "I imagine a new owner will ring these babies fast," he said as he squeezed first one tit and then the other until the slave shuddered and a tear spilled out of his eyes. "Sensitive, I see," David said as he noticed the tears spilling down the boy's cheek and squeezed even harder to see if the slave would break stance. When he never moved, David looked pleased and ordered the slave to bend over with his ass open for inspection. The slave's large brand was prominently burned into one cheek. David examined the three number brand and knew it wasn't uncommon on African slaves. When slaves were first captured they were typically branded with a three digit number by the slave catchers. It allowed for easy sorting with the vast numbers involved and it told the slave immediately, with a great deal of instructive pain, that he was now just a numbered property and always would be. When David jammed his forefinger up the boy's hole forcefully, the slave gasped but never flinched, even when David added the next two fingers and drove them up the boy as far as he could. The slave moaned deeply but never moved. "Nicely trained," David commented as he jerked his fingers out of the distended hole and told the boy to resume posture. "He's the type any owner would likely tit-ring and then band his genitals so they're on full display all the time. Be a shame not to with a slave equipped this well."

"How'd you like to be a display slave, boy?" David asked as he again began stroking the boy's long, thick shaft.

"Don't really know what a display slave is, master, but I'd like it fine if that's what my master wanted," the handsome slave replied in utter humility. "If it means wearing those rings and bands you mentioned, master, it's their body to decorate I reckon, if they buy me."

Exactly," David said as reluctantly let loose of the pulsating shaft he was stroking.

That brand on his butt won't hurt his value much, especially since everyone expects it these days on the Africans usually just sold in big lots. I guess they've branded newly captured slaves for at least a thousand years now and tradition dies slow, I guess. They'll probably be branding butts for the next thousand years," David laughed as he turned to the third slave.

"Is this the Kurd you told me about, Forrest?" David said.

"This is the one, David. You haven't lived until you bedded this one down."

"The body's great and that face is about as handsome as men get, especially with those big blue eyes of his sunk so far back in his head and that gold nose ring between his nostrils is strangely appealing. Makes him look totally controlled despite his size," David commented as he reached up and twisted the small ring to see if it was just clipped on for show or permanently installed through a pierced hole in the connecting tissue between the nostrils and a firm weld on the ring itself. He was happy to see it was the latter.

"His sex is huge but not freakish and it's very nicely shaped. I like the way his big balls hang close to his body and force his shaft up and out for a good natural display. But you and I have both seen slaves with those qualities," David said as he began wrapping his hands around the huge shaft and began stroking the slave, already fully erect and dripping. "I do like the way his nose ring is small enough not to hang down over his lips. That way he can still suck properly but it's installed so you can easily clip a leash to it for great control."

"But you said he was phenomenal. What's phenomenal about him?"

"He's indefatigable," Forrest said flatly. "This slave boy can keep going forever it seems and you can milk him repeatedly and get a full load every time. He'd be perfect in a whorehouse catering to women. He'd keep going all day long no matter how many customers they had lined up. Or a perfect stud for a slave breeding farm – no telling how many new slaves you'd get out of him before he died of old age. Or as a stud for our older clientele who'd like to have a boy they can milk over and over so they drink down their 'youth nectars' that are so popular now – this boy can produce gallons of cum every day – hell, they could bottle it and sell it on the open market probably."

"Fine, but all I wanted to do was just play around a little," David laughed. "I didn't want to start a bottling factory. How does he take a simple fuck, or did you have him fuck you given his qualifications in that area?"

"Both," Forrest said. "I couldn't resist having him fuck me just to see what it was like – after I got bored fucking him. You should try him out, David – both ways. He's great taking it or giving it."

"Forrest, I haven't been fucked myself since we were here in Rome several months ago to talk to Mr. Broadley. You couldn't wait to fuck me then, as usual, but I admit it was memorable. You think this slave can fuck that well? Remember, I'm stacking him up against you, you old bastard."

"Even better, because this slave follows your commands down to the last breath. He'll do it exactly like you want – that's more than I ever promised," Forrest laughed. "This boy even shoots off exactly when you want and will pull out any time you want – he seems to be perfectly trained in that area. I can't imagine who trained him or how, but here it is. Too bad we can't buy him as a trainer for THE FIRM. Maybe he could share his secrets with thousands of new slave boys being trained for their master's beds as slave studs."

"Not a bad idea if he's half as good as you claim," David said as he continued stroking the boy's pulsating shaft which was steadily leaking copious amounts of sticky white cum. "Looks like he's going to shoot if I don't stop."

"Oh, he can hold it in, but with him, you don't have to worry about him draining dry. If he shoots, he'll be ready to go again in a few minutes."

"Well, we'll let him hold it until I get him back to the apartment," David said as he let loose of the Kurd's swollen shaft. "No use wasting good cum. After we get back to the suite, I'm going to fuck the American blond just to see what he's like and it might be fun to see the black swallow the full load of the Kurd."

"David, as soon as we get back, I'm going to fuck the black slave again, but I want to make sure you have that Kurd slave fuck you silly. It's an experience you won't forget. Remember, these three go back to their dealers tomorrow. Twenty-four hours from now they'll probably be on all fours or flat on their backs being fucked by their new owners the first of many, many times," Forrest laughed.

But things didn't quite work out that way. Neither Forrest nor David were willing to wait to get back to the apartment to start using the three slaves. Forrest ordered the black slave to his hands and knees right there in the parking lot and proceeded to fuck him vigorously, while David had the blond slave get on his back with his legs spread wide apart for a good fucking of his own. The Kurd stood watching the two couplings taking place right in front of him with a smile on his face and an ever-dripping erect prick that simply quivered in excitement, knowing he would be used by both masters just as soon as they got back to the apartment. Soon, all three slaves were again crammed back in the trunk, one with an oozing prick and two with cum oozing out of their asses. All three slaves fully understood this was just the beginning of a long night!

— — — — —

"There's more here than ever," Forrest commented as David and he strolled through the huge warehouse some distance outside Rome. It was remarkable how such a large facility had been kept so private from prying eyes over the years except to the select buyers who had discretely congregated for the big sale.

"Slaves or buyers?" David asked.

"Both, David. The world market is just growing leaps and bounds. THE FIRM's sales are already up 58 percent from last year and remember there are a lot of small dealers cropping up all over to handle the lesser stock. Oh, look, David, there's the Kurd from night before last – God, I'm surprised he can even keep his eyes open at this point," Forrest said with a wink to the Kurd who, although rigidly chained on an inspection stand at this point, brightly smiled at the two men he recognized.

The two men walked over the stand, one of hundreds and hundreds set up in that hall alone, and as one gently lifted the Kurd's balls and massaged them in his hand, the other walked behind him and began finger fucking his well lubricated hole.

"God, this slave's just as hard as he was two nights ago," David said in amazement as he saw the mammoth prick quiver as it dripped pre-cum. "You were right, Forest, this slave is phenomenal – truly indefatigable. I wonder if his new owner will appreciate what he or she's bought."

"I'm sure the dealer is already spreading the word. My guess is he'll bring well over a million at the auction and whoever buys him will primarily use him for stud. He's just too valuable to waste any other way. Probably a breeding farm or some billionaire who likes to get fucked any time he wants."

"What about THE FIRM, Forrest? Do you think we should snap him up for one of their breeding operations."

"I'm not sure what their needs are right now. We better check in with Mr. Broadley and see if we need a stud slave or whether he knows of any of THE FIRM's special customers who'd be interested in something like this," Forrest said as he again wrapped his hand around the huge organ and begin pumping the shaft. "We probably should buy him for the MaleServe contract – Lord knows he's exactly what they're looking for in their 'salons'."

"Come on, Forrest. We can't play with this slave any longer. There's loads of stock to look over yet," as he jerked Forrest's hand off the slave's shaft. "But we should bid on him up to a million at least. He's way too expensive for the MaleServe contract, but I'm sure THE FIRM's New York office could find a home for him whether THE FIRM needs a stud slave or not at this point. He sure wouldn't need much training."

They strolled on and checked out hundreds or other slaves up for auction in the next few hours. Quality was high today and prices should remain high. Even slaves to be sold in ready lots, like the Nigerian they had 'sampled' yesterday, would bring reasonably high prices even though they weren't up for individual inspection and had to be bought in large lots or not at all. Forrest estimated the Nigerian lot of 500 would bring in an average price of at $250,000 each if the boy they had fucked 36 hours ago was representative. Slaves like the Nigerian were generally offered up for construction crews, mining, plantation farming, and other hard labor where they were worked long and hard under the whip. Only the very pretty ones spent their first few years of slavery in somebody's bed before their youthful vigor faded and they joined their less handsome brothers in hard labor. Gang slaves like these Nigerians were inexpensive enough, especially the ugly ones, that they were primarily utilized in labor situations that couldn't be automated in some fashion or another. Hence, they were generally worked in hard-to-fit situations, remote situations where fuel was expensive and hard to transport, or where some degree of intelligence was required such as picking and packing vegetables and fruits.

But most up for market today were not destined for gang labor. They were far too select for that. They were more like the American blonde the Mafia was selling today and who now stood proudly before the two procurers from THE FIRM. Ramrod straight on his display stand with bright lights highlighting his body, the slave's wrists were chained to the back of his thick neck collar so that all parts of his body were in full display, especially since each ankle was fixed to the floor as far apart as possible, leaving his sexual apparatus exposed from either the front or back. His shaved, oiled body glistened in the spotlights. His prick even now was semi-erect and his balls looked full and invited handling. The slave's eyes sparkled as he smiled in invitation as each potential buyer that passed his stand. When he spotted his recent users, his eyes literally danced in delight as he focused in on someone familiar out of a sea of strangers.

"Masters," he blurted out before he caught himself. Slaves weren't allowed to utter a sound while being inspected. Furtively looking around to see if the slave handlers had heard him, he blushed but thrust his pelvis out in full invitation as he risked another smile at the two men who had fucked him so thoroughly right before sending him back to the dealers so he could be prepared for auction display. He'd love being owned by those two but knew he had no choice in the matter.

Next to him were 12 others for sale from the American Mafia. All were good looking, well muscled, and heavy hung. All were fully erect, apparently eager to be sold, and undoubtedly well-trained since the Mafia rarely put anything on the market until it had been so trained the slaves quivered in fear of offending anyone at all, not just the ones who owned them. All 13 slaves sported the Mafia's tell-tale brand which guaranteed their quick return if they ever ran. Forrest and David had often bought Mafia slaves for THE FIRM and had never been disappointed. They checked the 12 other Mafia offerings they hadn't fucked over thoroughly and made some notes for the upcoming auction.

—————

"I'm going to call Mr. Broadley," David said as he reached for his cell phone. "I hate to see that Kurd slip away from THE FIRM."

"Great idea. I wanted to ask about that blond Aussie I bought for THE FIRM – I'd like to keep him for myself for a while before MaleServe has him fucked to death in their brothels."

David punched in Mr. Broadley personal number at THE FIRM's headquarters.

"John Broadley here," came the rich deep voice they were both so familiar with. "How may I help you?"

"Mr. Broadley, its David and Forrest here at the Rome auction warehouse. We needed some info about THE FIRM's needs before the bidding starts."

"First, David, it's great to hear from you. I want to congratulate you and Forrest for your fine work during the past month. We're easily going to meet our MaleServe contract, thanks to you two, with plenty of good looking slaveflesh left over for our own markets. There will be some bonuses for both of you along with your usual commissions," Mr. Broadley said in his usual well organized fashion. "David, the trainers in our European training center tell me some of the stock you bought up in Macedonia is far too good for MaleServe and they will be training them for our own sale here in New York at some future date. They've picked out 50 they thought would sell for at least one million each if properly trained to guarantee standards. And tell Forrest he did very well with his own stock acquisitions – the mestizos from Puerto Rico and the mulatto prisoners from Arizona and California prisons will fit into the MaleServe quotas fine as we were short in those areas, as will his Asian stock. But that means we need to pick up at least 50 more for MaleServe to make up for the transferred stock and, David, we're still short of pure blacks for the MaleServe quota."

"Got it," David responded. "Mr. Broadley, one of the dealers we've done business with before sent us some 'loaners' while we were waiting here for the auction to open for inspection. "One was a Kurd who's already very well-trained and would be perfect to serve stud at one of THE FIRM's breeding operations. Or THE FIRM could sell him off to a customer collecting a personal harem. The slave is inexhaustible, handsome as they come, built like Adonis, and obsessed with pleasing his owners. Frankly, I think after THE FIRM's training program has been completed with him, he'd make a damn fine trainer himself – especially for slaves destined to be sold as sex slaves. That slave knows tricks we've never even thought of."

"Sounds fascinating," Mr. Broadley laughed. "Forrest, I've never doubted your judgment. Buy him up for THE FIRM and ship him directly to our New York facility. I'm sure we'll find a good use for him."

"There's three lots of 500 Nigerians on the market today to be sold in bulk lots. One of them was sent over to Forrest and I as a 'sampler.' They're all branded, black as coal, super muscular, pretty well acclimated to being slaves and some of them are heavy hung and very good looking. I think if we approach the dealer before the auction we can cut a deal – the right to pick out the best 50 of the 1500 he's got penned and pay him double what he'll get selling them in wholesale lots. Most of them are destined for the plantations and mines anyway. We need pure blacks, the dealer would like to make a little extra, and the slaves themselves would be happier getting fucked in a brothel than sweating in the mines."

"Good thinking, David. We'd meet our MaleServe quota for pure blacks, and we could cull a few more of the very best out of that shipment for our own pens. Go for it – you'll probably still get the blacks dirt cheap considering today's market prices."

"There's 13 slaves here offered up by the American Mafia, Mr. Broadley. THE FIRM's had very good luck training that stock in the past and they've all brought top dollar once THE FIRM's sold them."

"You're right, David. We've never had a customer complaint on any Mafia stock we've sold. I think that Mafia brand and that heavy whip training they all experience with the Mafia does as much for their success as our own training here at THE FIRM," Mr. Broadley commented. "If they're good looking and well equipped, buy the lot of them for THE FIRM and have them shipped to New York for training. Hang the price they'll bring – buy them anyway. We'll still make plenty on them if past history is any indicator. Women seem to really like that Mafia brand on their slaves – sort of a status symbol with them. Matches their Land Rover's, I guess," he laughed. "I don't doubt those lady buyers use their Mafia slaves more than their Land Rovers. Poor boys probably get fucked half to death," he laughed uproariously.

"Will do, Mr. Broadley. Forrest would like to talk to you, sir."

"Fine, but before he does, I want to again tell you what a great job you're doing. I know you're earning over 15 million a year now, but money isn't everything. You take pride in your work and you're great at it. THE FIRM wouldn't be what it is without you."

"Thanks, Mr. Broadley," David blushed. "But it's really not work to me – it's a privilege to work for THE FIRM."

"Well said. Now let me talk to Forrest."

"Forrest, you did a great job buying up that Asian refugee stock in Australia. The training center they are at now tells me they're all very handsome, well hung, and eager. They felt they could be trained to guarantee standards in a relatively short time. And making an example of those two the handlers bungled was about all you could do under the circumstances. We'll keep an eye on those particular handlers as we deduct the cost from their pay, but they've probably learned a good lesson. We'll watch they don't go too easy on future stock without harming them permanently – it's a delicate balance as you pointed out in your report."

"Thanks, Mr. Broadley. I overheard what you told David about buying up the best of the Nigerian stock to even out the color balance of our MaleServe contract. That should do it."

"What did you want to talk to me about, Forrest?"

"Well, as you probably already know, I bought up this blond Australian prisoner right before I left Australia. Could I have him for a year or so after he's finished THE FIRM's training program? I'll trade in one of the boys I keep for him when he's available?"

"It can be arranged, Forrest, as long as we get him back for sale eventually. Of course, we'll sell off the one you turn in for him quickly, so we won't be out too much."

"David is too shy to ask, Mr. Broadley, but I'm sure he'd like the Nigerian boy that was loaned out to us here before he's shipped off to MaleServe."

"Tell David he's insatiable when it comes to bed bucks, but I'm sure one Nigerian slave, give or take a few, isn't going to be missed for a while. Of course, that Nigerian slave will have to go through THE FIRM's training program first you understand."

"Sure, I know that. But David would really like him all the more by then. He's got a thing for blacks and I can tell he's really enjoying that boy's body."

"You'll get the Aussie blond and David will get his Nigerian fuck boy. Serving you two should be a training program in itself," Mr. Broadley laughed.

EIGHT MONTHS LATER:

"We sold that Kurd for $1.8 million to a woman's resort in the Caribbean. Well, leased him, actually. We get him back after two years and then we'll 'retire' him to stud at one of our big breeding operations. He'll have to fuck his brains out at that resort, but he seems to enjoy that sort of thing," Mr. Broadley reflected. "He was quite a find, David. You and Forrest spotted him in the Rome auctions, I believe."

"All of the American Mafia boys you bought up at that same time completed training in record time and all brought top dollar. As I predicted, most of them were sold to women who seem to have a thing for Mafia products. We duplicated their Mafia brands on their rumps and also added one on their upper back. We found it only adds to their value. Strange. Most of the time it lowers the value because it always implies previous ownership, but not in this case. I suppose those boys are earning their keep keeping their mistresses happy around the clock – they love it, I'm sure. When their mistresses tire of them, they'll be right back here for sale probably, so we profit out of them again, although this time around we're probably direct them to male owners so they stay good and versatile like they were trained."

"David, those 50 we culled out of your Macedonia buy worked out fine. We picked the best of the lot and, although they certainly hadn't acclimated to their slavery when we got then, they adjusted well over the course of some heavy whip training. They finished their final stages of training just last week and each brought us top dollar. They were marketed as pleasure slaves and most of them were sold for that purpose. A few, due to their sheer size and strength, were sold as pit fighters, gladiators, and work overseers. Doesn't matter, they'll all be worked hard – whether out in the sweat shops or in someone's bed. Probably both. They brought us top dollar no matter what usage they were destined for with their new owners."

"And, Forrest, I'm glad you continue to enjoy the Australian blond. He completed training in a record six weeks – a natural slave as you predicted. We sold that Greek boy you turned in for him within the week – a Russian millionaire bought him for his own private harem."

"David, are you still enjoying the Nigerian slave we sent you once his training was complete – the very one that served as a 'sampler' for that lot of 50 Nigerians you bought to fulfill the MaleServe contract?"

"He's a keeper," David smiled. "At least for a while longer. THE FIRM's training really added the icing to that cake."

"Make sure he's well used, David," Mr. Broadley counseled. "It will only add to his value when THE FIRM auctions him off. That slave you turned in for him was sold within a week – a very rich Polish businessman bought him. I think he runs a string of brothels throughout Poland. I suppose a good looking pure black is a novelty there – especially when you can fuck them anyway you want."

"I've got a little surprise for you, "Mr. Broadley smiled at both of them as he pushed a button on his desk and two naked slaves of indescribable masculine beauty lithely glided into the room. Each had a gold envelope tied to their slave collars.

"In each envelope is your quarterly paycheck – 10.8 million you two have earned this quarter alone with your hard work and exquisite good taste. The messengers are yours to keep: both have completed THE FIRM's training and are fully guaranteed. The black is for you, David, and the blond slave is yours, Forrest. They'll each bring over 1 million on the open market. It's THE FIRM's way of saving thank you for a job well done. Let's just say it's the bonus I promised you two when we so easily met the MaleServe contract."

David reached out and hefted the black's huge swollen balls while Forrest began to stroke the blonde's protrusive ringed tits. Both slaves smiled at their new owner's attention and each thrust their pelvis out further to show their appreciation.

"Oh, their ownership papers made out to you are also in the gold envelope," Mr. Broadley laughed. "Of course, you can get to that detail after you've had your fun with them," Mr. Broadley winked as he gestured toward the bedrooms adjoining his huge office. "The trainers tell me fucking them is at a 'higher level,' whatever that means," as he winked again and quietly left the room.

ABOUT THE AUTHOR

Bill Smith is a prolific writer of homoerotic novels which receive critical acclaim for their tightly constructed plots, their believable characters, and their writing craftsmanship. Four books already available from Nazca Plains are "Bates Training Center," "The Brazilian," "Guiliano Imports," and "The Marketplace."

BATES
TRAINING CENTER

A NOVEL BY
BILL SMITH

SMITH

BATES TRAINING CENTER

GUILIANO
IMPORTS

A EROTIC TALE OF SATISFACTION GUARANTEED BY
BILL SMITH

SMITH

GUILIANO IMPORTS

THE BRAZILIAN

BILL SMITH

SMITH

THE BRAZILIAN

THE
MARKETPLACE

BILL SMITH

www.ingramcontent.com/pod-product-compliance
Lightning Source LLC
Chambersburg PA
CBHW051655260626
47170CB00004B/1516